"You were mad about a lot more than me not bringing that plate back pronto."

"Oh, dear. I should have known. But then I thought—"

She stopped, blushed.

"You thought…?" Witt prompted, fascinated by the mix of emotions that washed across her face.

She bit her lower lip, shook her head. The color in her cheeks was rapidly changing from rose to scarlet.

She had *very* kissable lips.

He bent closer. He couldn't help himself. She drew him like a magnet drew iron. "Yes?"

"I thought you thought I was too…forward. That I was…"

Closer still. *"Yes?"*

"Chasing you." The words escaped on a gasp.

Witt's head spun. Molly Calhan? Chasing him? *Him?*

He liked the thought. *A lot.*

* * *

The Lawman Takes a Wife
Harlequin Historical #573—August 2001

Praise for award-winning author Anne Avery's recent works

The Bartered Bride
"Rich in historical detail and lush in characterization…Anne Avery takes her place with the best."
—*Romantic Times Magazine*

Summer Fancy
"…laugh-out-loud funny and sweetly sensual… if you're looking for a book to lift your spirits, this is definitely the one!"
—Under the Covers Web site

"*Summer Fancy* is a funny, engaging, sexy love story…a wonderfully told story to read…anytime you want to fall in love."
—*The Old Book Barn Gazette*

ANNE AVERY

THE LAWMAN TAKES A WIFE

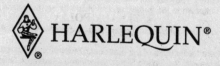

HARLEQUIN®

TORONTO • NEW YORK • LONDON
AMSTERDAM • PARIS • SYDNEY • HAMBURG
STOCKHOLM • ATHENS • TOKYO • MILAN • MADRID
PRAGUE • WARSAW • BUDAPEST • AUCKLAND

ISBN 0-373-29173-6

THE LAWMAN TAKES A WIFE

Copyright © 2001 by Anne Holmberg

Visit us at www.eHarlequin.com

Printed in U.S.A.

This book is for Dame Agatha and Phinneas T. Dogg,
who have stuck by me from the first.
And in loving memory of Osa, the Wonder Bear,
who tended to shed.

Chapter One

"What'd I tell you? That's him."

"You sure?" Bonnie Calhan frowned down at her eight-year-old brother. With the superior perspective of her eleven years, she'd learned to be cautious—even making Dickie cross his heart and hope to die wasn't always a guarantee you could believe him. Now that he'd grabbed hold of this latest wild notion of his, there was just no telling at all.

Dickie wasn't paying her any mind, anyway. He was standing on tiptoe, face pressed against the tall, narrow front window of Elk City's sheriff's office, straining to see inside.

"Are you sure?" she insisted, poking him to make him listen.

He grudgingly backed away from the window and dusted his hands on the seat of his overalls. "Certain sure. Saw him come in on the train last night. He was carryin' a rifle an' a saddle an' askin' for the mayor. An' I heard him sayin' somethin' about the sheriff's office. Honest. Couldn't be nobody else."

"Anybody else."

He shrugged, irritated. "See for yourself if you don't believe me."

Bonnie eyed him doubtfully, then cupped her hands around her eyes and peered through the rain and dirt-blotched window. The effort was wasted. What with the grime, the natural distortions in the crude glass, and the sharp contrast between sunlit street and shadowed interior, she couldn't see anything except a dark bulk hunched over a desk at the back of the room.

But it was the sheriff's office, and they'd been expecting the new sheriff for weeks, now. Much as she hated to admit it, Dickie was probably right.

"All right," she said, reluctantly giving in as she usually did, sooner or later. "But if you're wrong..."

"I ain't. You'll see."

"Yes, I will. And don't say *ain't*. You know Mother doesn't like it."

She tried to take his hand, but he scowled and dodged out of reach. "Don't you go bossin' me, Bonnie Mae Calhan! Just 'cause you're bigger'n me an'—"

"Oh, come on. If we're going to do this, there's no sense dawdling."

His scowl deepened. "You sound just like Mother." But when Bonnie moved toward the door, he was a half step ahead of her.

Bonnie halted on the threshold, blinking against the sudden transition from sunlight to shadow. Dust coated the raw plank floor and hung in the air like a gauzy curtain, obscuring details. Not that there was anything worth seeing except the desk and the man behind it.

He looked up at their entrance, but she couldn't make out much more of his features than she had outside.

"Yes?" His voice was deep, pleasant to the ear.

"Are you—" The words stuck on her tongue like molasses.

All of a sudden, she was even less certain of the wisdom of this visit than she'd been when she'd given in to Dickie's pleading. What if he laughed at them? Or gave them a tongue lashing for wasting his time like old Mr. Garver was always doing? Or worse, told their mother?

Bonnie blenched at the thought of what her mother would say if she found out.

Dickie had no such reservations. "You the new sheriff?" he demanded, boldly stepping forward.

"I am."

Dickie threw her a look that clearly said, *told you so!* and edged a little farther into the room. "You really a gunfighter, like Freddy Christian said you was?"

The man's mouth abruptly thinned to an intimidating straight line. "No."

The single word rumbled in the dusty air like distant thunder. He deliberately set aside the papers he'd been reading, then shoved back his chair and came around the desk toward them.

Seated behind the battered old desk, the man had looked impressively large. On his feet and up close, he was downright intimidating—more like a mountain on legs than a man. The floor jumped with every step he took.

Bonnie backed up a foot.

Her brother didn't budge, but he hunched his shoulders and stuck out his chin so he could swallow. If his eyes opened any wider, his eyeballs would pop out.

The sheriff loomed over them. Bonnie had to tilt her head back to meet his gaze. Her throat tightened. There was an awful lot of jaw on that sharply carved face of his.

He stared down at her unblinkingly.

Bonnie backed up another step and clasped her hands behind her, where he wouldn't see their trembling.

The sheriff turned to Dickie. "Who is Freddy Christian?" His voice seemed to shake the walls around them, despite its mild tone.

"A friend," said Dickie in a very small voice. He gulped and added, a little louder this time, "He's a year younger'n me, but he knows 'most everything 'cause his dad, see, he's the editor of the paper."

The sheriff considered that a moment, then, "How old are you?"

Dickie rubbed his hands on the sides of his overalls. "Me?"

The sheriff nodded.

"Eight. Nine come October." Dickie hesitated, then cocked a thumb in Bonnie's direction. "This here's my big sister, Bonnie. She's eleven."

Those coal-black eyes turned back to her. After a moment's sober study, the sheriff politely ducked his head by way of acknowledgment. "Miss Bonnie."

Bonnie flushed. She'd never had a grown-up gentleman call her Miss Bonnie before. And now that she'd had the chance to study him a bit more, the new sheriff didn't seem nearly as hard as he had a minute earlier.

On the other hand, he didn't seem any smaller, either.

"I'm Dickie," her brother announced, drawing the sheriff's attention back to him. "Richard James Calhan. Named after my dad and granddad. My mother—"

"Our mother," Bonnie snapped. She was happy to leave the talking to Dickie, but she didn't care to be left out altogether.

"*Our* mother, then," Dickie conceded, annoyed. He wasn't willing to interrupt his recital to argue with her about it, though. "She runs Calhan's General Store. Guaranteed best store in town! If we don't have it, we'll get it, no extra charge."

The sheriff mulled over that bit of information, too. "If your ma runs the store," he asked at last, "what's your pa do?"

Dickie's face fell. Over four years had passed since their father had died in a coal mine cave-in and he still had nightmares at times. For that matter, so did Bonnie, though she would never admit it. Mother already had enough to worry her.

"Da's dead," Dickie admitted reluctantly.

That admission was usually enough to launch a dozen questions about how he'd died and when, and how they were getting along without him. At the very least it got an "I'm sorry to hear that" kind of response, regardless if the person was sorry or not. But this man mountain neither asked rude questions nor offered false sympathy. He accepted the statement with the quiet composure that seemed as much a part of him as his broad shoulders or big feet. Bonnie found his calmness strangely reassuring.

With one smooth motion, he squatted on his heels in front of them. The change in position brought him to eye level with her.

"So," he said. "What can I do for you?"

Bonnie looked at him, then she looked at Dickie. This was all Dickie's idea, not hers. She'd only agreed to come with him because, if he was right, she didn't want to be left out of the excitement. But that didn't mean she wanted to take the blame if he got into trouble, instead.

"Dickie'll tell you. This was his idea, not mine."

Dickie, ever the showman, swelled with importance. "It's this," he said, pulling a rolled-up newspaper out of his back pocket and holding it out to the sheriff. "We wanna report a bank robbery."

Calhan's General Store was filled near to bursting with ladies who had gathered to inspect the new collection of winter dress goods. Since it was unthinkable that any self-respecting woman in Elk City would let the other ladies get a jump on her in the matter of selection, each of them had made a point of arriving early, only to find that everyone else had been possessed of the exact same thought. By the time Molly opened the door at 9:00 a.m. precisely, the boardwalk in front was jammed. It was eleven now, and while the lengths of cloth and ribbon and lace had shrunk, the crowd appeared to have grown.

As she always did, Molly had gotten up early so she could arrange the new bolts of cloth and boxes of buttons and trim in an attractive display on top of the broad oak counter that ran the length of the store.

It took her hours to set up the display, and hours more to straighten up after, but the ladies only needed a couple of minutes to create chaos out of her carefully constructed order. Molly suspected that was part of the attraction of this novel method of selling and the main reason she always sold three times more sewing notions and more yards of cloth than any other dry goods store this side of Denver.

Dealing with the ladies was never easy, however. Not only did she have to cope with their often heated competition for the more popular fabrics and notions, she had to sort their questions and requests out of the confusing babble of conversation and gossip that always reigned at these events. At the end of the day, she inevitably emerged with a headache and a satisfyingly well-stuffed till.

As long as the till was full, she never begrudged the headache. The store was Bonnie's and Dickie's future, after all.

And hers, of course. She tried not to forget that.

At the moment, though, she didn't have time to think about the future. It was all she could do to deal with the present—measuring and cutting and tallying orders while answering the dozens of questions being flung at her from all sides. The gossip and chatter she ignored, as much out of habit as out of necessity. No merchant could afford the luxury of gossip or of choosing sides, and her position as a widow and Elk City's only female store proprietor made her more careful than most.

That didn't stop the ladies, however—the latest rumors had been flying thick and fast all morning. At the moment, a recent arrival held undisputed center stage.

"The new sheriff's in town," Coreyanne Campbell said, loud enough for everyone to hear.

The announcement caused a gratifying stir. Even Molly put aside her scissors for a moment, intrigued.

"Arrived last night on the train," Coreyanne added, her vast bosom swelling with satisfaction at being the first with the latest news. "From what I hear, he was packing a saddle and a rifle and a bedroll and not much else."

"The sheriff's here already?" The large silk daisies on Emmy Lou Trainer's hat bobbed dangerously. "I'd heard he wasn't coming for a couple of weeks, yet."

"Wouldn't you know! And no one expecting him so we could give him a proper welcome."

Molly couldn't tell who had spoken.

"Probably Josiah Andersen's fault," the widow Thompson snapped. "He may be mayor, but he never could get anything right." Her sharp, narrow little face looked extra pinched with disapproval. "High time that man got here, though. Must be a month or more since the town council offered him the job."

As the crowd murmured agreement, she took advantage of the diversion to grab a length of blue-and-white Sheppard plaid she'd been eyeing for the past twenty minutes. She fingered it, judging the weight and feel of it, then brought it to within three inches of her pointy little nose and squinted.

"Weave's off. Be a tough job to get that straightened out." Without letting go of the cloth, she craned forward across the counter so Molly couldn't ignore her. "How much you asking for this, Molly?"

"Fifteen and a half cents a yard," Molly said, and braced for what came next. It didn't matter what price she quoted, Thelma Thompson would say it was too dear, and then she'd start to haggle.

"Fifteen and a half!" gasped the widow, scandalized. Her thin face flushed. "Ridiculous! It's not worth a penny over ten."

Molly ignored the protest and unrolled a bolt of a silk-and-wool blend for another of the ladies. "I remember you were talking about making yourself a new suit, Ida, so the minute I saw this, I thought of you. The green's just your color. Go with your eyes, you know."

"That's nice, Molly," Ida Walker said, smiling. "Trust you to remember. Though I don't know..." She slid her work-worn hand over the fine cloth doubtfully. "What with young Will growing out of his britches faster than I can think, and big Will talking about buying some land up Oh-Be-Joyful Creek...well..."

"Did you hear me, Molly Calhan?" Thelma sniffed and tightened her grip on the plaid. "Not a penny over ten. It's scandalous, the price of things these days. Absolutely scandalous!"

"You could probably get it for twelve and a half or thirteen cents a yard in Denver, Thelma, but then you'd have to pay for the train and your meals, you know. Don't forget, I can't buy things in quantity like the big Denver stores can, and that's besides having to pay for the freight. And you know how high freight charges are getting to be!"

"I still say it was wrong to bring in someone from outside," said Emmy Lou Trainer, dragging the conversation back to the new sheriff. The daisies quivered with her indignation. "Especially when we had perfectly good candidates for the job right here in Elk City."

Emmy Lou's husband had been one of the unsuccessful candidates, but the other ladies politely forbore to mention that fact. Three months ago, when there'd been no clear winner after four rounds of voting, the town council had decided to bring in a sheriff from outside the community rather than see the city split into factions. Everyone had thought the suggestion inspired except Emmy Lou.

"Josiah Andersen says he comes well recommended," said Coreyanne. Her husband was drinking partners with the mayor, so she got all the scoop on city hall goings-on. "Seems the town council from someplace up north had been talking to him about a job. According to Josiah, Elk City's lucky to get him."

The widow Thompson wasn't interested in new sheriffs or town councils. She especially wasn't interested in Josiah Andersen's opinion on anything since the two had been feuding for years.

"You know I'm too old to be making that trip to Denver if I don't have to, Molly Calhan," she protested. "And my widow's pension certainly won't cover something as dear as this plaid. Besides, Ben Dermott over to Gunnison always gives me a discount, me being a widow and all. I was just sure you would, too. You ought to understand how it is, not having a man around to provide, yourself."

"What did he look like?" Louisa Merton asked. "The sheriff, I mean." Louisa was nineteen and pretty and known to be on the prowl for a husband, and rumor had it the sheriff was still unclaimed. "Did you see him? Is he…nice?"

"I didn't see him," said Coreyanne, "but my Ed said he's big. Real big. And quiet. Didn't say much, Sam says, even when he was treated to a round or two in Jackson's saloon."

She shook her head, lips pinched shut in disapproval of anyone, and especially the new sheriff, being seen drinking in Jackson's Saloon. Especially if they were seen drinking with her husband. Ed Campbell had a fondness for drink that almost exceeded his fondness for his well-built wife, and Jackson's was far more likely to cater to his weakness than any other of the town's establishments.

Worries about her husband's drinking and the excitement of a new sheriff couldn't compete with the attractions of new yard goods, however.

"Could I take a look at that pink silk, there, Molly?"

Coreyanne said. "It looks like it'd be just the thing to go with my old gray suit. Sort of spruce it up, if you know what I mean."

"But what did he look like?" Louisa had a one-track mind when it came to men. "Is he handsome?"

"I'll give you thirteen," said Thelma grudgingly.

"Now, Thelma." Molly passed the pink silk down the counter to Coreyanne. No one paid any attention to Louisa.

"Thirteen cents a yard," said the widow, pulling the plaid out of Ida Walker's reach. "That's my final offer."

Molly repressed a sigh. "Let me think about it, Thelma."

She'd give in eventually. Both of them knew it. None of the other women would touch that plaid until they were sure Thelma had either gotten what she wanted or given up the hunt—and Thelma never gave up. The woman could wear down rock with her nagging if she set her mind to it.

"What's his name? Is it true he's not married?" Louisa asked of nobody in particular. "I heard he was at least thirty. If not older!" Her face went white at the thought of still being single at the advanced age of thirty.

"His name's DeWitt Gavin, and he's thirty-three, Sam says," Coreyanne informed them with satisfaction. She started to say something else, then bit back the words.

"What else have you heard?" demanded Emmy Lou, leaning closer. "Is he married? I'd heard he was going to be living in that room at the back of the sheriff's office. There's not enough space there for a cat to turn around in, let alone a family.''

"Nooo," said Coreyanne, still uncertain. "He's not married.''

"Well, then?'' said Emmy Lou. All the other ladies stopped breathing so they wouldn't miss a word of whatever came next.

Coreyanne glanced at them nervously, but it was clear to everyone present that her information was simply too good not to be shared.

"I told Sam I wouldn't say anything, but I know he didn't really mean I couldn't tell you ladies. After all, you're my friends.''

"That's right,'' said Emmy Lou. "We are. You know you can trust us!''

"Well…''

"Oh, for heaven's sake, Coreyanne,'' Molly said sharply, yanking on a piece of wool felt that had gotten tangled around a bolt of flannel. She tugged the fabric to straighten it and started to roll it back up. "If you promised not to tell—''

"You can tell us!'' Thelma interrupted. Even talking Molly down on the price of the plaid took back seat to the pleasurable possibility of scandal.

Coreyanne caved in.

"He's divorced!'' she said in a theatrical whisper loud enough for all to hear.

A collective gasp shook her audience.

"Can you imagine?''

No one said a word. The news was just too thrillingly awful to treat so lightly.

Molly knew the silence wouldn't last long. "I can imagine, but it's none of my business to try.'' She flipped the bolt over another turn, giving a snap to the fabric as she did so it lay straight and taut.

"No, but—"

"No buts, Coreyanne!" she snapped. She kept her gaze fixed on the bolt. She'd never liked confrontation or conflict, but sometimes it couldn't be avoided, no matter how much she wished it could. "I won't listen to gossip of that sort! You know that."

"Well, I will," Emmy Lou said. Nothing fazed Emmy Lou, especially not Molly's straitlaced notions of propriety and good manners. *Especially* not when it came to dirt about the man who'd taken the job that rightfully belonged to her husband.

"What did she do that he'd divorce her? It must have been something pretty bad."

"Mmm," said Coreyanne doubtfully. She cast a nervous glance at Molly, then at her friends. There wasn't a chance she'd get out of the store without sharing whatever juicy tidbit her Sam had shared with her. "Well, according to what my Sam heard, he didn't divorce his wife. She divorced him!"

"No!"

"Yes!"

"Well, I never! In all my born days, I never!"

Molly glanced at the avid faces in front of her, every one of them focused on Coreyanne. There was only one way to get the ladies' attention off the sheriff and his disreputable past and back on the business at hand.

"Tell you what, Thelma," she said to the widow. "I'll let you have that plaid for fourteen cents a yard. I can't do better than that, and neither can you. And Coreyanne, did you want the silk? If you don't, Sally, here, was interested."

A discount and competition for a coveted fabric! As one, the ladies abandoned the sheriff and plunged back into the fray. The distraction wouldn't hold for long, but it was the best she could do under the circumstances.

Distraction or no, as she measured lengths of fabric and rang up sales, Molly couldn't help wondering—what could the new sheriff possibly have done to make his wife take the scandalous step of divorcing him?

Witt Gavin had no trouble finding the store little Dickie Calhan had mentioned. It was a good-sized clapboard building with a one-and-a-half story false front facing the town's main street. From the busy cross street running alongside the store, Witt had a clear view of the sign painted in big red letters on the whitewashed siding: Calhan's General Store. Guaranteed Best Store in Town! If We Don't Have It, We'll Get It, No Extra Charge!

At least the boy had gotten that part right.

As for his wild tale about strangers who skulked down alleys and loitered around the town's main bank whenever the mine payrolls were delivered…

Witt propped his shoulder against the building opposite Calhan's, crossed his arms across his chest, and studied the scene before him. From where he stood, Main Street stretched north through town, headed straight toward the Elk Mountains that gave the town its name. The street's unpaved expanse was lined on either side by false-fronted wood buildings and a dozen impressive brick ones. Saddle horses and teams hitched to a variety of buggies and wagons were tied at rails on either side of the thoroughfare. Several blocks up, a covered public well occupied the middle of an intersection, readily accessible to any citizen who lacked the convenience of a private one.

Nearer at hand, catercorner to Calhan's General Store, stood a substantial brick building with an aura of sober respectability that immediately identified it as Elk City's main financial institution. The sign over the door said Elk City State Bank in bold gold letters. It was more a concession to convention than an absolute necessity—the place was impossible to miss.

If there'd been any suspicious goings-on, a sharp-eyed, intelligent boy on the boardwalk in front of Calhan's would have spotted them right off.

And if there weren't any suspicious strangers, Calhan's boardwalk was the ideal place for a boy with an overactive imagination and a taste for the lurid tales in dime novels to dream some up.

Elk City was a decent, workaday place that boasted good railroad connections, coal, lumber, water and some of the finest grazing range in the state of Colorado. It was also well off the more traveled roads and rail lines that laced the state. Payroll or no, the town wasn't the sort of place he'd expect to find a bunch of desperadoes intent on a shoot-'em-up bank heist.

Witt watched as an old woman with a shopping basket over her arm made her way along the opposite side of Main. Every man she passed doffed his hat. Several exchanged a few pleasant words, as well. There was something comfortable about the scene, as if the folks he saw were glad to be right where they were. That wasn't something you could say about every town he'd ever been through. Not by a long shot.

With hard work and a little luck, Elk City just might

be the spot where he could finally put down roots, buy some land, some cattle. Maybe even get married. He was almighty tired of boarding house meals and narrow beds for one.

At the thought, the old, familiar hollowness came back. Witt shoved away from the building, disgusted with himself and his mush-headed daydreams. There wasn't a woman in her right mind would want him, even if he'd had more than a dream to offer her, which he didn't. Besides, if Clara hadn't been able to abide him, it stood to rights nobody else would want to try.

He'd might as well not waste time reminding himself. The mistakes he'd made were well-plowed ground, yet for all the time he'd spent working that field, thinking it over, worrying about it, he'd never yet gotten a crop of anything but weeds out of it.

He'd do better to tend to his work, and right now that meant introducing himself to Mrs. Calhan and finding out if she'd noticed anything to indicate her son really had seen something, no matter how improbable the boy's tale sounded.

As he crossed the street, Witt was conscious of a number of curious glances directed his way. Word had obviously gotten around that Elk City's new sheriff was somewhat oversize. He ignored them. Over the years, he'd gotten used to the attention even if he'd never learned to like it.

He'd even gotten used to checking an unfamiliar boardwalk before he stepped on it to make sure it would hold his weight. Calhan's boardwalk was sturdy enough and neatly swept, which was promising. The broad front windows were so clean they gleamed, which was even better.

Witt glanced at the display behind that glass and stopped dead in his tracks.

The proprietors of dry good stores generally had two ways of filling their front windows—either they stacked their excess supplies higglety pigglety on the broad display shelves built under the windows, heedless of appearance, or they crammed in as many unrelated items as they could until it was next to impossible to sort out anything from the heaps and piles and mounds of merchandise.

Mrs. Calhan had done neither. Instead, she'd constructed an intriguing arrangement of boxes of various sizes, then draped a length of shiny, bright-red cloth on top. The fabric spilled over the boxes and gathered in glistening folds in the spaces between them, for all the world as if it had been carelessly flung there, then forgotten. Yet there was something about the arrangement, something about the way the cloth caught the light, that drew the eye from one displayed item to another and then another, so that Witt felt as if he were being irresistibly drawn into the store.

Of course, it was possible the secret to the display's attraction was that it offered nothing but candy—and Witt had a sweet tooth whose roots went all the way down to his toes.

He moved closer, studying the riches laid out before him. There were peppermint sticks in a tall glass jar, and chocolate creams in a box lined with shiny gold paper. There were licorice jawbreakers, and bright-yellow lemon drops, and candied nuts, and cream balls, and lady kisses, and an assortment of chocolate biscuits and bars arranged on a silver tray. There was a bowl of candied peanuts and another of mouthwatering pecan pralines. There was a little metal pirate's chest stuffed with French bonbons that were as tempting to Witt as pieces of eight would be to a pirate. And there, right in the middle of it all, was an enormous glass jar tied with a bright-red ribbon and filled to overflowing with gum-drops in every color of the rainbow.

Witt let out the breath he'd been holding, and licked his lips. And then he pulled open the broad screen door and walked into paradise.

Chapter Two

A shadow claimed half the light in the store.

Molly looked up from straightening the disaster the ladies had left in their wake and found a mountain standing in her doorway. The mountain held out a hand to make sure the screen door didn't slam shut behind him, then took a cautious step forward, squinting against the change from the bright sunlight outside.

Slowly, she set down the drawer of buttons she'd been about to put away. Coreyanne Campbell had said the new sheriff was big, but Molly hadn't pictured anyone quite *this* big. Who would have? The man stood six three in his oversized stocking feet, maybe more. He'd have to have his clothes special made for him—those broad shoulders wouldn't fit into any ready-mades she knew of, and she'd done her best to scout out all the options for her customers.

And his face…

Molly's fingers closed around the edges of the drawer.

If the man himself was a mountain, the core of him had been made out of granite. His face was all hewn slabs and hard lines, like the stark, gray rock that jutted out of the nearby Elk Mountains. Life had slashed grooves at the side of his mouth and the corners of his eyes, but it hadn't softened one angle of the sharp-edged nose or that uncompromising jaw.

There was an awful lot of jaw.

Slowly, deliberately, Molly raised her gaze to meet his.

Gray eyes gleamed from beneath heavy lids. Even with the light behind him, shadowing his face, they seemed alive and bright and warm. Wary, almost. She had the odd sense that he took in more in one glance than most people saw in an hour of looking.

"Good afternoon, Sheriff," she said, "What can I do for you?"

He snatched his hat off and, squinting, lowered his head to look for her in the shadows at the rear of the store. "Ma'am?"

When he came forward, his movements were quiet, controlled, but that didn't stop the floor joists from creaking in protest at the weight. She could feel the jouncing with each step he took.

The glass in her display cases rattled softly.

"You're Mrs. Calhan, the proprietor of this store?" His voice rumbled up from somewhere deep in that big chest like distant thunder over the Elk Mountains. Just like the thunder, it sent a shiver of charged awareness down her spine.

"I am. And you must be Sheriff Gavin." She smiled. "The ladies were talking about you just this morning."

Too late she remembered what they'd been saying.

His expression didn't change, yet she sensed a tension in him that hadn't been there a moment earlier. To cover her gaffe, she extended her hand over the counter.

After a moment's hesitation, he gingerly took it in his own large, callused paw.

The warmth and the hard, masculine strength of that hand wrapped around hers made something inside her squeeze tight. It had been four years since Richard had died. Four long, hard and often lonely years.

"Welcome to Elk City, Sheriff." She slid her hand free, palm tingling from the contact. "We're glad to have you here at last."

"You've had trouble?" The question came too quickly, as if he'd had it prepared beforehand.

"Oh, no," she hastily assured him. "No trouble. Not really. Not *that* sort of trouble. Only, if there *were* trouble, we'd rather have a sheriff around than not."

He nodded, glanced at the disordered counter, then let his gaze slide along the shelves of goods that lined the walls behind her.

Nervous, she nudged a couple of the button boxes in the drawer on the counter in front of her. The faint clack of the buttons shifting was comfortingly normal.

"I take it you're introducing yourself to the shop-keepers?" she said. "That's very commendable, such dedication to duty. And on your very first day, too."

That came out a little more stiffly than she'd intended. She was used to men who weren't much on conversation—a couple of her customers shopped mostly by grunting and pointing—but she wasn't used to being quite so *aware* of the male on the other side of the counter. It was…unsettling. And strangely intriguing.

"We—the shopkeepers here in town, I mean—we're very glad to have you. Things were getting to be so…difficult. Arguments, you know, about who was going to be sheriff and—" She smiled. "Well, let's just say there was a good deal of discussion before the town council agreed we'd be better off getting a man with your...er, your experience.''

Heaven help her, she'd been about to say ''your reputation.'' Surely it was her imagination that his shoulders stiffened as if he were expecting a blow.

''I'm not sworn in yet,'' he said, deliberately not looking at her.

''I'm sure Mayor Andersen will take care of that little matter just as quickly as he can.''

''Mmm.'' His gaze slid from the table in the center of the store with its eye-catching stacks of tinned fruits, to the glass-fronted case where she kept the sweets, to the rack made of antlers that displayed a range of ropes and twine, then over to the artful arrangement of tin washtubs and willow baskets that she'd hung on the wall at the back.

At the sight of a man mannequin with a rolled theatre bill in its waxen hands and sporting a ready-made suit, stiff-collared white shirt and bowler hat tipped at a rakish angle, he blinked and glanced back at her, clearly surprised.

''Never seen a store quite like this.''

His eyes were blue, Molly realized, not gray, as she'd thought. She wrenched her gaze from his face before it became obvious she'd been staring.

''It's proven very handy, putting things on display like this.'' There was an odd little catch in her throat. She cleared it, tried again. If she hadn't known it was mere foolishness, she'd have sworn she could feel the heat of him clear across the counter. ''This way, folks can find what they're looking for without me having to fetch it off some shelf or dig it out of some drawer first. Saves a lot of time for everyone.''

She didn't tell him it also increased her profits significantly. With so much right out in the open where customers could get their hands on it, more often than not they walked out of the store with at least one or two things they hadn't intended to buy but hadn't been able to resist. Sometimes they bought so much they forgot what they'd originally come for and had to come back to buy that, too.

Molly smiled at the mannequin. Since she'd installed it in the store, she'd doubled her sale of men's hats and fancy dress clothes. Sales on cravats and ties had more than tripled and showed no sign of slacking. She'd already started to look for a child-size mannequin to go with it.

She hadn't bothered with a female form since there were cheaper ways of tempting her women customers.

The sheriff wasn't interested in mannequins any more than the rope and twine. His gaze swung back to the glass-fronted display case where she kept her candies and sweets.

Without speaking, he walked over, making the floorboards groan at every step. Staying safely on her side of the broad counter, Molly followed.

"Saw your display out front." He bent forward, forehead furrowing as he studied the array of riches behind the glass.

From this angle, she could see the back of his neck. His hair was too long and poorly trimmed. It brushed over the top of his collar in a ragged ruffle that made her itch to set it right. She'd always trimmed Richard's hair, just sat him in a chair and gone to work with her scissors until he was neat and presentable. Better than any barber, or so he'd always said.

Her hands twitched at the memory of how a man's

hair felt sifting through her fingers, of the heat and texture of his skin.

She smoothed her palms down the sides of her skirt, cleared her throat. "Did you like it?"

Confused, the sheriff glanced up from his perusal of the case's contents. "Like it?"

"The display. In the window out front. Did you like it?"

"Oh." His jaw worked as if he were chewing on the question. "It was…nice. Real nice."

"Thank you."

If he heard her, he gave no sign of it. His attention was riveted on the display. After a moment's careful consideration, he pointed with a blunt-tipped finger. "Those chocolate drops, there. They the bittersweet kind?"

Molly craned to see what he was pointing at. "No, that's milk chocolate. But I can get the bittersweet if you'd rather."

He shook his head but didn't take his gaze off the collection of sweets. Molly had seen that look in the face of children who couldn't decide how to spend their precious pennies, but she'd never seen a grown man take it so seriously.

"Try one of these chocolate creams," she said on impulse, moving behind the case. She slid open the glass door at the back and plucked a cream in its paper nest from the box. "They come all the way from New York. Try it."

He eyed the chocolate on her open palm, then glanced at her, clearly embarrassed.

"Think of it as a welcome to Elk City," she said.

Delicately, frowning in concentration, he plucked the chocolate from its nest, then popped the thing into his mouth whole. She watched his mouth work as he tongued the confection, fascinated in spite of herself. His eyes closed and an expression of bliss softened the hard lines of his face.

"Good?"

He blinked back to an awareness of where he was. "That's...fine. *Real* fine."

He said it reverently, like a man who'd experienced a small miracle. She wasn't sure, but that looked like the faintest trace of a blush under his dark tan.

"Told you!" Smiling, she impulsively slipped a half dozen into a little paper bag. "Have some more."

He glanced at her, then the bag, then backed away, shaking his head.

Molly waved the bag slightly, just enough so he could hear the shifting of the paper-wrapped sweets inside. "It's not a bribe, you know. And it's rude to refuse."

His eyes locked with hers.

"Please," she said.

Reluctantly, he reached to take the sweets. "Thank you, ma'am. That's...very kind."

She laughed. "Not at all. It's plain good business. If I get you hooked on them, you'll *have* to come back, now won't you?"

There was no mistake this time—that really was a blush under the tan.

It wasn't until the screen door to Calhan's General Store had banged shut behind him that Witt realized he hadn't thought to ask Mrs. Calhan about the bank or if she'd seen any suspicious strangers lurking in any alleys. Nothing but that one question if she'd had any trouble, then he'd shaken her hand and whatever smarts he'd ever had had flown out the window. All he could think of was how cool and strong and feminine her small hand had felt encased in his, and how pretty her hair was, especially those soft strands that had pulled free to drift along her cheek and the back of her neck.

It'd been all he could do to keep from staring. Seemed like he'd looked at darned near every single box and bag and bale in the place rather than look into those cool green eyes that seemed to throw off sparks every time she smiled.

So much for tending to his proper business.

Disgusted, he tugged his hat low over his brow, propped his hands on his hips, and scowled at a hip-shot bay lazily twitching away flies at the hitching rack in front of him. The packet of chocolate creams in his pocket rustled with his every move. The taste of chocolate lingered on his tongue, rich and sweetly heavy.

Hell of a way to start a new job.

So what did he do next? Besides make a damned fool of himself?

He scanned the street, trying to decide if it was worth the effort to follow up little Dickie Calhan's tale, or if he ought to just do what Mrs. Calhan had thought he was doing in the first place and introduce himself to a few more of the storekeepers and businessmen along the street.

Nothing to say he couldn't do both at the same time. And then there was the meeting with the mayor and the town council. Six o'clock, the mayor had said, and don't be late.

Shifting his gun belt a little so it rode more comfortably on his hip, Witt stepped off the boardwalk and headed toward the bank.

* * *

From the shadowy safety of Nickerson's Riding Stable six doors down and on the other side of the street, Bonnie and Dickie Calhan watched the sheriff walk out of their mother's General Store. The sound of the screen door slamming behind him came like a distant thunderclap.

Bonnie poked her brother in the ribs with her elbow. "Now we're in for it. Told you, didn't I? Carrying tales like that. Mother will make us scrub the floor for a *week* because of this!"

"Weren't carryin' tales," Dickie growled, poking her back. "It's the truth and you know it!"

She watched the sheriff tug his hat lower on his brow, prop his hands on his hips, then scan the street from one end to the other. Slowly, like a man who was looking for someone. Or two particular someones.

Ignoring Dickie's squirming protests, she grabbed the back of her brother's overalls and tugged him away from the open stable door.

"I'm going home and if you know what's good for you, you'll come, too. Besides, Mother said we were to clean the lamps and carry out the ashes from the stove."

Dickie dug in his feet and pulled free. "We don't gotta do it right now, do we? She didn't say nuthin' about right *now*."

"No, but look." She pointed toward the store.

Her brother turned just in time to see the sheriff hitch his gun belt on his hips, like a man who wanted to be sure it sat right in case he needed to go for the gun it carried. And then he stepped off the boardwalk, headed their way.

Dickie was right behind her when Bonnie scooted out the back door of the stable and ducked down the alley, headed toward home as fast as her feet could carry her.

* * *

A fair amount of money had gone into Elk City State Bank's fancy tiled floor and carved oak paneling and shining brass fixtures. The building wasn't overly big, but it was solidly built, exactly the respectable, prosperous-looking sort of place a man might think could be trusted to keep his hard-earned savings safe.

The clerk who guarded access to the bank's nether regions looked up at Witt's approach. When it became clear that Witt was not going to go away, he reluctantly removed his wire-rimmed glasses, folded them, and set them precisely in the middle of the enormous bound journal he'd been writing in.

"May I help you?" His thin lips pinched together as if the prospect of helping anyone with anything was bitterly distasteful, and helping Witt more distasteful still.

Witt couldn't help wondering if the fellow found it difficult to breathe. His shirt collar was the tallest, stiffest piece of torture Witt had ever seen, and it was cinched in place with a fussily knotted tie that would have strangled a lesser man. Witt's throat hurt just looking at it.

"I'm looking for the president," he said, forcing his gaze away from the clerk's neckware.

"Mr. Hancock is busy at the moment." The man's voice was as pinched and tight as everything else about him.

"Tell him the new sheriff would like to talk to him."

"The sheriff?"

Witt nodded, meeting the man's disapproving stare impassively.

When he showed no sign of budging, the clerk sighed and got to his feet. "What name shall I say?"

Judging from the way the fellow walked, his shoes pinched him even more than his collar.

However much the clerk might resemble a dyspeptic fish, the bank president was a handsome devil who looked like he belonged in big-city boardrooms and expensive men's clubs, not workaday coal mining towns like Elk City.

He looked, in fact, a lot like Clara's fancy man, Witt thought, and felt his hackles rise.

"Sheriff Gavin!" The man smiled and extended his hand over the low railing that fenced off the office area from the lobby. "Gordon Hancock. Welcome! Speaking as the president of Elk City State Bank *and* as a member of the town council, I'm damned glad to meet you! And you're already on the job! Excellent! Excellent!"

The clerk sniffed, slipped his glasses back into place and pointedly buried his nose in his journal.

Hancock opened the railing gate with a theatrical flourish. "Come on back, Gavin. Let's talk.

"Drink?" he added a moment later as he waved Witt to a chair in his office and closed the door behind him. "I know it's still a little early in the day, but—"

Witt glanced at the bottles of expensive whiskey that stood atop a low cabinet, then set his hat on one of the two chairs in front of the desk and deliberately claimed the other. "Thanks, no."

Hancock shrugged and came around the big oak desk to take his seat. He shot his cuffs, rested his perfectly manicured hands on the leather blotter and leaned forward, smiling.

Witt had to fight to suppress his irritation. "You're on the town council."

Hancock's smile widened. "That's right. As president of Elk City's largest and most important bank, I regard it as my responsibility to help guide this fine city of ours into the future. There's great things happening here, Sheriff. Great things! And you'll be a part of them, I promise you.''

He flipped open a brass-trimmed humidor and extended it across the desk. ''Cigar? Cubans, straight from Havana.''

The sweet, rich smell of expensive tobacco filled the air.

Witt shook his head. He liked a good cigar as well as the next man, and a good Havana didn't come his way every day, but he didn't like Hancock and he didn't like the idea of being charmed as the banker was obviously trying to charm him.

''No?'' Hancock chose a cigar, sniffing at it appreciatively. ''Gold and silver now, they go up and down. But Elk City's built on coal, and coal…''

He paused to pull a small, silver-handled pocketknife out of his pocket. Frowning in concentration, he neatly cut off the tip of the cigar, then lit it with a match from a fancy glass holder and puffed the cigar into glowing life.

Witt kept his expression impassive.

''Ah!'' Hancock tilted back in his chair. He blew a cloud of smoke toward the ceiling, then smiled in satisfaction. ''Nothing quite like a good cigar. Unless it's a good woman, heh, sheriff?''

''Coal?'' Witt prompted. He didn't like men who made leering references to women, either.

''Ah, yes. Coal.'' Hancock took another deep drag. ''Coal's going to be around for a while, Sheriff. You can take my word on that. A long while. The faster the state grows, the more we're going to need it. It's not very glamorous, of course. Not like gold or silver. But, oh! the things you can do with it!''

Behind his big cigar, he smiled, and his eyes glittered. Watching him, Witt was reminded of a hungry wolf he'd once faced, years ago.

Hancock lowered the cigar to study him. ''Ever thought about it, Sheriff? All the things you can do with coal?''

Witt shook his head. He'd never been much of a talker, but Hancock didn't want a response. He wanted somebody to talk at, somebody to show off for.

''Railroads, Sheriff! Think of 'em! And that big steel mill down in Pueblo. And the electric plants going up around the state. There's not much of that yet, but someday electricity will be for more than just a factory here and there, you mark my words. And our homes! Where would we be without coal to heat our homes and cook our meals, eh, Sheriff? People might give up buying gold and silver, but they still have to eat and keep warm, don't they?''

Hancock punctuated his remarks by stabbing at the air with the glowing tip of his cigar. With the last point, he glanced down at that bit of fire in his hands, and smiled, a small, secret smile just for himself. He leaned back in his chair and took a deep draw, held it, then pursed his lips and slowly exhaled.

''Yes sir, Sheriff, coal's going to be around for a while, and that means Elk City's going to be there, too. Growing, expanding, getting richer every day, by God!''

''And you want to make sure someone's here to keep those riches safe for you.'' The dryness in Witt's voice wiped the smile off the banker's face.

''That's right.'' His eyes glittered coldly. ''Not that

there's much to worry about in the way of trouble around here. A few drunks on payday, a quarrel between a shopkeeper and a customer every now and then. That's about it. We'd like you to keep it that way.''

Witt gave a small, noncommittal grunt. *It's because of Clara,* he told himself. I'm thinking of that smooth-talking fancy man she fell in love with. It has nothing to do with Hancock. Nothing.

''Paydays for the mine,'' he said, remembering Dickie Calhan's tale. ''Gotta be a lot of money coming in for those payrolls.''

''True.'' Hancock smiled in wolfish satisfaction. ''A very great deal of money, and we take good care to keep it safe, I can assure you. Only a few people know what train the money's coming in on. Even some of the railroad and bank people aren't informed. That way, there's less chance of the train being stopped and robbed. No sense in stopping a train when all you might get is a few wallets and women's purses for your troubles.''

Witt remained silent, waiting.

''This bank is solid, too, of course. You saw. Solid brick, bars on the windows, and the best safe money can buy. The mines, of course, have their own guards for when the money is actually being paid out.''

''Are you the only bank that handles the payrolls?''

Hancock shook his head, took another drag, blew the smoke toward the ceiling. ''No, but we handle the majority. All the big mines, certainly.''

''And you've never had an attempt on the bank or the payroll?'' Witt persisted.

''No, I told you. Nothing like that.'' Hancock was growing irritated. ''Watch the saloons. A few of the men get drunk and rowdy, but that's as far as it goes.

We've never had more of a problem than that. But if we do…'' He stared at Witt across the desk, his eyes hard and unblinking. "If we do, then you've proven you're the man for the job. That's why we hired you, you know. Because you proved you knew how to deal with *real* problems.''

A chill swept down Witt's spine. "What do you mean?''

"Oh, come now, Sheriff. There's no need to play the silent hero here, between the two of us. Frankly, that little incident with those two bank robbers over in Abilene is what convinced us to hire you. Convinced me, anyway. I had to do some arguing to talk some of the other council members into the idea. They weren't sure they liked the idea of a gunfighter serving as our sheriff.''

"I'm not a gunfighter.''

Hancock looked skeptical. "You're not trying to tell me you didn't kill those two, are you? We checked into that incident pretty thoroughly, and—''

"No, I'm not going to say I didn't kill those men. I did. But I'm not a gunfighter.'' After five years, he still found himself sweating, just thinking of it.

"But you faced them down, right there in the street, didn't you?''

"It happened outside the bank, yes. They—''

He stopped. He didn't owe this man an explanation, but he should have known the minute that little Dickie Calhan asked him if he was a gunman that he would have to face it. Like divorce, the fact that he'd killed two men—two *boys,* dammit—wasn't the sort of thing people forgot.

"I'm not a gunfighter.'' He shoved to his feet. "If

that's what you and the town want, Hancock, hire someone else.''

"No, no. Sheriff!" Hancock was on his feet, hands raised, palms out, the still smoking cigar between his fingers. He smiled. "Please. Forgive me if I've offended you. My choice of words was…ill-considered."

Witt's hands twitched with the urge to punch that handsome face.

"I'd best get going." He bent to retrieve his hat.

Hancock deliberately set the cigar on the rim of a massive polished stone ashtray. "You know about the council meeting tonight?"

"Six o'clock."

"In the town hall. You know where that is?"

It wasn't because of Clara. "I'll find it."

"Good. Good." Hancock came around the desk. "I'll see you there, then."

Witt gave a curt nod of acknowledgment. He didn't trust his tongue for more.

The instant they stepped out of the office, the clerk looked up, face squinched in disapproval. "Mr. Hancock? There's Mr. Dermott here to see you." His face pinched a little tighter. "*And* Mrs. Thompson."

"Mrs. Thompson." Hancock turned pale. "What—"

A thin, stooped little woman popped up from one of the chairs set near the office railing. "My accounts, Mr. Hancock! I want to speak to you about my accounts!"

"Mr. Dermott was here before you, Mrs. Thompson," said the clerk, peering at her disapprovingly from over the rims of his glasses.

A stout, middle-aged gentleman occupying the chair farthest from Mrs. Thompson's waved his hands to indicate he'd rather wait than be dragged into the discussion. Both the combatants ignored him.

"There's absolutely nothing wrong with your accounts," the clerk insisted. "I reviewed them myself, just last week. Accurate to the penny and so I told you."

The woman sniffed. "As if that makes me feel one whit better, Hiram Goff! You're so tight your shoes pinch, but that doesn't mean you've the wits God gave a goldfish or you would know a two from a twenty at the back end of the day."

Gordon Hancock's smile was getting a little forced around the edges. He cleared his throat. "I'm sure if Mr. Goff says your accounts are accurate, there's no need for you to worry, Mrs. Thompson. In fact, now we have Sheriff Gavin on the job, you can stop worrying about anything."

She looked Witt up and down. "So you're our new sheriff."

The corner of Witt's mouth twitched. He could make two of her, with some left over, but that didn't bother her in the least. He'd seen banty roosters that weren't half as feisty. "Yes."

"Sheriff Gavin—" Hancock began.

"Can speak for himself, I shouldn't wonder," the old lady snapped. She leaned closer. For a moment, Witt had the feeling she was going to poke him, as if he were a smoked ham and she was judging the balance of meat to bone.

"Well?" she demanded. "You *can* speak for yourself, can't you?"

Witt stifled the grin that threatened. "Yes, ma'am."

"That's it? That's all you have to say?"

He nodded.

"Huh!" she said, and skewered Gordon Hancock with her stare. "Hired yourself a fool for a sheriff, did you? Trust the mayor for it. Isn't a thing in the world that Josiah Andersen can't foul up, including hiring a sheriff.''

"Mr. Dermott..." Hancock began, a little desperately.

"Though if it's a choice between a fool and Zacharius Trainer, I'd rather have the fool. At least there's a bit more of this fellow than that old windbag, Zacharius.''

"Mr. Dermott," said Hiram Goff with a pinched little frown, "has left.''

Witt clapped his hat on his head and sidled toward the railing gate. "Ma'am." He glanced back at Hancock. "Six o'clock.''

"I'll just see you out." Hancock darn near trod on his heels following him out to the boardwalk in front. "Good of you to drop by, Sheriff. I'm glad we had this little chat, just the two of us.''

Witt gave a noncommittal grunt.

"Not real talkative, are you, Gavin? But that's all right. We hired you because you're a man of action. Proved that in Abilene." Hancock beamed, then clapped him on the shoulder as if they were old friends. "You do the right thing at the right time, we won't care how few words you use to tell us about it. Guaranteed!''

From the shadowed safety behind her storefront windows, Molly watched Gordon Hancock escort the new sheriff out of the bank. Hancock was a handsome fellow and by far the best-dressed man in town, but it wasn't Hancock she was watching.

From the looks of it, DeWitt Gavin didn't have much more to say to the bank president than he'd had to say to her. That made her feel a little better. Not a lot, but a little. For a few minutes there, she'd been fool enough to think he'd been rather more dangerously aware of her as a woman than most of her customers ever were.

She watched as Hancock slapped the sheriff on the back, just as if they were good friends and had known each other for years. The sheriff's expression was so impassive, she couldn't tell what he thought. When he stepped off the boardwalk and started up the streets, she shifted to get a better view.

Despite his size, he moved with a deceptively lazy ease that got him from one place to another quicker than it seemed. Scarcely a minute had passed since he'd stepped out of the bank before he disappeared through the post office door.

Just as well, she told herself, regretfully abandoning the window. She had better things to do than get interested in a man. Any man, let alone one with nothing more to his name, it seemed, than a saddle and a rifle and a bedroll. A woman her age with two children to worry about should have better sense than that.

But still she couldn't help pausing in front of the tall, narrow mirror she'd mounted on the outside of one of the storage cabinets for the convenience of her customers.

The sight was enough to make a grown woman cry. If this was how she'd looked when Sheriff Gavin had walked into the store, it was no wonder the man had had a hard time looking her in the face, then run as soon as he could.

Blushing, she hastily tucked up the tendrils that had escaped her bun, scrubbed the pencil smudge from her cheek, and tugged her shirtwaist into place. And then she sternly turned away to finish the task of putting up the rest of the notions and yard goods.

No matter what the town gossips might say behind

her back, she was doing just fine without a man in her life. Richard had been a good husband and a kind lover, but he was dead and the dreams they'd shared and the children they'd had were her responsibility now, and hers alone. So far, she'd done all right by both the dreams and the children, but there were times…

Molly sighed, remembering the brief feel of her hand in Sheriff Gavin's, the comfortable, solid, eminently masculine bulk of him.

Sometimes it was awfully hard to be a widow when she was still young enough to hunger for the pleasures of the marriage bed. The prospect of years of cold sponge baths in the middle of the night was too grim a possibility even to consider.

Chapter Three

As the broad double doors of Jackson's saloon swung closed behind the last of their party, Witt surreptitiously checked his pocket watch. Almost nine. He sighed and snapped the case shut.

That six o'clock meeting in the town hall had lasted just long enough for a brief swearing-in and handshakes all around before they'd adjourned to the Grand Hotel's private dining room—at the taxpayers' expense, no doubt—for dinner and drinks and a sometimes heated political debate.

Three hours later, their political differences temporarily discarded under the mellowing influence of the Grand's best whisky, the council had adjourned again, this time to the livelier environs of Jackson's saloon.

Only Hancock had bowed out, saying something about a widow and the attentions due her that had roused good-natured laughter from the other council members and a strong urge on Witt's part to flatten the man's pretty nose. It was none of his business to wonder who the widow might be, but Witt found himself hoping it wasn't Mrs. Calhan.

Mayor Andersen clapped him on the shoulder, driving out the thought of the woman and her smile and the tempting way those stray locks of hair had drifted against her cheek and throat.

"Move on in, man, move on in! Can't stand in the doorway blockin' traffic, you know!"

Witt slipped his watch into his vest pocket and stepped to the side, out of the way. Bert Potter swayed after him.

"Good place, Jackson's," he said with only a faint slurring of his sibilants. He cast a slightly bleary gaze over the room. "M'wife hates it. Won't speak to me for a week after I've been in."

"That so?" said Witt.

"Yup." Bert looked around in satisfaction. "I try'n come once a month, at least."

As Elk City's only pharmacist, Bert had inquired right off into the general condition of Witt's stomach, bowels and liver. The assurance that all Witt's organs were in good working order and in no need of a reviv- ifying tonic had been met with a resigned sigh. Since then, the man had been industriously trying to pickle his.

As the mayor stalked to the bar to order a bottle of whiskey and some glasses, Billie Jenkins, proprietor of Jenkins Hardware and one of Elk City's leading busi- nessmen, sidled closer.

"Don't tell my wife about this, will you?" he said in what he no doubt thought was a low voice. He hic- cuped solemnly. "She thinks I'm at a council meeting."

Bert frowned. "Hell, Billie. If she don't know what you're up to by now, I'll eat my boots."

"Damn good thing there ain't a chance in hell of that, Bert," a man at a nearby table jeered good-naturedly.

A rancher from the looks of him, rather than a miner. "Them's the damned ugliest boots I've *ever* seen."

"Savin' yer own, Tony!" his victim returned. "And mine ain't caked with that peculiarly odiferous stuff that's adornin' yours!"

Tony laughed and rose to his feet, gesturing to the empty chairs at the opposite side of his table. "Pull up a chair and join us."

He eyed Witt, grinned, and stuck out his hand. "Judgin' from the size of you, you'd be the new sheriff. Heard you were in Jackson's last night. Zacharius Trainer must be some put out."

Witt took Tony's proffered hand. Before he could ask who Zacharius Trainer was and why he should be some put out, Josiah Andersen returned, loaded with glasses and a bottle.

"Don't let Trainer worry you, Gavin," he advised. "He don't mind we didn't elect him sheriff. It's the missus Trainer you gotta look out for, not ol' Zach. She's twice as mean as he is, and carries a grudge, besides."

Laughter swept the table. While Josiah passed the glasses round, Witt studied the room around him. Last night had been a workday night and the place had been relatively quite. Tonight, however, was Friday and the place was crowded.

According to the mayor, there wasn't much else in the way of entertainment in Elk City except two smaller, less popular saloons at the opposite end of town and the Women's Christian Temperance Union's reading room. And that, thank God, Josiah had said, was closed of a Friday evening.

Though there were a few women scattered here and there through the crowd, none of them had the look of trouble. They were with their men and it didn't take much looking to realize that an invisible and unmistakable hands-off sign had been posted on every one of them.

The men in Jackson's didn't seem to mind. The ones who wanted a woman had already taken the last train into Gunnison, twenty miles away. According to Josiah, who'd said his wife would have a stick to him if she ever found out he'd dare think such a thing, Elk City's one lack was a good whorehouse.

The respectable ladies of the town had long since forced the closure of the two brothels that had provided the early miners' entertainment. Josiah admitted the establishments had never been all that impressive, but they'd been Elk City's own, and he missed them.

There were still a couple of women who entertained visitors privately, though, and the mayor had taken pains to tell Witt exactly who they were and where they worked. He hadn't come right out and said it, but Witt had the feeling it would be as much as his job was worth to drive the last of those enterprising females out of Elk City. So long as they minded their business and didn't disturb the peace, he didn't have any intention of trying.

A checkers game in the corner had drawn a few onlookers, all of whom were more than willing to tell the players what they *ought* to have done and to argue over the differing strategies. In the opposite corner, a burly miner sat picking out a song on a battered, out-of-tune piano that didn't look as if it had ever had much in the way of better days.

The pianist's friends were urging him to play something else, *anything* else but that same, damned "Clementine" with which he'd been assaulting them for hours. Impervious to their pleas, he simply played louder. He couldn't possibly have played worse.

The air reeked of cheap whiskey and cheaper cigars, and the language coming from a couple of the patrons would have gotten the ladies of the church going something fierce. A freckle-faced boy kept busy moving the spittoons and cleaning up the spills, and so far as Witt could see, there wasn't anything other than the foul language that a boy his age shouldn't be seeing or hearing.

Friday night at Jackson's was remarkably peaceful. Provided the checker players didn't turn violent from a surfeit of advice, Witt decided he could stop worrying about trouble. If this was the wildest Elk City had to offer, his tenure as sheriff was going to be a mighty peaceful one.

He settled comfortably back in his chair while a dozen threads of conversation swirled around him. Beneath the noise, he caught the faint rustle of the paper bag of chocolates in his shirt pocket as he shifted.

He stilled, but not soon enough to stop the sudden itch in his palms, and the bigger itch a little lower down.

Maybe not so peaceful, after all.

The Elk City Ladies' Society biweekly meeting was in full swing. The group, which was presently engaged in making quilts for a church-sponsored orphanage in Chicago or New York—there was some disagreement about which, though they were all agreed it would be one or the other of those licentious hellholes back East—had assembled in Elizabeth Andersen's parlor for this week's session.

"The new sheriff's been busy," Coreyanne Campbell said approvingly. She finished pinning the fabric she was piecing and reached for the spool of thread on the table in front of her. "Already been to half the stores in town, introducing himself around. My Sam ran into him coming out of Potter's Pharmacy this afternoon. Had a nice talk, the two of them, or so Sam said."

Everyone tactfully refrained from mentioning that Sam and the sheriff already had a basis for friendship since the two of them had spent the previous evening drinking in Jackson's saloon.

"Heard he visited you first, Molly," Emmy Lou Trainer commented. Above the gold-rimmed glasses perched on the tip of her nose, her eyes narrowed. "That true?"

"He visited me," Molly replied noncommittally. "I have no idea if I was the first, but he did stop by."

After he'd left the bank, she'd watched him work his way from store to store down the street. Which was sheer foolishness, and probably due to her having been so tired and suffering from the headache generated by that morning's free-for-all. At least, that's what she'd told herself when she'd caught herself staring out the window for the dozenth time that afternoon, waiting for him to reappear. Simple curiosity. It had nothing to do with the cut of his jaw or the breadth of his shoulders or the way he'd looked, savoring that chocolate.

Becky Goodnight, whose husband ran the smallest and least profitable general store in town, reached for the scissors that lay on the table beside her. "My George wasn't impressed. The man didn't have much of anything to say for himself, or so George said."

Emmy Lou's mouth pinched into a frown. "He's certainly big enough. MayBeth Johnson said the floor shook with every step he took."

"It would, as rickety as the Johnsons' old building

is.'' The *snick* of Becky's scissors seemed viciously loud.

Molly winced. George Goodnight had been spending most of the small profits from their store on a fancy woman down in Gunnison lately, so Becky was awfully touchy these days. It was easier to take her resentments out on her flourishing competitors than to admit that her husband wasn't much good as a storekeeper, and an utter failure as a husband and father.

Sometimes, when she started thinking about remarrying, Molly remembered George, gave a little prayer of thanks for the good years she'd had with Richard and made herself think about something else entirely.

Nineteen-year-old Louisa Merton sighed, oblivious to Becky's problems. ''I was in the Johnsons' store when he came in. I swear, I was never so disappointed in all my life! He looked so...*old.* He wasn't at all handsome and he didn't say two words when MayBeth introduced us.''

Old? thought Molly. She frowned down at the pieces of the wedding ring quilt in her lap. DeWitt Gavin wasn't *old.* And only a mooney young girl like Louisa would think he wasn't good-looking.

''And on top of it all, he's divorced,'' Louisa added, heaving another, deeper sigh. ''At least Mr. Hancock's always been a bachelor.''

''Don't tell me you've gone chasing *him!*'' Emmy Lou protested, clearly shocked.

''Wouldn't have done me any good if I had. The only lady he ever looks at is Molly, and she's always turning him down.''

''*Really?*''

All eyes turned on Molly.

Molly bristled under their stares, but managed to say

evenly, "Louisa is mistaken. Mr. Hancock has not come courting me and never will."

Which was the truth. Though he'd never been so crass as to say so outright, Gordon Hancock was interested in gaining her bed, not her heart.

"But he asked you out to dinner at the Grand, Molly. I *heard* him," Louisa insisted.

"A business discussion," she lied.

"Gordon Hancock never invited my Zacharius to dinner for a business discussion," Emmy Lou observed tartly.

"Probably because he couldn't afford the bill for the drinks," said Thelma Thompson.

Thelma didn't do much quilting—too expensive for a poor widow woman she often said—but that didn't stop her from showing up at the meetings. Especially when they were being held at Elizabeth's house. Elizabeth's cook made the best sweet biscuits in town, though it wasn't the quality so much as the quantity and the fact that they were free that was the main attraction for Thelma.

Elizabeth hastily passed the widow another plate of biscuits. "Well, I'm sure even a dedicated banker like Mr. Hancock likes to get out once in awhile."

"Then why doesn't he ask *me?*" Louisa demanded.

"Chit your age?" Thelma said, clearing the plate. "Why ever for?"

"At this rate, I'll *never* find anyone to marry," Louisa wailed. "Never!"

"I'm sure you'll find somebody eventually, dear," said Elizabeth. Before Louisa could demand to know just when that might happen, she added, "What I'd like to know is what the sheriff did for his wife to divorce him. He doesn't seem the type to have a miss—" She glanced at Becky. "Be a troublemaker. He just doesn't seem the type."

She looked around the circle. "I don't suppose anybody's heard the details?"

"You're married to the mayor." Emmy Lou stabbed her needle into her quilting pieces as if it could have gone straight to the hearts of those who had deprived her husband of the position he deserved. "Seems to me you, of all of us, ought to know."

Elizabeth stiffened. "You know I don't interfere in Josiah's business. Such things aren't appropriate for a lady."

"Huh!" said Thelma around a mouthful of sweet lemon biscuit. "*I* shay—"

"Watch the crumbs!" Without looking, Elizabeth slapped a napkin into Thelma's hand. "Besides, I'm sure Josiah and all the members of the council investigated the matter thoroughly before they agreed to hire the man."

"Doesn't seem right, bringing in a man we don't know anything about, a man with a scandal in his past when there was perfectly good candidates—" in the midst of battle, Emmy Lou's carefully cultivated grammar tended to desert her "—for sheriff right here in Elk City. Why, if the town council had had a brain among 'em, they would have seen straight off that my Zacharius was—"

"Are you accusing my husband of not knowing what he's doing?"

"Not only of not knowing, but of deliberately ignoring the good of Elk City just so he could—"

"But doesn't anybody know what Sheriff Gavin did to make his wife divorce him?" Coreyanne persisted, more to stop the brewing quarrel between Emmy Lou and Elizabeth than because she really wanted to know.

The would-be combatants breathed out in angry little huffs, torn between their personal animosities and the attraction of a scandal.

"Most likely he was a womanizer," said Emmy Lou with a challenging glance at her rival. Everyone in town knew Josiah Andersen had an eye for the ladies.

Elizabeth flushed. "Probably drank too much and beat her."

Molly set her sewing in her lap. She'd only just met the man, but already she felt sorry for DeWitt Gavin. "Maybe it was her fault."

Her calm statement got everyone's attention.

"*Her* fault? Ridiculous!" snapped Emmy Lou. "He'd have divorced *her,* if that were the case. And Coreyanne said it was definitely *she* who divorced *him.* No decent woman would divorce her husband if she weren't driven to it."

"Maybe she wasn't really a decent woman," Molly insisted. "Maybe she had a...a lover and wanted to marry him, instead."

"Or maybe she was really a criminal. A thief, perhaps or even a murderess!" Louisa Merton's eyes were shining at the thought. "I read a book like that once, where she was really wicked, but the hero was really good and loved her anyway and he convinced her to repent and—"

"Nonsense!" snapped Thelma, Emmy Lou and Elizabeth, all at once.

"You read too many of those trashy romance novels," Emmy Lou added quellingly, "and I've a good mind to tell your mother so."

The light went out of Louisa's eyes; her shoulders slumped.

"But even if it was his fault, that doesn't mean he couldn't make some other woman a good husband," said Coreyanne, ever the peacemaker. "Maybe he's settled down. Or maybe she drove him to it somehow. I'll bet the right woman could keep him in line."

Several heads around the room nodded in agreement. A couple turned Molly's way, expressions alight with keen-eyed speculation.

"Sheriff Gavin seemed quite respectable when he stopped in my store," Molly said, more sharply than she'd intended.

"Looks are one thing," said Elizabeth Andersen primly. "Respectable's quite another."

"And you should know," Thelma Thompson said.

One of the women at the far end of the room tittered.

"Respectable or not, he didn't look so bad to me," Coreyanne interjected quickly. She smiled dreamily, remembering. "Even if he is big enough to make two normal-size men. Those eyes, you know, and that deep voice, and that big, broad chest."

Even Emmy Lou paused respectfully a moment, thinking of his chest. Thelma reached for the second plate of biscuits.

Molly remembered all too clearly how big Sheriff Gavin had seemed, standing there in the sunlit doorway, remembered how the floor had bounced beneath his weight. She knew the rumors about his past, yet what she'd thought about all afternoon was not his size or his disreputable past, but how strong and safe he'd seemed, and how gentle his voice had been, and how he'd looked, blushing. And though she'd tried to forget, she could remember, all too clearly, just how warm his hand had been when it had closed so securely around hers.

The memories had been playing havoc with her good sense all afternoon. If she wasn't careful, they'd be wandering through her dreams, as well.

"Would anyone like more tea?" she said, picking up her cup.

Witt had rather liked the song, "Clementine." He could have sat through it without a word of complaint three, or even four times running, if he'd had to.

After a half hour spent listening to it being played, over and over and over, and badly at that, he was debating whether to shoot the piano or the piano player. Neither one would be considered a great loss, so far as he could tell, though the miners might miss the piano.

"He gets this way every now and then."

"What? Who?" Witt wrenched his gaze from the burly piano player.

"Crazy Mike." Fred hooked a thumb in the piano player's direction. "He gets this way every now and then. Decent sort when he's sober, and the best miner in five counties, but he's got a temper like a sore-footed mule when he's drunk and a kick to match when he starts throwing those fists around."

"Does he get drunk often?"

"Couple times a year, maybe. Maybe three."

"It's the melancholy, shee," said Billie Jenkins, leaning across the table confidingly. He was having a hard time keeping his head up. Jackson's whiskey wasn't half the quality of the Grand's, but it was a whole lot cheaper, and Billie had been enthusiastically saving money ever since he'd walked in the door.

"Ol' Mike, he had a girl, onct," he added by way of explanation. "Pretty girl. He was gonna marry her."

Fred grinned. "Named Clementine, if you haven't figured it out."

"She left 'im." Billie pooched out his lips in drunken frown. "Broke his heart, poor bashtard."

"Women'll do that to you," said Bert Potter, blinking and nodding sagely over his half-filled glass. "Every time, women'll do that to you."

"Only if you're damn fool enough to get hitched to 'em," said Josiah Andersen heartily. He winked at Witt. "Or if you can't get rid of 'em once you do."

Witt's jaw tightened. He shoved his chair back.

He'd shoot himself before he'd sit through another round of that damned song, and he wasn't about to try pushing his authority to convince the miner to stop.

"You'll excuse me, gentlemen," he said. "Work to do."

Whatever objections his companions might have made were cut short by a furious bellow from the direction of the piano.

"Gol durn it! Don't you go tellin' *me* what t'play!"

Crazy Mike surged to his feet like an angry buffalo, all snorts and dangerous, threatening bulk. The crash of his chair falling echoed loudly in the sudden silence.

One of his companions gave him a queasy grin. "Ah, now, Mike, you know we didn't mean nothin' by it."

Mike glared at the cringing men in front of him. "You told me t'quit playin'."

"Didn't tell yuh t'quit! Just t'play somethin' differnt."

Mike advanced a step. The miners retreated two.

"You din't like my song."

"Not t'say we didn't *like* it," said one of his hapless friends.

"'Clementine's' a *fine* song, Mike, just fine," the other hastily assured him. "But dammit! You been playin' it fer God knows how long an'—"

"Don't cuss!" Mike roared. "You know I don't approve uv cussin'!"

Three steps in retreat. "Sure, Mike. Sorry about that. Din't mean t'— That is—"

"Ah, hell," said the man beside Witt. "That'll about do it for tonight, I'm thinking."

The patrons nearest the door abandoned their drinks without a backward glance and escaped into the night. The freckle-faced boy, who'd been collecting empty glasses at another table, slowly set the ones he held back down, then sidled closer, eager for a better view.

The sharp crack of a pistol made even Witt jump. Crazy Mike wasn't wearing a gun belt—most men didn't even own a gun—so he must have carried it shoved in the waistband of his pants. Right now the weapon was pointing at the floor, which had a new hole in it and a number of fresh wood chips scattered across the surface.

Witt quietly got to his feet.

"Ain't *nobody* tellin' me what to play," Crazy Mike insisted, swinging around to confront the saloon's wary patrons.

"Put the gun down." Witt didn't raise his voice, but in the silence, his words carried clearly.

The miner's eyes narrowed suspiciously. "Who're you?"

"I'm the new sheriff, and I'd appreciate it if you'd put the gun down."

Mike grunted. "Make me."

Witt studied him for a moment, then slowly unbuckled his own gun belt. He set it on the table, much to the consternation of his drinking companions, then held up his hands, palms out.

"Put the gun down, Mike."

Mike shot a hole through the painted tin ceiling.

"Watch the damned chandelier!" warned the outraged proprietor.

This time, Mike deliberately aimed at that battered brass fixture. His shot sent bits of paint flying from a new hole in the ceiling a good four feet to the right of the first.

"God dammit!" Jackson roared.

Mike swung toward him, the gun wobbling in his unsteady hand. "Don't cuss. Ain't right t'cuss."

A warning gesture from Witt stopped Jackson from fishing beneath the bar for the gun that was undoubtedly hidden there.

"Sure, Mike. Sorry," Jackson said through gritted teeth.

"Whyn't you come back and play fer us, Mike?" one of the miner's friends suggested.

Mike shot the piano. Twice.

He would have shot it again, but he was out of bullets.

Moving slowly, with both hands up where Crazy Mike could see them, Witt worked his way toward the angry miner. The crowd happily moved out of his way. No one offered to help.

For that small favor, Witt was devoutly grateful. He'd dealt with enough Crazy Mike's over the years to know that "help" of that nature only made things worse. To men like Mike, one man coming after them was a joke.

Half a dozen eager citizens was a threat that provoked more violence and got a lot of people hurt.

And it would take half a dozen normal-size men to stop someone as big as Mike.

He hadn't met many men even as big as he was, but Witt was willing to bet Mike topped him by a good two inches or so and outweighed him by at least fifty pounds. The man had arms that looked like tree trunks and fists the size of a nine-pound sledgehammer.

Five feet from the miner, Witt stopped.

"Nice night out, Mike," he said conversationally. "Let's you and me go for a walk, shall we?"

Crazy Mike tossed aside the useless gun and came at him like a bear, roaring with rage, shoulders hunched, eyes glittering with the light of battle.

Witt sidestepped, then punched him in the gut as he passed. Hard.

The miner's roar died in a choking grunt as he doubled over, clutching his middle. He staggered, tried to straighten.

Witt hit him again.

Crazy Mike sagged, then slowly toppled onto the floor, face first. The floor shook when he landed.

Witt could hear the crunch as Mike's nose smashed into the wood. He winced and ruefully rubbed his knuckles. The damn fool was so drunk, he didn't have the sense to roll.

Silence held Jackson's saloon in a grip of iron.

One of Mike's friends stepped forward, fists half raised in the wary, defiant stance of a man who felt obligated to defend his friend but wasn't all that happy about it. Witt looked at him, raised one eyebrow in silent inquiry. The fellow wavered for a moment, then lowered his fists and sheepishly slunk back into the crowd.

Witt scanned the rest of the gaping patrons. "A couple of you gentlemen want to help me get him to the jail?"

"You're gonna put Crazy Mike in *jail?*"

"Well, I'll be a—"

"Damn straight he's going to put Mike in jail," said the mayor, pushing through the crowd. "It's about time Mike realized he can't go around doing as he damn well pleases."

"You might want to watch your language," Witt advised, suppressing a grin. "The gentleman clearly objects to vulgarities."

The gentleman in question groaned and tried to shove to his knees. Witt reached to help him up. Mike's head bobbled. He stared at the proffered hand for a moment, bleary-eyed, his mouth working like a dying fish's. In the end, drink and the effects of a broken nose won out. He glared, grunted, then his eyes rolled up in his head as he quietly slumped to the floor in a dead faint.

Chapter Four

It was nearing ten when Molly called good-night to the last of her friends. This late, most of the town had settled peaceably behind their doors. Lamps shone through windows, but here and there the houses were dark, their inhabitants long since tucked into bed.

A few people strolled past her—a man alone, head down and hurrying home; two men laughing; a couple, arms entwined, oblivious to anything outside their world of two.

The sight of them only reinforced her sense of isolation.

Four years. That's how long she'd been a widow.

Sometimes, especially whenever she glanced at the photograph of Richard that hung in her small parlor, it seemed like only yesterday that he'd gone out to work and never came back. There were still times, usually when she was tired and her thoughts had wandered, when she would hear a sound and look up, expecting to see him walk in the door. And sometimes, in the night, she'd turn in her sleep and reach for him, wanting his warmth and his strength, needing to feel his lean, angular body curled around her, shielding her from the world outside their door.

There were even times when she was wide-awake, without the distraction of wandering thoughts or a weary body, when she would find herself physically aching for his touch and the glory of what they'd shared in bed.

Especially what they'd shared in bed.

She had never been one of those simpering misses who blushed at the mere thought of kissing a man, but she knew, now, that she had been fortunate in her choice of husband, for Richard had been kind and more than willing to teach her the secrets of what was possible between a man and a woman who loved each other. She'd never asked him where he'd learned his secrets, and he had never told her. She'd never thought it mattered, for once he'd married her, he had given everything to her—his heart and soul; his dreams. Eventually, even his life.

It was his dying that made her angry. He had gone into the mines because he wanted to earn more money to pay off the debt they'd incurred to start the store and a little extra to put aside for the future. Richard had always been impatient, eager to move ahead, and he'd seen the mines as the fastest way to get what he'd wanted. They'd quarreled about it horribly.

She regretted the quarrels. She regretted even more that, in the end, she'd been proven right.

Immediately after Richard's death, when creditors were pressing her to close the store and sell off the inventory, she'd spent long, sleepless nights scheming how to save Richard's dream and her children's future.

Calhan's would be different from all the other dry

goods stores, she'd decided. Better. Bigger, someday, when she could manage it.

Richard hadn't been buried a week before she began changing things. At first, the changes were more for distraction from her grief than for the work itself. Eventually, however, the new ways had taken on a life of their own, challenging her and helping to make the long hours and sometimes exhausting routine more bearable.

She'd started with a few eye-catching displays on the counters and tabletops. Gradually, as her confidence in herself and her ideas had grown, she'd ordered more merchandise that her competitors didn't carry and tried more adventurous approaches to displaying what she had.

The man mannequin had been the talk of the town. People had wandered in just to have a look at the thing, and often as not they'd wandered out again with something else they hadn't planned on buying. She'd paid for it in three months with the profits from the extra sales.

What she had realized, and none of her male competitors had yet understood, was that women were the ones who controlled the money in most households, not the men.

Oh, men were quick enough to buy tools and hardware and an occasional pouch of tobacco—they were, she'd found, particularly fond of fancy patent tools— but they were generally happy to pass responsibility for everything else to their wives. Women bought the family's food and shoes, chose their clothes or the cloth to make them, and decided which medicines and tonics to stock to keep them well. It was the women who selected the furniture and decorated the home, then bought all the supplies to keep that home swept and polished and functioning as it ought.

It was an insight that had changed her life because once a woman was in her store, Molly knew how to hold her attention long enough to tempt her to open her pocketbook.

She hadn't looked back since.

Sometimes she thought she didn't dare. Though four years of hard work had paid off the debts and allowed her to put a little money aside, she couldn't help worrying about the future. She still needed an occasional loan to finance her expansion. Was, in fact, considering her largest loan yet for a move that would increase the size of Calhan's by half again. But what if the state was hit with another panic like the one in '93, when the price of silver plummeted and nobody had any money for anything, even sometimes the essentials? What if the coal ran out and the mines had to close? What if something happened to *her?*

What if, what if, what if. There were so many things that could go wrong and so little she could do to stop them if they did. And, oh! how much easier it would be if only there was someone to share the worries and responsibilities with her, someone on whom she could depend, no matter what.

Molly drew her shawl closer about her shoulders, shivering a little in the cool night air. She didn't usually waste time thinking about such things, but tonight, somehow, she couldn't stop.

When she reached Main Street, rather than crossing it as she usually did, then walking down Elm Street to get home, she turned to the right. She'd pass the store on the way.

And the jail, a small voice inside her said.

She stifled the voice and kept walking.

This time of night, even Main Street was quiet, the buildings dark except at either end of the street where Elk City's three saloons were lighted and open for business.

A burst of masculine laughter coming from somewhere ahead of her made her stop. When the jail door opened, spilling the faint light of an oil lamp across the walk, she muttered a word she would have washed Dickie's mouth out for using and shrank into the shadowed doorway of Dincler's Barbershop.

A moment later, half a dozen men stepped out, laughing and joking among themselves. They clumped off the boardwalk and into the street, clustered like reluctant partygoers leaving the fun.

"You take good care of your guest, now, Sheriff, you hear?" one of the men called.

"Don't let his snoring keep you up!"

The attempt at humor brought more laughter from the men, but not a word from the sheriff. He stood, a silent presence in the faint wash of lamplight, watching them, neither friendly nor distant. Simply...*there*.

The laughter died. A couple of the men shuffled their feet.

"You did good, Gavin," someone said at last. "Just want you to know that. You did good."

The others murmured agreement. They would, she knew, have been more comfortable if the sheriff had laughed or joked right back at them, or made one of those vulgar comments men were prone to when they thought ladies weren't present.

One among them broke the spell by clapping a companion on the back.

"Come on, boys. The night's still young. Wouldn't

want to upset the missus by comin' home too soon, now, would we?''

To Molly's relief, they headed away from her, down toward the other end of town and the two saloons whose lights shone in the distance. She hadn't worried that any of them would bother her if they did discover her huddling in the shadows, but men were as gossipy as women, no matter how much they denied it. The last thing she needed was word going round that she'd been hiding in the shadows outside the jail at an hour when a sensible woman would have been home and in bed.

To her dismay, the sheriff lingered in the open doorway.

He propped his shoulder against the frame, crossed his arms over his chest, and tilted his head to stare at the star-swept sky. The light behind him outlined the broad shoulders, deep chest and long, powerful legs, but left his face in shadow.

Why didn't he just go in?

Why didn't she just walk past? a mocking little voice inside her head demanded. A polite nod, a friendly greeting. *Good evening,* maybe. Or maybe just, *Sheriff.* And he'd say, *Ma'am,* or, *Evening,* and that would be it.

And if he *did* say something, she'd just explain that she'd been startled by the men suddenly emerging onto the street, which would be true. He'd nod, and maybe he'd apologize for having startled her, and then she'd say she had to get home, and he'd say, *Of course,* and maybe, *Good night,* and then maybe he'd go in and shut the door and forget all about it. Forget all about her.

Her stomach twisted, just at the thought.

Molly peeped out of her hiding place. The man hadn't moved an inch.

He made a compelling figure standing there, his big, powerful body cast half in golden lamplight, half in shadow. She still couldn't see his face, but she remembered with disconcerting clarity the strong lines of cheek and jaw, the piercing clarity of those blue-gray eyes that seemed to take in everything at a glance.

From the look of him, he might have been a thousand miles away.

Was he thinking of his wife? she wondered. Or of another woman, perhaps? A woman he'd loved so much that his wife had chosen to divorce him rather than live with the constant reminder that he had set another before her?

It had to have been another woman. She'd scarcely met the man, but she couldn't imagine anything else he might have done that would have driven a woman to the scandal of divorcing him.

Yet if he'd loved another, why hadn't he remarried the instant he was free of his first marriage?

Whatever it was that haunted him, he evidently found no solace in those cold, distant stars for he straightened suddenly and, without a glance to either side, turned and stepped into the building. An instant later, the door clapped shut behind him, throwing the street back into darkness.

Molly sank into her own shadows, heart pounding, fighting against a sudden urge to knock on the door and ask if she could help, if there weren't something she could do to fill his yearning silence.

The thought was utter madness.

She forced herself to wait a minute, then two, to be sure he wouldn't return. When she could stand the wait no longer, she tugged her shawl more closely about her and hurried across the street, turned toward home and walked as fast as her feet could carry her.

Witt picked up the oil lamp he'd left on his desk and carried it back to the single, windowless cell that served as Elk City's jail. His first guest was a great deal too large for the lumpy, metal-framed bed. Crazy Mike's big feet, still clad in their heavy miner's boots—no one had been the least inclined to make him more comfortable by removing them—stuck out over the end by a good eight inches. His head was propped at the other end with only the single thin pillow to cushion the steel frame.

He looked like hell, but his broken nose had stopped bleeding long ago. One of his friends, an unprepossessing gentleman rejoicing in the name of Gimpy Joe, had washed off the worst of the blood, but that was as far as anyone had been willing to go.

Mike hadn't roused to any of it. Having at last yielded to the influence of all the whiskey he'd consumed at Jackson's, he'd gone from a faint to a dead sleep from which the angels would have a hard time rousing him before he'd slept it off.

Witt made sure the cell's chamber pot was within Mike's reach if he did wake up, checked the lock on the cell door one last time, then retreated to his own small room beside the cell. The only real differences between the two spaces were that the walls of his room were painted wood, not raw metal bars, and he had a window and a door that wasn't anywhere near thick enough to shut out the sound of Mike's snoring.

Eventually, he'd have to find a proper place to live, but for right now, this would serve. So long as he didn't end up with too many guests like Crazy Mike, that is.

Slowly, he undressed. Hat, vest, gun belt he hung from nails driven into the wall beside the bed. His boots, side by side, claimed the floor at the foot. With every movement, the soft rustle of the paper bag in his shirt pocket reminded him that there were other things in life besides barren rooms and drunken miners.

Slowly, he pulled the small bag of chocolates out, then set it on the rickety table beside his bed. In the lamplight, he could see the stains where the oil of the chocolate had seeped through the paper.

He'd already eaten three of them, and with every slight rustle of the paper, with ever sweet bite of the chocolate, he'd found himself thinking of Mrs. Calhan.

She'd laughed at him, there in the store. He'd felt it, even though she'd clearly taken pains to cover her amusement beneath that sweet, friendly smile of hers.

The thought made him droop. He did that to women, made them laugh. A big man like him, clumsy and hulking and likely as not to get his tongue tangled around every other word, at least when pretty women like Mrs. Calhan were around. He'd often wondered why Clara had married him, knowing how she liked everything around her to be just so. But, then, they'd grown up together and she hadn't had much to choose from, so maybe he'd just been the best of a bad lot.

The thought never brought much comfort, but it was better than admitting she had used him until she had a better offer, then discarded him as easily as she'd have tossed out an old shoe.

Strange how he never felt a fool when he was with men. Not that he'd ever been what you could call talkative, but at least he didn't mumble and stumble, and God forbid, turn red at every other word. Not when he was with men.

And not when he was around children, either. He liked children and he usually found, once they'd gotten over their dismay at his sheer size, that they liked him and were comfortable around him. Kids never expected much of a man except that he be a man. But a woman, now...

Witt frowned, then picked up the bag of chocolates, turning it in his hands, remembering.

Women like Clara—pretty, marriageable women— seemed to think a man should have a tongue that worked slick as silk and always had just the right words on the tip of it. His tongue had never worked that way and he didn't expect it ever would.

He knew he'd made a fool of himself in Calhan's this afternoon.

He'd been staring at Mrs. Calhan and thinking how smooth her skin looked, and how pretty her hair was— brown like a thrush's wing, with a dozen colors all mixed in so subtly that you couldn't really say it was *brown,* but you couldn't say exactly what it was, either. Maybe if he saw it in the sun, free of that neat little twist she kept it in—

Witt bit his lower lip, cutting off the thought, and gently set the bag of chocolates back.

The thought of that drift of hair on her cheek and nape had plagued him something fierce. Even as he'd gone about his business, introducing himself to the businessfolk up and down Main Street and getting the lay of the land, he'd been thinking about those wayward strands of hair and how soft they'd feel, brushing against his fingers.

The thought of Gordon Hancock's fingers sifting through her unbound hair had been enough to make him grind his teeth.

But there was no sense thinking thoughts like that. It wasn't right, and all it would do would be to lead him into trouble.

It was only with Clara that he'd ever gotten up the courage to go courting, and that because he'd known her all his life, and she'd been pretty and willing, especially once he'd inherited his father's house and his father's savings. But once she'd seen what married life was like with a clumsy brute like him, she'd started looking around for something better.

There were times when that made him angry, but mostly it just made him ashamed that he hadn't been able to keep her happy, that he hadn't pleased her as a man was supposed to please a woman.

She'd certainly never taken any pleasure from his lovemaking, no matter how careful he'd been to make things comfortable for her, to not put his weight on her or drive into her too hard. At times he'd ached to let go and simply enjoy what everyone else seemed to find a pretty straightforward and simple act, but he never had.

He could remember her lying beneath him on the bed, staring up at nothing while he'd tried to rouse some feeling in her. He'd tried kissing her, but he wasn't much of a kisser—Clara had taken pains to tell him so, not long after they were married—and even as he'd shuddered with pleasure at the feel of her soft skin, at the warmth of it beneath his lips, he'd cringed at how she'd turned away, or sighed, or, worse, gritted her teeth and forced herself to kiss him back.

He'd loved her breasts, so heavy, full and soft, so white beneath his sun-browned hand. She didn't often let him touch them—she said his hands were too rough and callused. She'd never let him kiss her there. He'd never tried, though sometimes just the thought of them had been enough to make him sweat and ache with yearning.

Always when he'd finished, she'd rolled away from him and gotten out of bed to wash herself as if his touch had dirtied her. And always he'd lain there listening to the sounds of her bathing, burning with his shame and his need and his hunger. He'd never touched her afterward, but while she slept he'd often lain awake for hours, listening to her breathe and wondering, if he just took her and used her as his blood urged him to, would she cry out then in pleasure and delight?

It had to be him, some lack within himself that made him incapable of pleasing her.

Oh, he'd heard the tales that women didn't much care for such things, but he knew there were decent women who loved their husbands and took as much pleasure from the marriage bed as did their men. His own father had told him once that if he was kind and took the time to please his wife before he took his own pleasure, that she'd respond by giving him back more than he could imagine.

But then, his father and mother had loved each other, while Clara— Well, if she'd ever loved him, his own oafish need had killed it, and driven her to another.

Samuel Kroshak had been the kind of man he'd never be. Sleek and gentlemanly, well dressed and of a size to fit in a lady's parlor without making the chairs creak or the floorboards groan. Kroshak hadn't looked like an outsize fool if he picked up one of the fine china teacups that Clara had taken such pride in and he'd known about the theater and dining out and just what to say to a lady to make her laugh.

Clara had met the man at a dance. Witt had been on

duty and hadn't much wanted to go anyway, knowing
he'd make a fool of himself lumbering around the dance
floor and stepping on her toes as he always did. So
Clara had gone alone and had danced the waltz with
the handsome stranger who was visiting with friends in
town. She'd discovered that folks sat up and noticed
when she whirled around the floor on Samuel Kroshak's
arm instead of laughing and taking bets on how long
her toes would last, as they did whenever Witt reluctantly led her out.

Kroshak had come visiting the day afterward, then
the day after that. Witt blamed himself. He'd been such
a blind fool that he hadn't seen what either of them
were about until it was far too late to stop it.

He remembered clearly the day Clara had told him
she wanted a divorce, that she didn't care what it took
but she wanted out, wanted to be done with him. Her
demand had shamed him, but it hadn't surprised him.
Not by then. He'd agreed to take the blame, even agreed
to perjure himself and say he was the adulterer, not her.
He'd thought of it as payment due for all his other failings as a husband and a lover.

In the five years since, he'd occasionally considered
the possibility of remarrying—assuming he could find
a decent woman who wouldn't expect too much of him,
that is—but the thought of such a cold union had chilled
him to the bone. Occasionally he'd taken comfort with
a whore, but it had been shallow comfort, and fleeting,
and he'd paid far more for it in guilt and shame than
he'd ever paid in gold.

Now here he was, little more than a day in town and
already having troubling thoughts about a woman
who'd been kind to him. A decent widow woman with
children to raise and a reputation to protect.

Witt eyed the small, crumpled paper bag on the side table, remembering Mrs. Calhan and the way she'd looked when he'd opened his eyes after tasting that first chocolate. As if she were going to laugh, not at him, but with him. As if she understood exactly how he felt with that sweet chocolate melting on his tongue, spilling all that gooey filling. Like he'd been given a taste of paradise, right there in the middle of Calhan's General Store.

The memory alone was enough to start him wanting.

With a curse, Witt roughly turned down the lamp until the flame winked out, plunging the room into darkness.

Chapter Five

"An' then he grabbed the gun, an' you all know just how crazy ol' Crazy Mike can be! Mike tried to shoot 'im again, but that didn't scare him none. Nosirree! Mike got off a half dozen shots, mebbe more, but the sheriff, he just went a'wadin' in there an' grabbed that gun, an' then he clobbered ol' Mike. Wham! Straight to the jaw!"

Tom Seiffert, at twelve the envy of all his peers because he swept out Jackson's saloon, a known den of vice and depravity, was holding court in the alley behind Dincler's Barbershop.

Dickie, relegated to the far edge of the circle because he was the smallest and youngest, tried to squeeze between two of the older boys so he'd be close enough not to miss a word Tom said.

"But then ol' Mike, he got up, mad as a gut-shot bear, a'roarin' an' a'ragin', an' he goes at the sheriff again."

"What'd the sheriff do?"

"What'd he do?" Tom looked around his crowd of awe-struck admirers, clearly relishing the attention. "Why, the sheriff hit'im again, that's what he did. Pow!

Right to the chin. Laid ol' Mike out flat on the floor, just like that!''

"Oooh!"

"He really flattened *Crazy Mike?*"

Tom nodded. "Flatter'n a mackerel!''

Seven boys' eyes went wide with awe and envy that one of their number should have witnessed such a memorably heroic deed.

"Ain't nobody ever done that before,'' said one, looking around him as if for confirmation. "Leastwise, not that *I* ever heard of!''

"An' you got to see it *all?*"

"Yup.'' Tom's skinny chest expanded with the sweet air breathed by those who held their audience in the palm of their hand. "Saw every single bit of it, first to last.''

Dickie forgot that, as the littlest, he was supposed to keep his mouth shut. "And Crazy Mike really shot at the *sheriff?*"

Tom's head bobbed. "Yup. That first shot just missed the sheriff by a hair. An' the second went whistlin' right by me!''

"Weren't you scairt?''

As one, seven boys swayed forward to hear the answer. Dickie almost stopped breathing.

"Scairt? Me!'' Tom grinned. "Heck, yes, I was scairt! What d'yuh think? I ain't never had no one shootin' at me before. I ducked under the nearest table so fast you'd'uv thought I was a jackrabbit.''

"And that's when Mike shot the piano?''

"Yup. Blewee! Jus' like that! An' that *really* made the sheriff mad.''

"He got mad because of a *piano?*"

"Musta been, 'cause he didn't do nothin' when Crazy

Mike shot at *him*. But then Mike shoots the piano an' *wham!*''

Dickie let out the breath he'd been holding on a long sigh of delight. He'd known from the minute he saw him that the sheriff was the kind of man that heroes were made of, but he hadn't expected to have his judgment proved right so quickly, or so marvelously well.

''Didn't nobody else try an' get in the fight?'' one of the other boys demanded, clearly hoping for more.

''There was a few others thinkin' about it,'' said Tom. ''You know, Fat Sam and Gimpy Joe and them. Four or five, anyway. But they took one look at how the sheriff had laid out ol' Mike so quick, and they snuck outta there like whupped puppies.''

''Whupped puppies? Really?''

A collective sigh of delight and envy escaped Tom's audience.

''Whupped puppies,'' breathed Dickie, awed.

Dickie shared the tale over lunch that afternoon.

''An then ol' Mike, he got off about a dozen shots, bam, bam, bam!'' A spoon wasn't much of a substitute for a gun, but a fellow had to make do with what was available. ''Bullets flyin' everywhere. Tom says he didn't hardly know which way to run, so he just dived under a table and stayed there. Tom says the sheriff never even blinked. Just like Deadwood Dick, he said, or maybe Jesse James.''

''Put your spoon on your plate, where it belongs.'' His mother frowned. ''You know I don't like you listening to those tall tales that Tom Seiffert tells.''

''But what happened then?'' Bonnie demanded.

''Well, then, see, some of the other miners came at him. Dozen, maybe more.''

Bonnie, ever the stickler for accuracy, frowned. "How many exactly? Didn't Tom say?"

Dickie gave his sister a superior look. "He was too busy dodgin' bullets and fists to waste time countin'. But it was *lots*."

"*I'd* have counted, if *I'd* been there," Bonnie said.

"Bet you wouldn't've!"

"Bet I would!"

"No, sir! You'd've been screamin' an'—"

"Would not!"

"Would, too!"

"Children!"

One glance at their mother's face was enough. They guiltily subsided.

"We do not quarrel at the table. In fact, we do not quarrel ever. If you can't discuss a topic calmly and rationally, then you don't discuss it at all." She frowned, first at Dickie, then at Bonnie. "Is that understood?"

"Yes, ma'am," said Bonnie, glaring at her plate.

"Yes'm," Dickie mumbled.

The minute she looked away, Bonnie made a horrible face at him. Dickie made a worse one right back. And stuck out his tongue for good measure.

If their mother noticed, she gave no sign of it. She was frowning at her bowl of soup and for a moment seemed to have forgotten they were there. She tugged at the edge of the tablecloth, cleared her throat, and said, "So then what happened?"

Dickie tried to remember where he'd left off in his tale. It was kind of hard, because Bonnie had distracted him and the details Tom had shared were getting a little blurred. Fortunately, he'd read enough to know exactly how these things were supposed to play out.

"Well, so then there's all these big, big miners comin' at him, see, so the sheriff, he ducks when the first one swings. And then he hits the next guy, an' the next. Wham! Pow!"

"And then what happened?" Bonnie insisted when his imagination ran out of steam.

"And then nothin'. That was it. The sheriff won an' Tom, he says most those miners spent the night in the town jail."

"All of them?" Bonnie demanded. "In the *jail?*"

"It's no more than they deserved," said their mother. She abruptly shoved back from the table. "You two hurry up. I have to be back at the store at one and there's still the dishes to wash."

"Heard there was some trouble at Jackson's Saloon last night," Emmy Lou Trainer said a couple hours later, rather more loudly than was necessary.

She'd come in for a packet of pins and a bottle of blueing, or so she said. Everyone present—and there were a great deal more people than could usually be found in Calhan's on a Saturday afternoon—knew what had really brought her into the store: exactly the same thing that had brought them.

Molly bit her tongue and bent to dig a packet of pins out of the drawer where they were kept. There were so many people in the store they were tripping over each other, but nobody was buying much of anything. All they wanted was to talk about the sheriff and Crazy Mike and that stupid piano.

She'd heard all she wanted to about all three of them. Last night she'd scarcely slept for thinking of how empty and echoing the house seemed, and of how the sheriff had looked, standing alone in that open doorway, staring at the stars. This morning, common sense had prevailed. She wasn't going to waste time thinking of DeWitt Gavin and his exploits.

That resolution would be a lot easier to keep, however, if others would tend to their business at least half as much as she tried to tend to hers.

"I told the town council, didn't I?" Emmy Lou continued, raising her voice a little more. "Don't get a sheriff that doesn't know the town, I said. That little incident last night just goes to prove I was right. Scarce one full day in town and there's that new sheriff the council hired, brawling in Jackson's while a madman shoots it up. Mr. Trainer wouldn't have stood for it. *He—*"

"Would have been hiding under a table pretending he didn't hear anything at all," muttered Thelma Thompson under her breath.

Thelma had been trying to talk Molly down on the price of some blue ribbons to go with the Sheppard's plaid she'd bought the day before, but without success. Being balked on a bargain was making her peevish and eager for a fight.

"...would have seen right off that trouble was brewing!" So far as Molly could tell, Emmy Lou hadn't paused for breath. "After all, he's been here long enough to know which troublemakers to watch out for. Especially when they're drinking. Let men like that get a little liquor in them and there's just no telling what they'll do."

"Huh!" said Thelma, a little louder this time. "Since when did that ever stop you from telling it?"

Emmy Lou bristled. "I beg your pardon?"

Old man Fetzer, who was pretending to inspect a coffee grinder, perked up at the prospect of a catfight.

Molly slapped the packet of pins on the counter. "What kind of blueing did you want, Emmy Lou? The powdered? Or the one in a bottle?"

"The powdered," Emmy Lou said, glaring at Thelma. "I'll have you know that my Zacharius—"

"Large or small?"

"Small. My Zacharius would never—no, make that large—he'd never have let things get out of hand like that. Imagine! Letting that man shoot the piano!"

"What's so bad about shooting the piano?" Thelma demanded, the ribbon entirely forgotten. "It isn't as if we ever borrowed it for church services any more. Not since we got our own, anyways."

"Blew it to smithereens. That's what *I* heard," Mr. Fetzer said with satisfaction.

Emmy Lou cast them both a fulminating glance, then turned to the room at large where she had all the audience her soul could want. By now, no one was even pretending to shop.

"It's not just the piano, you know," she said. "It's the fact that the town council hired a perfect stranger for sheriff—a *divorced* stranger, I might add!—and what's the first thing that happens?"

"Here's your blueing, Emmy Lou. Will that be all?"

She might as well have talked to the wall. No mere box of laundry blueing could stop Emmy Lou Trainer in full cry.

"Why, a shoot-'em-up brawl in the worst dive in Elk City, that's what happens!" Emmy Lou threw her hands wide, inviting the others to share her outrage.

"Not a *brawl*," Davey Zellerhoff objected from over in men's haberdashery. "I heard there was a few shots fired and only two miners in the fight. For sure not enough to count as a *brawl*."

"Half a dozen shots or more, and nobody knows how many in the fight," said Harry Nickerson, who'd left the livery stable to take care of itself for "a minute or two" a good half hour ago. "And they shot Jackson's chandelier, too! *And* the bar! I heard there was spilt whiskey all *over* the place!"

The news of the spilled whiskey brought frowns from all the menfolk present.

"Eleven shots," piped up Dora Beidlebaum, happily abandoning her perusal of the cookbooks. "My neighbor was there and he said eleven shots, besides the ones to the piano. And four miners and the sheriff having it out, right there in the saloon."

"It's a wonder no one was hurt!" said someone at the back of the store.

Old man Fetzer cackled happily and gave the coffee grinder an extra spin. "Wonder is old Mike ain't kill't someone afore now. I seen 'im in a drunk and I'm here t'tell you it ain't a purty sight."

Molly had a sudden mental picture of DeWitt Gavin sprawled lifeless on the floor, bright-red blood staining his broad chest. The thought made her feel queasily light-headed. She gripped the edge of the counter, fighting against nausea.

Thelma eyed her, frowning. "You all right, Molly? You look almighty pale of a sudden."

Before Molly could get a word out, the screen door swung open and the sheriff himself walked in. A stifling silence fell over the store.

The man who, according to which tale you listened to, had faced a hail of bullets and a roomful of drunken bullies without flinching, stopped dead in the doorway. A lesser man would have turned and fled. DeWitt Gavin, however, was the stuff of heroes.

He set his jaw, squared his shoulders, then politely tugged at the brim of his hat. "Ladies."

Only the meanest faultfinder would claim there was a little more white to his eyes than there ought to have been.

Emmy Lou's mouth pinched tight shut.

Thelma grinned. "Sheriff. Good to see your hide's still in one piece."

He said something indistinguishable at the back of his throat and nodded to the men, who solemnly nodded back.

The air in the room was so thick you could have ladled it out for soup.

Molly swallowed against a mouth gone suddenly dry. "Good afternoon, Sheriff."

"Ma'am." With a wary glance at the silently disapproving Emmy Lou, he sidled over to the counter.

And then he just stood there, staring at her.

Embarrassed, she told herself. Tongue-tied to find himself in a roomful of people who'd obviously been talking about him.

Which didn't stop her from feeling a strange, half-forgotten heat work its way through her like a warm breeze after a long, cold, bitter winter.

It was Mr. Fetzer, craning his scrawny, wattled neck to get a better look, that reminded her of their audience.

"Can I help you, Sheriff?" she said.

DeWitt Gavin cleared his throat and looked away, toward the back of the store. "I need a bucket."

"A bucket," said Molly blankly. He was even bigger than she remembered. Much, much bigger.

"Yes, ma'am. For the jail."

She had a sudden vision of herself cradled against that broad chest, sheltered in those strong arms. The vision was dangerously close to what she'd imagined in all those sleep-robbing dreams she'd suffered through last night. What little air was left in her lungs slipped out with a throat-tightening squeak.

His gaze swung back to her. Molly forced herself to breathe.

His eyes were definitely more piercing than she remembered.

"A tin bucket," he said. "With a handle?"

"Of course." She forced herself to smile. "They're here at the back. If you'll just follow me…?"

She had to come out around the counter, which brought her so close she could easily have touched him. She was almost positive the hem of her skirt brushed against his trouser leg. It troubled her she'd even noticed. If he had, he gave no sign of it.

The combined gazes of a dozen curious townsfolk kept them company all the way to the back of the store where the buckets were stacked against the wall. Blindly, she snatched up several samples. Their tinny clatter covered the sound of her own pounding heart.

"We have several sizes. The ten-quart size here is forty-six cents." She thrust one at him and almost dropped two others.

The rolled wood handle spun off the tips of his fingers, sending the bucket crashing to the floor. They both froze.

"Need any help back there?" Mr. Fetzer's sly offer drew appreciative snickers from the crowd.

Molly stiffened. The heat in her cheeks was reaching dangerous proportions.

She held up another bucket. "This one's fifty-four cents. This is sixty-five."

This close to him, air seemed in dangerously short

supply. She held up the largest, breathless. "And this one's twenty quarts for eighty cents."

DeWitt Gavin stooped to retrieve the one he'd dropped. "This'll do fine."

"Great," said Molly. She stared, fascinated, as his hand slid into his pants pocket. The tops of his knuckles were raw, as if they'd recently connected with something rough. Something like a miner's unshaven jaw.

"Fifty-four you said?" He pulled out a badly crumpled dollar bill.

Molly stared at his open palm, caught by the image of her hand resting in that big, strong, eminently masculine one. "What?"

"Fifty-four cents, right?"

She drew in a shaking breath. "Forty-six," she said, and turned away to drop the other three buckets back where they belonged, *clank, clank, clank.*

The noise didn't quite cover up the sound of more snickering.

Molly turned back to find his hand still stretched toward her.

"You don't want me to bill the mayor?" she said, strangely reluctant to take the money from his hand.

He shook his head. "I'll be the one that's using it."

She had no choice. Taking care not to touch him, she plucked the bill from his palm. As she headed back to her place behind the counter, she was conscious of Emmy Lou and Thelma watching them, expressions sharp with disapproval on the one hand, and avid speculation on the other.

Everyone else pretended to be fascinated by whatever object was closest to hand. Molly wasn't fooled. Davey Zellerhof was a bachelor with absolutely no use for the babies' nightcaps he was frowning over, and Harry

Nickerson had as much use for that music box he was eyeing as his horses had for hats.

Her hand fisted around DeWitt Gavin's crumpled dollar. They were nothing but a pack of prying busybodies. The minute the sheriff was gone she'd send them about their business so quick their heads would spin.

With every step he took behind her, she could feel the floor give a little, then spring back.

Molly slid behind the counter, but before she could ring up the sale on the cash register, the sheriff was pulling the screen door open. "Ma'am," he said, with a quick nod in her direction. "Ladies."

By the time the screen door swung shut behind him, the only thing left in the doorway was sunshine.

Old Mr. Fetzer scuttled over to the front window, craning to watch the sheriff until he was out of sight. He gave a snorting little cackle. "Moves awfully fast for such a big feller, don't he?"

Davey Zellerhof tossed aside the nightcap he held. "I'm beginning to think you might be right after all, Harry. He's big enough to take on half a dozen fellows if he wanted."

"Four," said Harry Nickerson, abandoning the music box and heading for the door. "It was four. That's what Billie Jenkins said."

"First time in my life I ever felt inclined to believe old Billie," Davey said, thoughtfully following Harry out.

One by one, reluctantly, the other customers followed suit until only Thelma and Emmy Lou and Mr. Fetzer were left.

It was as she turned to deal with them that Molly realized she still had DeWitt Gavin's crumpled dollar in her hand. She hadn't even rung up his purchase, and now she would have to chase him down to return the fifty-six cents she owed him.

She wasn't sure if it was annoyance, or a leaping excitement at the excuse to see DeWitt Gavin again that made her palms sweat suddenly. She shoved the bill deep into her pocket, then surreptitiously wiped her palm on her skirt.

"Now then, Emmy Lou," she said, forcing her attention back to business. "Pins and blueing. That's it, unless you want something more."

Emmy Lou glanced at the blueing, then frowned. "That's powdered blueing, Molly. You know I always use the liquid kind."

Molly drew a steadying breath. "Large or small?" she said from between gritted teeth.

"Large. No, small. Small will do me fine."

"Take the large," Thelma said helpfully. "I was thinking your mister's shirts were looking just a bit dingy, last time I saw him."

"If you weren't blind as a bat, Thelma Thompson, you'd see that Mr. Trainer's shirts are white as an angel's wings."

"Good-lookin' feller, the sheriff," said Mr. Fetzer, companionably propping an elbow on the counter. "Wouldn't you say he was good-lookin', Missus Calhan?"

The diversion worked. Emmy Lou and Thelma's heads snapped around to study her reaction. Molly would have preferred their quarreling.

She forced a teasing smile, but her heart wasn't in it. "Not bad, Mr. Fetzer," she said. "Not bad. But not near so handsome as you."

That brought a wheezy guffaw. "If I were twenty years younger—"

"You'd still be too old," snapped Emmy Lou. She pulled out her coin purse. "How much do I owe you, Molly?"

"That's twenty-two cents, total," Molly replied, deliberately adding two cents for the aggravation. She'd had all the customers she could take for one day. Even the prospect of driving off the only one who'd bought anything didn't daunt her.

"Twenty-two!" Emmy Lou exclaimed. "My word, it's a scandal what things cost these days."

"That it is," Thelma said, more than willing to agree on that point, at least. "Now about those ribbons, Molly...."

All the frustrations and confusions that had been bubbling just beneath the surface since Molly had watched DeWitt Gavin stare at the stars suddenly came to a boil.

"Six cents a yard, Thelma," she said, sharply enough to make the older woman flinch. "And, so help me, you nag me one more time over the price and I'll double it, just for you!"

Old Mr. Fetzer's snicker died in his throat under Thelma's baleful gaze.

Chapter Six

Grimly trying to forget the stares of the townsfolk who'd been assembled in Calhan's, and even more grimly determined to squash the memory of Mrs. Calhan and how pretty she'd looked, and how surprisingly easily she'd blushed and how she hadn't smiled, even once, at his own inarticulate clumsiness, Witt filled his new bucket at the public well, then hauled it back to the jail. His previous evening's guest was gone, having roused to remorse and a pounding headache just before noon and been released shortly thereafter.

To Witt's surprise, Crazy Mike had been more admiring of the blow that brought him down than resentful.

"It's good to meet a man knows how to use his fists," he said, grinning a little, then wincing at the effort. "You and me, we oughta have us a little sparring match, just for the fun of it."

It had been Mike's approach to bathing that had convinced Witt to buy a new bucket. Rather than pour the water out into the basin Witt had provided, Mike had simply stuck his head into the bucket, sloshed it around a bit, then pulled it out and shaken it like a dog after a dunking.

The floor was still wet where the water had slopped over the rim and flooded the bare pine plank flooring.

Since Mike had seemed genuinely repentant and sworn to pay for the damages he'd caused, and Jackson himself hadn't bothered to come down to the jail to lodge a formal complaint, Witt had let the miner go with a warning. His promise of better behavior had sounded heartfelt, and Witt hadn't believed a word of it.

His overnight lodger had, however, reminded Witt of one of the many items that had to be dealt with soon: he needed to find someone to clean the place on a regular basis.

It wouldn't be much work, just sweeping up every few days and hauling his sheets and dirty clothes to the Chinese laundry at the far end of town on Fridays. Maybe a good mopping once a month. A boy like the one who'd been working in Jackson's saloon, retrieving dirty glasses and cleaning up after the patrons, would do just fine. All he had to do was find one whose parents wouldn't mind their darling paying regular visits to the town jail.

A boy who could also clean the windows, Witt thought, squinting at the dust-begrimed panes. They were so dirty that he almost needed to light a lamp to work by in the middle of the day. And there'd be meals to arrange for anyone who took up more than a night's residence and—

His thoughts were interrupted by the sound of footsteps on the boardwalk outside. An instant later, Mrs. Calhan walked in.

Witt was on his feet so quickly that his chair almost tipped over. He grabbed it just in time, sweating a little at the thought of what she must think of him, as clumsy and inarticulate as he was every time he was around her.

"Ma'am."

She smiled, a rather anxious little smile that instantly made him forget the sorry figure he cut.

"Is anything the matter?"

"You left before I could give you your change." She held out her hand. Coins glinted in her palm. "I brought it over before I could forget."

In his eagerness to escape, he'd forgotten entirely.

"Oh," Witt said. He held out his hand, palm up; she tilted her hand and let the coins spill into his. They didn't come close to touching.

"Thanks." He shoved the coins in his pocket and tried not to stare.

She really was a fine-looking woman. Tall and dignified, despite the faint blush, and though her eyes weren't sparking with laughter at the moment, they were still warm and clear under thick, brown, downcast lashes. Not a single hair had come loose from her neat arrangement.

Foolish to be disappointed that she'd been so carefully tidy.

He tried to think of something to say that would keep her there a little while longer, but nothing came. She'd given him his change and that, unfortunately, was that.

If only he'd been born with the clever tongue of a man like Hancock! He would have liked Mrs. Calhan to linger.

"Is Mr. McCord gone?" she asked, glancing at the empty cell.

"Who?"

"Crazy Mike." She smiled. "He's really rather a nice man when he's not drinking, you know."

"You know him?"

She nodded. "He comes into the store now and then. Always very polite. Rather sad, too."

Witt tried to picture a sadly polite Mike in Calhan's. His imagination failed him. "Someone said he'd had a girl."

"Clementine. Smith, I think. Clementine Smith. He was planning to marry her, but she ran off with another man." She looked a little sad at the thought. "Mr. McCord's never been quite the same since."

Witt went still. He hadn't taken to drink when Clara had left him, but he understood the temptation.

"At least he doesn't swear."

Like sunshine from behind a cloud, her smile came back, sparked with a glint of amusement in her eyes.

"Crazy Mike never swears. He's broken up every saloon in town, one time or another, but he never swears. He says his mother wouldn't approve."

Witt couldn't help but smile back. There was something so comfortably right about seeing her smile and listening to the laughter in her voice.

She didn't notice his smile because she was looking about her, a little more relaxed now than at first, and obviously curious.

"I've never been in a jail before," she admitted.

Her gaze fixed on the rapidly drying damp spot on the floor where Mike had slopped half the contents of the bucket. The dirt and dust that had covered the floor before the deluge was rapidly turning into a solid layer of dried mud. Her nose wrinkled in disapproval.

"Too bad Mrs. Morganthau's moved away. She used

to sweep out the place for the last sheriff every now and then.''

"I was thinking about hiring a boy to sweep out. I—'' Witt paused, suddenly struck by a dangerously tempting thought. "I don't suppose your son would want the job?''

"Dickie?''

"I know he's young and you—''

"He'd love it.''

"—probably don't want him hanging arou— What?''

She smiled, and he'd swear the room brightened. "Dickie would love it. He hasn't stopped talking about you since you arrived. Says you're a real-life dime novel hero.''

Witt blinked, frowned. A dime novel hero?

"He's going to be disappointed when he finds out I can't measure up to Buffalo Bill or Deadwood Dick.''

That made her flinch. "I suppose you think I let him read too many dime novels.''

"No!'' he said, surprised. "Smart boy like him is bound to have an imagination.''

"Too much, sometimes.'' A shadow crossed her face. "He misses his father.''

Witt's fingers twitched with the urge to touch her, to smooth away the shadows. Foolish thought. As if any touch could ease the lingering pain at the loss of a beloved husband and father, let alone his clumsy fumblings.

He cleared his throat, instead. "Has to be hard, losing a husband like that. Dickie told me,'' he explained when she looked surprised. "Said his father died in a mine cave-in. That has to be hard.''

"Yes,'' she said in a very small, tight voice. "Yes, it is.''

After a moment, she forced a smile back on her face, but she couldn't force the light back into her eyes.

Kicking himself for a fool, Witt retreated to safer conversational ground.

"Could he start tomorrow?" he said, a little more stiffly than he'd intended. "Your son, I mean? I was thinking to pay four bits a week, maybe a little extra at the first, since there's so much to do."

"So much? Surely—"

"Four bits," Witt said firmly.

In the end, after a little haggling over the details, she agreed. Mostly, Witt suspected, because she'd realized she couldn't wear him down if she'd tried. One of the advantages of not talking too much, he'd found, was that you didn't end up arguing much, either, or following your tongue into trouble because you didn't stop to think before you opened your mouth.

For a long time after she left, he remained right where he was, staring at the open door, thinking of her and her children and wondering what he'd gotten himself into. He'd find out soon enough, he supposed, and then he'd wish he'd kept his mouth shut while he had the chance.

Then again, maybe he wouldn't.

He thought of Mrs. Calhan, of her laughter and the sadness that it hid, and decided that maybe, just maybe, he wouldn't regret it after all.

What had she gotten herself into? Molly wondered as she walked back to her store.

Nothing, she tried to assure herself. Absolutely nothing. She'd given the man the change he was due and arranged a job for her son, that's all. A lot of boys had a job by the time they were Dickie's age. No one could criticize her for agreeing to the sheriff's proposal.

Or could they?

She sighed. Of course they could, and would. But she'd never let that stop her before.

It was just a job. A good-paying job. She could make sure Dickie saved most of what he earned. She'd let him keep enough to buy a treat now and then, maybe one of those dime novels he was so fond of, but that's as far as it went. The rest would go into a bank account so he could start saving for the future.

But he was only eight! If she hadn't been so dazed at being so close to DeWitt Gavin, she'd never have agreed to it in the first place.

But she had agreed, and she couldn't go back on her word.

Or could she? *Should* she?

She thought of the expression that had flitted across his face when she'd mentioned Crazy Mike's lost love. The shadows she'd seen in those changeable eyes of his had struck right to her heart. DeWitt Gavin had lost a love, too, she thought. And the loss still hurt.

She remembered the smile that had followed. Just a little one, but it had softened the hard lines of his face and made him a little less intimidating.

DeWitt Gavin, she thought, was a nice man. A kind man. She was as sure of it as she was that the sun would come up tomorrow. He'd be good to Dickie. He'd be good *for* Dickie. Her son needed a man in his life, a good, kind, decent man.

She'd have to check on Dickie now and then, of course. Make sure he was doing the work he was paid for. And if Sheriff Gavin was there when she did—

The thought stopped her in her tracks. What was she

thinking? She was a respectable widow woman, the mother of two children and proprietor of Elk City's most prosperous general store. She didn't have time to go mooning after a man just because he was good-looking and available. And had a nice smile. Or because his voice could send little shivers up and down her spine even if he was talking about the weather and blushing and saying "ma'am" just about every other time he opened his mouth.

And she wouldn't think about his mouth, either, or the way it might feel pressed against hers in a passionate kiss.

She yanked open the screen door of Calhan's, and froze, her attention caught by her own display of sweets in the front window, especially the chocolate creams and candy kisses.

With an effort, Molly wrenched her gaze away, then sailed into the store without bothering to catch the door before it banged shut behind her. It was, she decided, high time she changed the window display.

Witt's new cleaning boy showed up at a quarter to eight the following Monday morning with his mother in tow. Mrs. Calhan looked as neat and tempting as she always did, though he'd swear there was a stiffness about her that hadn't been there when she'd brought him his change.

He had to force himself to look away, to concentrate on the boy.

Dickie's eyes were round as saucers and he made sure to keep close to his mother's side. From the way his right hand kept clenching into a fist, then unclench-ing, then clenching again, Witt suspected the boy was fighting against the urge to cling to his mother's skirts.

Reporting bank robbers was evidently one thing, applying for his first job quite another.

The boy was clearly determined not to let his fears get the best of him, however. He shuffled his feet and shoved his fists into his pockets, then as quickly pulled them out again before his mother had to remind him about his manners.

"I'm here, Sheriff," he said with only a little waver in his voice. "Just like you said."

Witt squatted on his heels, bringing his gaze more on a level with the boy's. "Your mother told you what I expect?"

The boy nodded, eyes wide.

"Dickie?" Dickie glanced up at his mother warily. "Speak up, son."

Dickie squared his shoulders. "Yes, sir. She said I was to sweep the floors three times a week—" Witt had suggested twice a week "—and take your clothes to the laundry on Fridays and mop out every other Wednesday."

Witt was trying to concentrate on the boy, but it wasn't easy with his mother standing so close. Squatted on his heels like this, he had a tempting view of her bosom and the intriguing way it curved out, then in again and down into a neat waist that just begged for a man to wrap his hands around it. Worse, he was uncomfortably aware that beneath the full, dark-blue skirt were two long legs that he suspected would be just as well-shaped and intriguing as the rest of her.

Just the thought of her legs was enough to make him sweat.

At this rate, he'd have to be making that trip down to Gunnison whether he wanted to or not.

He forced his gaze back to the boy. "That's right. I'll pay you four bits a week."

Dickie's eyes went wide as saucers. "*Fifty cents? Really?*"

Witt grinned, remembering the time his pa had hauled him into Mr. Ledbetter's livery stable with the firm intention of getting him a real, wage-paying job. Ten cents a day and his midday meal with the Ledbetter family. It had seemed a fortune, way back then, and Witt remembered all too clearly how he'd had to fight to keep from shouting for joy at the thought of all those riches.

"That's right. Every week. And an extra four bits this week if you'll clean the windows, too."

"Sure! I do 'em at home sometimes."

"But no streaks!" his mother warned.

The warning scarcely registered. "I do 'em *real* good. You'll see!"

"I do them well," his mother corrected. "Occasionally."

Dickie nodded. "That's right."

His mother sighed.

Witt grinned and shoved to his feet. "All right, then. If your mother doesn't mind, you can start right now. There's a broom at the back."

Dickie left a dust cloud in his wake, he was moving so fast.

"Is there a mop to go with the broom?" Mrs. Calhan asked. "Or anything at all to clean the windows?"

Witt's grin vanished. He hadn't gotten past the broom in any of his calculations.

She rolled her eyes, then shook her head and smiled at him—the amused, indulgent smile of a woman wondering how a man ever survived without a female around to do his thinking for him.

"You'd best come on to the store with me," she said.

Witt meekly followed her out the door. He wasn't sure whether to be relieved or disappointed when she refused to take his arm out on the boardwalk.

It wasn't far between the sheriff's office and the store, but Molly was uncommonly aware of every step.

She was also conscious of the interested stares of a couple of passersby. That brought the heat up to her cheeks, which only irritated her more. She hadn't blushed this much since Richard had come courting all those years ago.

The sheriff didn't say a word. He waited politely while she unlocked the door, then held it open for her and followed her in. Her shoulders tingled with her awareness of his presence behind her.

"Vinegar and ammonia," she said, carefully unpinning her hat and setting it aside, then pulling on the big apron she always wore when she was in the store. "Mix them in water. They'll take the grime right off those windows. I don't suppose you have any rags?"

She glanced at him when he didn't speak. He hadn't moved three feet from the door.

At her querying look, he shifted his feet. "No, ma'am. No rags."

She gave a small inward sigh. It must be her. He hadn't been so stiff and formal with Dickie. He hadn't even been this formal yesterday, when she'd returned his money, but then, they'd been on his turf, not hers.

All she said was, "I have some cloths I'll sell you, then. And you'll probably need another bucket just for mopping and cleaning. A bigger one than the one you bought yesterday.''

"Yes, ma'am.''

She wondered, suddenly, what her name would sound like spoken in his deep, soft voice. A shiver went down her spine at the thought.

"The mops are in the back," she said, grateful for a chance to put some distance between them.

Five minutes later she'd gathered everything he needed, and he'd moved as far as the display case that held the chocolate creams.

"Did you want some more of those chocolates?" she asked, moving behind the case. The memory of how he'd looked as he'd tasted that first cream was surprisingly vivid.

He shook his head. "No creams." His voice sounded oddly thick. "Thank you," he added an instant later, remembering his manners.

"Some horehound drops, perhaps? They're in fresh this week."

"Peppermints," he said firmly. "And lemon drops. A nickel's worth each."

She caught him eyeing the chocolate creams as she turned away.

A few minutes later, as she rolled up two small paper sacks of candy, the screen door swung open and Gordon Hancock, president of Elk City State Bank, walked in.

Molly repressed a frown. No matter how little she liked the man, or how much she mistrusted his motives, she couldn't afford to antagonize him. He had the power to refuse the occasional loan she needed to keep her business running, and he was the kind who would be vindictive if she crossed him.

Besides, he was a very profitable customer. He ordered expensive Cuban cigars by the box, bought count-less trinkets and trifles to give as gifts to special bank customers, and once he'd discovered she could bring in his favorite and very expensive linen shirts, he'd or-dered a dozen from her, just like that, with a promise to order a dozen more when the first showed signs of wear.

His shoes and tailored suits he bought in Denver, however. It helped, he'd once confided to her, to share the same tailor as the governor and three state senators. According to him, you never knew when that sort of connection might come in handy.

It was just her imagination that DeWitt Gavin tensed at the sight of him.

Molly put on her best storekeeper's smile. "Mr. Han-cock, good morning."

"Mrs. Calhan. You're looking especially lovely this fine morning."

She ignored the compliment. "I'll be with you in a moment."

"Of course. Got to take care of the sheriff!" He clapped Gavin on the back with the ready familiarity of an old friend. "Especially one who's as good at his job as this fellow is, hey?"

The sheriff's mouth thinned, but he gave a curt little nod of recognition. All he said was, "Hancock."

"I'm sorry I didn't join you at Jackson's the other night," Hancock continued, oblivious. "I hear I missed a fine show."

"One drunk."

"Oh, but Crazy Mike's not just any drunk. Isn't that so, Mrs. Calhan?"

Molly was busy toting up the sheriff's purchases, which gave her an excuse not to reply.

"That's a dollar-six, Sheriff," she said. She packed the bottles into the bucket and padded them with the cleaning cloths while he counted out the coins to pay for them.

"Going to do a little housekeeping, are you, Gavin?" Hancock had a talent for sneering without being too obvious. It was one of the many things Molly disliked about him. Most people, when they wanted to sneer, made no effort to pretend they were doing something else.

"Sheriff Gavin has hired my son to sweep out his office." She pushed down the cash register's keys with rather more force than necessary. *Kaching!* "You should *see* the dirt the last man left!"

Outwardly, DeWitt Gavin was calm, oblivious to the insult and the rejoinder on his behalf, but Molly caught the hard glint in his eyes. He wasn't oblivious at all, and he didn't like Gordon Hancock.

Somehow, knowing Gavin didn't like the banker, either, made her feel a little more secure.

"The town won't pay for that sort of thing, you know," Hancock warned. "The cost of cleaning the jail comes out of your pocket if you don't do it yourself."

"That's what the mayor said." The sheriff picked up his purchases, politely touched the brim of his hat. "Mrs. Calhan."

"Sheriff."

She couldn't help smiling. There was something endearing about a man his size, with a gun belt strapped around his hips, toting a mop and a bucket filled with cleaning supplies.

"I'll be over later to make sure Dickie's done a proper job of it," she said. "And don't hesitate to tell me if he doesn't do the work or starts to bother you with all his chatter.''

He smiled at that. It wasn't a big smile, but it lit up his face. ''He won't annoy me.''

The smile vanished. He nodded at the banker. ''Hancock.''

Hancock casually leaned against the counter like a man who thought it was his. ''Sheriff. Good to see you.''

DeWitt Gavin was halfway out the door when she said, ''Mr. Gavin?'' He turned to look back at her questioningly.

''Thank you. For myself, as well as Dickie.''

He hesitated in the open doorway, then gave a curt, almost embarrassed nod. ''Ma'am.''

If it hadn't been for Hancock's presence, Molly would have run to the window so she could watch him until he was out of sight.

Chapter Seven

It wasn't fair, Bonnie thought. She was eleven, and Dickie was only eight, but *he* had a job and she didn't. Fifty cents a week pay, too!

Her head spun at the thought of such wealth.

It didn't help to know that he'd just spend every penny he could on dime novels and licorice whips, while here she was with not a dime to her name and almost dead with envy of Fanny Simpson and her fancy new lace collar.

Worse, last night at dinner he'd made a point of rubbing it in. Mother had been so preoccupied that she hadn't even noticed. Not, that is, Bonnie thought darkly, until Dickie had goaded her to the point that she'd *had* to pinch him, just to keep him in his place.

At his squawk, Mother had finally roused enough to notice what was going on, but instead of punishing Dickie, who was the cause of it all, she'd said, "Bonnie! Stop picking on your little brother. If you can't act more your age, you can do the dishes all by yourself tonight." And then Dickie had made a face, and she'd made the mistake of making one right back, and they'd both ended with extra chores.

It really, really, *really* wasn't fair!

Frustrated, Bonnie kicked at a pebble and sent it spinning. She was supposed to be home starting lunch soon, but right now she wouldn't mind going hungry if it meant Dickie went hungry, too. It just wasn't *fair*.

She kicked another pebble. This one hit the edge of a hitching post, ricocheted under the boardwalk in front of the Elk City *Courier* and Print Shop, and roused an indignant yowl from a startled cat. The cat shot out from under the boardwalk, raced across the alley, and dived under the boardwalk in front of Potter's Pharmacy.

Guilt-stricken, Bonnie hurried after it. She crouched to peer under the walk. The cat, a scrawny stray, cowered against the back close to the corner of the building.

"Here, kitty, kitty," she called softly. "I didn't mean to scare you. Here kitty."

The cat snarled and arched its back, ready to fight. Its tail had fluffed to three times its normal size.

Bonnie moved around to the back of the walk, right at the corner of the pharmacy. "Here, kitty, kitty, kitty."

The cat spat, swiped at her, claws bared, then shot out from under the boardwalk like a Fourth of July rocket and disappeared down the street.

"Well, poop," said Bonnie, slumping down on the stubby grass at the side of the building.

Nothing was going right and it just wasn't *fair*.

The screen door to the pharmacy creaked open. Bonnie tensed, then sank down into the shadows under the walk. The last thing she needed was for one of her mother's friends to spot her and give her a lecture about how young ladies weren't supposed to be crawling around under the boardwalks.

Footsteps echoed on the planking, followed by the

slap of the screen door closing. When the footsteps turned her way, Bonnie slid under the walk, heedless of the scolding she'd get when her mother saw the dirt on her dress.

"I was that shocked. I can't tell you how shocked I was."

"You don't need to tell me, Emmy Lou. I can just imagine!"

The first voice obviously belonged to Mrs. Trainer. Bonnie couldn't identify the owner of the second. Not Mrs. Thompson, anyway. Mother said those two ladies never talked to each other but what they got in was a quarrel, and from the eager note in these ladies' voices, they were a long way from quarreling. She daren't risk looking for fear of being seen.

The footsteps clunked across the boards over her head.

"There she was," Mrs. Trainer continued, voice thick with smug satisfaction, "first thing this morning, in the jail with her boy. I couldn't help but worry. You *know* how she lets those kids of hers run wild and boys, especially, will get into trouble if you don't watch them. I can't help but wonder what it was that had her down at the jail so early."

"Well if you can't guess, Emmy Lou," the second voice said, "*I* certainly can! Elizabeth Andersen told me she saw Molly Calhan and the sheriff together right after. The two of them were as good as walking arm in arm, she said, and him not one full week in town! Imagine!"

"I'd just as soon not!" said Mrs. Trainer.

Which meant, Bonnie thought sourly, that she was picturing all sorts of whatever wickednesses it was that grown-ups got into, and enjoying the thought of every one. And if what she thought up wasn't bad enough, Mrs. Trainer would probably make up something worse, and then she'd tell everybody she saw about it, just as if it *were* the truth.

She might be only eleven, but Bonnie knew a tall-tale teller when she heard one. Hadn't she had to put up with Dickie and his wild stories all these years?

But still… Her mother? And the sheriff?

The women's footsteps on the steps leading off that section of boardwalk brought her attention back to the present.

"She certainly hasn't wasted any time, has she?" Mrs. Trainer said.

"Maybe she was afraid Louisa Merton would cut her out."

"Louisa? Not a chance. Though she *was* talking about him…"

The women's voices faded into the distance.

As soon as she was sure she wouldn't be spotted, Bonnie slid out from under the walk. A good shaking and a few slaps at the back of her skirts was enough to get rid of the worst of the dust, but nothing served to dislodge the doubts those two old biddies had planted in her mind.

Her mother and the *sheriff?* Surely not! Mother had just gone to the jail so Dickie could get the job of sweeping out.

Hadn't she?

The questions dogged her all the way home.

"Four candles and a bar of Pearson's best soap, please, Molly. A jar of carbolic salve. Small size. And a roll of twine." Dora Beidlebaum frowned at the list in her hand. "Now did I mean hankies," she murmured, puzzled, "or hairpiece?"

Molly craned to see. It was hard enough reading Dora's cramped handwriting when it was right side up. "Could that be hairpins?"

Dora brightened. "Of course! That's it! Trust you to know just what I needed. I'll take two packets, if you have them, please."

"Certainly." Molly was already headed toward the far end of the counter to collect the twine and the salve.

She was bent over, fishing the roll of twine from a drawer when Dora said in the most innocent of tones, "I heard you had your son in at the jail this morning."

Molly jerked upright so fast she dropped the twine. "Where did you hear that?"

"Oh, here and about," Dora said with spurious innocence. "I hope he's not in any trouble. Is he?"

"No," Molly said curtly, bending again to retrieve the twine. "He's not in any trouble. Four candles, didn't you say?"

"That's right. And the Pearson's soap." A moment's pause until she was occupied in climbing the step ladder to fetch the candles from their box on a high shelf, then Dora added, "So what *were* you doing in the sheriff's office?"

Molly squeezed the candle box so hard she bent the edge. "Business." She climbed down, slapped the candles on the counter in front of her customer, and went off in the other direction to retrieve the hair pins.

"What *kind* of business?" Dora persisted, leaning across the counter so she could watch Molly's every move.

"*Private* business," said Molly repressively.

Dora mulled that one over for a minute, then tittered.

"With your son along? Though maybe that's wise because he *is* awfully good-looking, isn't he? I couldn't help noticing, you know."

"That's very kind of you," said Molly, deliberately misunderstanding. "As his mother, I suppose I'm partial, but I do think my little Dickie is quite a handsome boy. Like his father."

She shoved the drawer that held the different packets of hairpins back in with more force than was absolutely necessary.

Another titter. "I meant the *sheriff's* good-looking. Even Thelma said so, and she *never* pays attention to things like that, you know."

"Neither do I."

If Dora heard the frost in her voice, she gave no sign of it.

"Now, Molly," she said coyly. "Don't tell fibs. You know you noticed. We all did."

"Did you?" said Molly, even more repressively.

Dora nodded. "And no matter what Emmy Lou says, we all think he'd be a fine catch for you."

Only long practice at ignoring the nosey parkers of Elk City prevented Molly from saying something that would cost her a customer and be repeated over every cup of tea in town for a week.

"There's your pins," she said. "Will there be anything else?"

Dora frowned at the pile of goods in front of her, then consulted her list. "The soap?"

"Soap," said Molly. She'd forgotten the soap. "It's on that table behind you."

Too bad you couldn't wash out some people's brains the way you could a small boy's mouth.

"I wouldn't worry about the divorce if I were you,"

Dora assured her, retrieving the desired item. "These things happen, you know, and it really is time you were thinking about marrying again."

"That will be a dollar-eleven, Mrs. Beidlebaum," Molly said coldly, tossing the woman's purchases into the string bag she'd brought.

Dora's eyebrows shot upward. "So much? Are you sure?"

Molly's response was a narrow-eyed look that sent Dora scrambling for her purse. She didn't wait for Molly to finish ringing up the sale, just picked up her bag and headed toward the door.

"Scandalous, the price of things these days," she muttered, bustling away. "Simply scandalous."

It was only after Dora disappeared past the front window that Molly realized she'd dug grooves into the wood counter with her fingernails.

"It's not fair," Bonnie said as she set the table for supper. "It's just not *fair*."

"What's not fair?" Molly asked, distracted. The heat from the stove had turned the kitchen into an oven in its own right. She shouldn't have bought so large a roast, but the butcher, whose wife still owed her six dollars and thirty-seven cents for a living room suite she'd ordered special, had given her a good price for it. The thought of having enough leftovers so she wouldn't have to cook for a couple of days had been too tempting to resist.

"Dickie having a job before me," Bonnie grumbled. "It's not fair."

Molly glanced at her daughter, startled by the surly tone. Bonnie was usually the cheeriest and most willing to please of children. She never complained of anything.

"I didn't know you wanted a job," she said, desperately trying to think of something that would be suitable for a girl Bonnie's age. "There's Mrs. Donnagan, who just had a baby, and—"

"I don't want a *girl's* job," Bonnie retorted, disgusted. "Besides, with all her brats, Mrs. Donnagan would make me work a *lot* harder than Dickie is, and she wouldn't pay me fifty cents for it, either!"

Molly sighed. She should have realized this might happen. "You couldn't work in the jail, you know. It wouldn't be proper."

"Is it proper for Dickie to be there? He's only eight and I'm eleven. Twelve come August. Remember?"

Twelve? Her Bonnie was going to be *twelve?*

"I remember," she lied.

"Besides, I heard Mrs. Trainer and some other lady talking, and they didn't think it was right for Dickie to be working there, either. And that's not all." Bonnie's chin had an unfamiliar, mulish set to it. "They said you were walking arm in arm with the sheriff. And they *laughed* about it." Her brows dipped in a disapproving scowl. "You *know* how Mrs. Trainer laughs."

Molly knew, and she felt a hard, angry twisting in the pit of her stomach at the thought that her daughter had heard it.

Before she could collect her wits to respond, the sound of footsteps on her back steps diverted her attention. She easily recognized Dickie's light, quick tread. It needed only a second longer to identify the heavier, more measured tread that followed.

Her son charged into the kitchen with all the energy of a fizzing firecracker. DeWitt Gavin was two steps behind and looked as if he'd rather have been a lot farther than that. At the sight of her, he stopped dead in the doorway, then hastily dragged his hat off.

"Mrs. Calhan," he said. "Miss Bonnie."

Bonnie frowned at him, then at Dickie, then at the plates she was setting on the table. "Hello."

Molly stared, too surprised at seeing DeWitt Gavin in her kitchen to think of anything except that it seemed so right to have him there. "Good evening, Sheriff."

With an effort, she wrenched her gaze away and turned to her son. The bottom of her stomach fell away with a lurch.

"Dickie! What in the world? How—?"

The neat, scrubbed little boy she'd left in the sheriff's office that morning was now a grimy, disheveled ragamuffin. He'd pulled a button off the right shoulder of his overalls, his hair looked as if it hadn't been combed in a week, and there were smudges of dirt on his cheek and chin that no day of hard cleaning should have produced.

"I finished cleaning the jail!" he announced with a triumphant grin. "Even the windows! And then guess what? I got *another* job!"

"Did you?" Molly glanced at the sheriff. Guilt was branded on his face and evident in the nervous way he clutched his hat.

He swallowed. "I'm real sorry about that. I didn't—"

"At Drury's!" said Dickie.

"Drury's?" Molly groped for a chair. "Drury's *saloon?*"

"Dickie!" Bonnie stared, aghast. "You didn't!"

"I did!"

"Did not! You couldn't!"

"Did, *too!* An' Frank paid me ten whole cents to do

it, too!'' Triumphant, he dug into his pockets and pulled out a handful of coins. ''See?''

The sheriff looked like he'd have welcomed a noose around his neck before this kind of confrontation.

''I didn't know about Drury's until it was too late,'' he said weakly.

Molly wrenched her horrified gaze from him back to her son. ''Who's Frank?''

''Frank Caldwell. He sweeps out Drury's most every afternoon. Like Tom does Jackson's. But there was this baseball game, see, an' Frank—''

''Mr. Drury didn't hire you?''

Dickie shook his head. ''I didn't see him. Only Frank.''

''I see,'' said Molly weakly. Her son. Her eight-year-old Dickie, sweeping out a saloon. That Mr. Drury hadn't been party to it didn't help matters much. Already, she could hear Emmy Lou's acid comments on the shameful way some parents neglected their children.

The eager light went out of Dickie's eyes. He looked up at her anxiously.

''I didn't think you'd mind. It was just cleanin' up. There weren't any customers or anything. I was just sweepin' floors, like in the jail.''

''But it's a *saloon*,'' said Bonnie waspishly. ''You know we're not supposed to be around any of *those*.''

''We're not supposed to hang around the jail, either,'' her brother shot back, ''but Mother's letting me work *there*.''

The sheriff winced.

Molly's stomach churned. Had she been wrong in letting Dickie sweep out the jail? Worse, had she let him do it because she wanted an excuse to see more of DeWitt Gavin?

She held up her hands for quiet. Right now, what was needed was a little parental authority. She'd worry about her own guilt later.

"All right, all right. There's no need to quarrel." She frowned at her daughter. "Bonnie, this is none of your business."

Bonnie glared, but resentfully subsided.

"And you," Molly added, pinning her son with another hard stare, "go get cleaned up for supper. We'll talk about this later."

Dickie dejectedly shoved his precious coins back in his pocket. "Yes'm."

Head hanging, he trailed out of the room.

"He didn't get into any trouble, Mrs. Calhan," the sheriff earnestly assured her. "And the saloon *was* closed. I—"

"Let's go into the parlor, Sheriff Gavin, shall we?" Molly deliberately didn't look at him or her daughter. "We can discuss it there."

It wasn't a big parlor, but it seemed a whole lot smaller with DeWitt Gavin filling it up. Or maybe she was just more aware of him than she was of most visitors.

Pushing aside that troubling thought, Molly gestured to the armchair that had been her husband's favorite. "Please, sit down."

He sat. Gingerly. Even when the chair showed no sign of giving way under him, he didn't relax. Instead he leaned forward, elbows propped on his knees, fingers wrapped around the brim of his high-crowned Stetson.

"I'm sorry about Drury's," he said. "I found the boy coming out of the place a quarter of an hour ago when Drury was opening up for business. He was so excited about earning that extra dime, he couldn't wait to tell me all about it.

"He was strutting a little and checking his pocket every minute or two just to be sure the money was still there. He'd got a big boy's job all by himself and he was just proud to busting about it." His mouth softened into the beginnings of a smile. "I swear he didn't stop talking about it until we walked in the door here."

Molly flinched. DeWitt Gavin understood Dickie's feelings with the instinctive sympathy of a man who liked children and hadn't forgotten what it felt like to be a child. It wasn't an insight she wanted to deal with right now.

She sighed, suddenly tired and more than a little confused. Her children came first. She couldn't go mooning around after a man she scarcely knew, no matter how tempting it might be.

He took her sigh for disapproval. The smile vanished. "I truly am sorry, ma'am. If I'd known—"

"I'm not blaming you, Sheriff. If anyone's to blame, it is I. I shouldn't have let him take the job with you in the first place."

The big hands stilled. "Because it's the jail? Or because it's...me."

"Because he's only eight years old. If he'd been twelve or thirteen..." Her voice trailed off.

Eight *years*. Her baby was eight years old, yet he'd been without a father for half his life. And when he was twelve...

"He's only eight," she said again, firmly cutting off that train of thought. "Too young to be working, and certainly too young to be working in a jail. I should have thought of that right from the start."

The sheriff's gaze dropped. His eyes narrowed as if

he were displeased with the roses and ivy leaves trailing through the carpet. "He did a good job. As good as a boy twice his age would do."

"I'm glad to hear that. I wouldn't like—"

"He was proud of what he accomplished."

"Well, yes, but—" The words died under his suddenly fierce gaze.

He straightened in the chair, squared his broad shoulders. "If you have a problem with me, Mrs. Calhan, say so. You didn't seem to yesterday."

"It's not— I don't—" She stopped, dragged in air. The stricken look on her son's face when he'd been met with disapproval rather than the cheers he'd expected was painfully clear in memory.

"I'm sorry. It's just…hard, sometimes. His father's dead and I worry. Maybe more than I should, but I do. I can't help it."

The instant the words were out, she wished she hadn't said them. Too late to call them back now.

"I'm sorry. I didn't mean to inflict my worries on you."

Somehow, the hard lines of his face and jaw didn't look quite as hard as they had a moment ago.

"A woman alone, with children to raise," he said softly after a moment, "it'd be hard not to worry."

"Yes." The single word was scarcely a whisper.

She'd heard the same thing from so many sides, yet always before she'd thought she heard disapproval in the words, as if there were something wrong in her not remarrying when she had two children to provide for. There was none of that in his voice, though, just understanding and an unexpected sympathy that carried no hint of pity.

"Well," she said because she desperately needed to

regain her balance and couldn't think of anything else to say. "Thank you for bringing him home."

She ought to stand, offer her hand, show him to the door. Instead, she simply sat there staring at him, unable to move.

This time, he didn't look away. "If you don't want him coming by the jail, I'll understand."

"But I *want* to work. I did a *good* job!"

They both jumped, twisted to see Dickie standing in the doorway, his face drawn tight with dismay.

"You said I could clean the jail. You *said* I could!"

"I—"

"Dickie—"

"No!" His mouth set in an unyielding line. "I did the work. The job's *mine!*"

Startled by her son's unexpected defiance, Molly glanced at the man who was at the center of it. The sheriff was struggling to keep his expression impassive, but the glint of laughter in his eyes was almost as unsettling as Dickie's independence. His left eyebrow slid upward half a notch, just enough to let her know that he was waiting to hear how she was going to handle this rebellion in the ranks.

She'd never realized a slight lift of an eyebrow could be so…appealing. Or so dangerous. It made her feel like a conspirator, as if they shared secrets between them.

Just the thought unsettled her. The last thing she needed was to feel this close to a man she scarcely knew.

With an effort, she focused on her rebellious son. "We'll discuss it tomorrow, all right?"

His jaw hardened. "It's *my* job." He swung to the sheriff for support. "Right? You *said* it was my job."

"Only so long as your mother approves. And your

mother doesn't much approve of your having swept out Drury's.''

The calm, deep voice shattered the rebellion more effectively than either logic or stern parental warnings would have. Dickie's shoulders sagged. His mouth curved downward as his lower lip pooched out.

''And men take the orders like a man,'' the sheriff added.

Like a well-drilled Marine, Dickie snapped to attention.

''The biscuits are burning!'' Bonnie announced from the kitchen.

''Oh, dear!'' Abandoning all dignity, Molly raced to the kitchen.

''The roast's getting real dry, too,'' her daughter added with satisfaction, stepping back from the stove.

The biscuits weren't burned—Bonnie had taken them out of the oven before it had gone that far—but they were browner on the top than they should have been. The roast had survived, but the peas had turned into mush and the potatoes would have to be mashed since they were more than halfway there already.

Molly sighed, then moved the sheet of biscuits farther from the heat of the stove. The sound of a man's footsteps made her spin around.

''I'd best be getting,'' said the sheriff. He shifted the hat in his hands, his expression carefully neutral.

Bonnie looked relieved. Dickie, who had slipped into the kitchen behind the sheriff, looked anything but.

''He can stay for dinner, Mother, can't he?'' he said, looking from her to the sheriff and back again.

Molly frowned. The last thing she needed was to see DeWitt Gavin sitting across her kitchen table.

To her relief, he shook his head. "Got to go. Didn't mean to barge in on—"

"But there's plenty of food, sir. Isn't there? There's always plenty of food."

The eagerness in her son's voice stabbed Molly's heart. Dickie missed his father—she was only beginning to realize how much—but that didn't mean she wanted DeWitt Gavin at her kitchen table in his place.

"Please stay." The words were out before she could stop them. "There's plenty of food. More than enough for four."

He hesitated. She could see his fingers tighten around the brim of the hat he held in front of him like a shield.

"Yes, please!" Dickie insisted.

The sheriff glanced at Dickie and Bonnie, at the table set for three with an empty place where a fourth should have been. Then he looked at her, a long, clear-eyed look that made her throat tighten and her palms feel damp.

"I'd like that," he said at last. "Thank you."

After a moment's hesitation, he stretched out his hand and neatly hung his hat on the peg where Richard had once hung his.

Maybe the shoe-leather steak and overcooked beans that had been his lot for the past few days would have been a better idea, after all.

Witt stood on the back steps of Molly Calhan's house, a small, towel-wrapped plate of apple pie in his hands, and wondered if he'd left his good sense behind the day he'd first walked into Calhan's General Store.

Not that the dinner hadn't been fine. It had, in fact, been the best meal he'd had in ages, and that included the fancy dinner the town council had sprung. He'd had three servings of roast beef and mashed potatoes and made a damned pig of himself over the biscuits and strawberry jam. Only guilt and the pressure on his belt buckle had stopped him from eating more.

He'd hated to leave, but the last thing he'd wanted was to overstay his welcome. After so many years of boardinghouse meals and the often crude talk of hungry men who belched and scratched and cussed as if their mamas had never taught them better, Mrs. Calhan's tidy little kitchen and simple, tasty fare had been a gift from heaven. He'd almost forgotten how good a meal could be when there wasn't any rough conversation or the smell of unwashed male bodies to flavor it.

He'd even enjoyed the occasional bickering between Miss Bonnie and her little brother. It was, he thought, one of the essential ingredients for a family meal, like salt on meat or vinegar on greens. You couldn't have one without the other.

Mrs. Calhan hadn't said much except, "More jam, Sheriff Gavin?" or "Please pass the butter," or "No elbows on the table, Dickie." That hadn't bothered him, either. He hadn't managed much more than, "Thanks," or "Yes, please," when she'd asked if he wanted more biscuits. Too busy eating, for one thing. Too worried he'd say something he shouldn't, for another.

Too busy trying not to stare. He had a stomach-twisting feeling his dreams were going to be haunted by visions of a woman's face aglow in the lamplight for some time to come.

She'd looked so pretty sitting there, poised and soft-voiced with that delicate bit of lace at her collar contrasting so temptingly with the practical navy dress.

The faint shadows under her eyes had made him angry, made him wish there were something he could do to help. She worked too hard, a woman alone with children to raise and a store to run and a house to keep up. It couldn't be easy, but she was the type who never complained, just squared her shoulders and worked a little harder and a little longer because there was no one else to do it for her.

It wasn't right she should have to work so hard…and it also wasn't his business. He'd do well to remember that.

Which would be a whole lot easier, he thought, descending the step with the precious plate of pie firmly clutched in his hands, if he didn't think about chocolate creams and kisses every time he looked at her.

Molly hovered beside the kitchen window, listening to DeWitt Gavin's footsteps fading into the night.

Why had he lingered? He'd seemed in such a hurry to leave, then he'd just stood on her back steps, going nowhere. What had he been thinking?

She tugged at her collar, nervously smoothed her skirt. She'd probably looked a fright when he'd first walked in, cross and flushed from the heat of the stove, then gaping like an idiot at her bedraggled son.

Thank heavens he was a tolerant man. Bonnie's and Dickie's bickering must have driven him up a wall. Single men like him weren't used to the way brothers and sisters could snipe at each other despite their parents' warnings.

And what had he thought of her? Had she seemed brazen or unbecomingly pushy by inviting him to supper? It didn't matter that Dickey had broached the idea, she was the one who'd extended the invitation. A widow woman with two children—had he thought her calculating? Desperate? Determined to snag any marginally eligible bachelor who came her way?

She wasn't any of those things, of course, but did *he* know that? In town scarce a week and there she was giving him chocolates and pushing her son to work for him and inviting him to dinner. There were folks around here who regularly added two and two and got five, and they'd be bound to do it here, too. Would he think they were right?

Yet she'd swear he'd enjoyed himself.

Slowly, too lost in thought to be aware of it, she leaned against the old bureau where her pots were stored. In her mind's eye, she could still see him there at the opposite side of the table, the corner of his napkin tucked into the front of his shirt. She remembered the way he'd smiled when he'd accepted that first biscuit, the way his eyes had half closed with pleasure as he'd taken the first bite, heavy with strawberry jam. There'd been a drop of jam at the corner of his mouth as he'd chewed, and she'd found herself wondering how it would taste on his lips, and on hers.

After four years of looking at Richard's empty chair, that unfilled place at the table, it had felt good—deep-down good—to have a man sitting across from her again. A good-looking man who liked both her cooking and her beloved children and who had a shy smile that warmed her right through to her toes.

"Mother! Dickie says he's not going to do the dishes!"

Molly sighed, shoved upright. Her beloved children were glaring at each other like dogs circling for a fight.

"Do I have to?" Dickie demanded, looking aggrieved.

"Yes, you do. Bonnie cooked and set the table. That means you do the dishes."

"But I worked all day! I got a job now and—"

"And you still have your responsibilities here at home." She gave her son the steely-eyed stare that said she meant business. "If you don't think you can keep up your work here, then you'll have to drop the outside work. Is that clear?"

"Toldja," Bonnie jeered.

Dickie's hands balled into instant fists. "You did not! And it's none of your business, anyway!"

"Don't yell at your sister. And, Bonnie, mind your own business."

"So there!"

"Hah!"

"That's enough!"

The resulting silence wasn't promising. Hostility crackled in the air between them.

Molly drew in her breath, fighting for calm. "Dickie, do the dishes."

Dickie kicked a leg of the chair nearest him, not hard enough to earn another reproof, but enough to make his sentiments clear.

"Yes'm," he said, reluctantly picking up his plate.

"And, Bonnie," Molly added, turning on her eldest. "If you don't have a book to read or sewing to do, I'd be glad to find something to keep you occupied. If you're too tired for any of that, I suggest you go to bed early so you can wake up on the right side of it tomorrow."

Bonnie screwed her mouth shut and huffed out of the kitchen.

Dickie opened his mouth. Molly's warning stare shut it again before a word popped out. With a sigh of much suffering, he dragged over to the sink and dumped his plate in the wash basin, then dragged back to the table.

He'd be clearing the table one fork at a time as long as she was there, so Molly left him to his sulk. She had those accounts to work over yet tonight—she'd been thinking about asking Gordon Hancock for a loan that would enable her to expand her inventory and rent the back of the shop next to her so she'd have more storage—and there was all the mending that had been piling up. If she worked late enough, she'd be too tired to lie there in the dark, thinking of her dinner guest. Maybe.

Her daughter stood in the middle of the parlor, arms crossed over her chest, her expression thunderous.

"You shouldn't have invited him to dinner."

And how, Molly wondered, did a mother handle *this*?

"We've had guests to dinner before," she said mildly. "Including gentleman guests."

"Reverend James, who's *old*," her daughter grumbled in disgust. "And Mr. Fenwick, who's even older, and only because Mrs. Fenwick was off visiting her sister and all the ladies were taking turns feeding him. Mrs. Trainer would never say anything about *them*."

All true, and Molly knew it. She reached to brush back a stray curl that had worked its way loose from Bonnie's pigtails.

"Yes, dear, but—"

Bonnie jerked away. "Now those old biddies are *really* going to be talking about you and the sheriff, and there won't be anything you can say, will there?"

Before Molly could think of a reply, her daughter had darted out of the parlor and thundered up the stairs to her small room under the eaves.

Chapter Eight

Two days later Witt still had Molly Calhan's plate and the memory of the cinnamony-rich pie it had held. He'd washed the plate and folded the towel, but hadn't worked up the courage to return either. He hadn't been able to do anything about the memories.

He'd been right to be nervous. She *had* haunted his dreams. Continued to haunt them, in fact, and he didn't even have to be asleep for her to do it. He didn't dare risk making things worse by seeing her again.

The plate and towel would go home today, however, because Wednesdays were one of Dickie Calhan's sweeping-up days. Let Dickie take them, he'd told himself. He was busy and so was Mrs. Calhan. She wouldn't miss the things in the meantime.

Still, he'd felt guilty about not going back to thank her for the hospitality. His mama had brought him up better than that.

On the other hand, she hadn't raised a fool, and only a fool would court temptation. Which was why Dickie Calhan didn't get more than three feet inside the jail's front door before Witt had shoved the plate and towel into his hands and was pointing him back in the other direction.

"You take that plate right back to your mother and tell her I'm grateful. Never had a better bite of pie in my life, and that's a fact."

"I can take it when I'm done here," Dickie protested, puzzled.

"Take it now." Witt swung the door open wide.

"But—"

"*Now,*" said Witt, and shoved him out onto the boardwalk.

He waited until the boy passed by the window, then sagged against the door frame, limp with relief at having cleared his conscience so easily. Now maybe he could start forgetting Mrs. Calhan and start thinking about his job.

He turned back to the paperwork littering his desk, and wondered if she was wearing lace at her throat this morning.

It was just her imagination that she could feel the warmth where DeWitt Gavin's hands had touched, Molly told herself, clutching the plate and towel her son had just returned.

A dozen times over the past two days she'd thought about fetching the things herself, but each time she'd managed to talk herself out of it. She didn't need the plate or the towel. He'd remember eventually. It would be rude to ask and he might wonder if she were pursuing him if she did. Besides, she had too many other things to do to worry about one little plate and an old tea towel right now.

The longer she'd waited, however, the weaker the arguments had sounded until she'd just about worked up the courage to get them herself when Dickie had waltzed in the door and her best excuse to visit DeWitt Gavin had flown out the door he'd left open behind him.

Now that she had the plate, however, an irritation as unreasonable as it was intense grabbed hold of her. He couldn't be bothered to bring the things himself? The man eats her dinner and her pie, then doesn't even bother to drop by afterward to say thank you or how's the weather? She hoped he didn't expect her to feed him again, because his first dinner at her house was definitely his last!

Yet even as she fumed, she couldn't help thinking that he'd probably like her fried chicken even more than her roast beef. And everybody said she made the best cakes in town. She could do a devil's food, maybe. One with lots of buttery frosting and—

She set the plate down on the counter and forced a smile for her son's benefit.

"You tell Sheriff Gavin I'm glad he enjoyed the pie, and he's welcome to more any time he wants. And here!" she added on impulse, snatching a fat little paper-wrapped packet of candies out of a basket heaped with similar packets. "Take him this bag of sour balls. They'll be a nice change from those peppermint drops he bought before."

Dickie shrugged and pocketed the candies.

As she watched him walk past the front windows, she wondered if she should have sent chocolates, instead.

"Well, that's mighty nice of your mama, but she's been way too generous already" said Witt, dismayed. At this rate, there wouldn't be anything left that didn't remind him of her, and then what would he do?

He pulled a coin out of his pocket. "Here. Why don't you just take her this dime and say I'm much obliged?"

Dickie eyed the coin doubtfully. "She didn't say nuthin' about payin' her."

"That's all right. I don't want to trespass on her generosity. You just take the money."

"I can do it soon as I finish swee—"

"Now," said Witt, and shoved him back out the door.

"I didn't ask to be paid," Molly said, frowning at the coin her son had plunked down on the counter.

"I told him that," Dickie explained, "but he said he didn't want your generosity and—"

Her nostrils flared. "Oh he did, did he?"

Dickie eyed her warily.

"Well, if this is the way he repays it, I wonder anybody bothers to be kind to the man. You just take that coin right back and tell him I don't want it. If my kindness isn't enough…!"

"She doesn't want your money," said Dickie, holding out the dime.

"No?" said Witt. He was starting to get a bad feeling about this.

"Said it wasn't enough." Dickie tossed the coin down, then edged away. "I'll just start sweeping now and—"

"Oh, no, you don't!" Witt grabbed his sleeve before he could escape. "You just go right back to your ma and—"

"Do I gotta?"

"Yes, you gotta." No way *he* was going to confront

her! The expression on the boy's face told him all he wanted to know about Molly Calhan's mood.

He dug in his pocket and pulled out another coin. "You give her this two-bit piece and tell her I'd be much obliged if she'd just take whatever it is I owe her out of it. You can keep the change for your trouble."

Dickie just stared at the coin. "What if she won't take it?"

"That bag of sour balls doesn't cost two bits," Witt said grimly. "She'll take it."

Maybe.

Next time somebody sent him home with pie, he was by God getting up at dawn to get the damned plate back to them!

"He sent *more* money?"

Molly glared at the coin her son had tossed on the counter. She was tempted to throw it out the door. Didn't want her generosity, huh? Thought a few coins were enough to settle matters without one word of thanks for her kindness?

If it hadn't involved confronting the arrogant so-and-so, she'd march over to that jail right now, store or no store, and give him a piece of her mind. A large, sharp-edged piece of her mind.

Fortunately, she was a lady and above that sort of behavior.

She picked up the coin between the tips of her thumb and forefinger and handed it back to her son.

"You take this back there and you tell that man I don't want any of his filthy lucre, ever, and I'd be much obliged if he never darkened my doorway again. Understand?"

Dickie nodded miserably.

* * *

At the sight of Dickie Calhan reluctantly dragging through his doorway, Witt's heart sank.

"Your ma's a bit peeved at me, is she?"

Dickie nodded and held out the coin. His eyes looked haunted.

Witt grimaced. The proper thing to do would be to apologize in person, but he'd rather face a dozen Crazy Mikes, roaring drunk, than one strong-minded lady on her high horse.

Next time he wouldn't take a plate, regardless. To hell with returning it promptly.

"What'd she say?"

Dickie ducked his head and muttered something incomprehensible.

"What? Come on, tell me straight out like a man. What'd your mama say?"

"She said your money was filthy."

"What?" Witt shot out of his chair. "She said my money's *filthy?*"

The boy nodded miserably.

Well, hell! He didn't get mad very often, but this, by God, was beginning to get his dander up.

This time when he dug into his pocket, he pulled out a handful of coins, stirred through them for a minute, then selected the shiniest one.

"Here. You take this back to your mama and you tell her I'd gladly polish it for her if that's what she wants except I'm a tad short on polish. Got that?"

He'd seen men going to their own hanging who looked happier than Dickie.

Halfway between the jail and the store, Dickie rebelled.

Grown-ups! he thought, disgusted. At their best, they were usually unreasonable. Times like this, they were just plain impossible. Worse than impossible—they were downright *stupid*. And here he was, a kid caught in the middle of it.

Deadwood Dick wouldn't have put up with it for a minute. Even Frank Meriwell, who was so good that he got a tad annoying at times, wouldn't have put up with it. And if Dick and Frank wouldn't put up with it, then he didn't see any reason why he should, either.

Muttering words his mother would have washed his mouth out for using, he plopped down at the edge of the boardwalk and glared at the bald-faced roan tied to the hitching post. The roan blinked lazily back.

It didn't make any sense. His mama was mad at the sheriff for no good reason he could see, and the sheriff was mad right back at her, and here he was, smack in the middle with both of them shouting at him and telling him what to do. And all for nothing but a silly plate.

Or maybe, Dickie thought, frowning, maybe it wasn't the plate at all. Maybe it was something he'd done that had gotten them sniping at each other. But what? He hadn't done anything he wasn't supposed to lately. Not since he'd swept out Drury's on Monday, anyway, and he'd done that only because he'd wanted the dime and there hadn't seemed to be much difference between sweeping out the jail and sweeping out a saloon. Or sweeping out his mama's kitchen, for that matter.

Any other time, he'd ask Bonnie about it, but she was still mad about him getting the job when she didn't so she wouldn't explain anything, even if she knew. Tom Seiffert would have figured it out—Tom knew practically everything there was to know about anything—but Jackson's had been declared off-limits along with Drury's and a whole list of other places, so that wouldn't work. Which left…what?

Frustrated, he glared at the roan, which sighed, shut its eyes, and went to sleep.

Ah, to heck with it. If he kept his mouth shut, the sheriff'd probably think he'd delivered the money. His mother would never know, one way or the other.

Dickie squeezed the quarter in his hand. The sheriff had said he could keep the change, but if he never—

His head came up, his attention caught by two men who were sauntering down the other side of the street. He almost stopped breathing.

It was them. He was sure of it.

He watched as they paused at the end of the block where they'd have a good view of the bank. For a minute they just stood there, casually looking around as if taking in the sights, then one—a tall, scrawny guy with a walrus mustache—gave a little jerk of his head in the direction of the alley that led behind the bank. The second fellow, shorter and more solidly built than his companion, nodded and stepped off the walk. A moment later the two had slunk out of sight down the alley.

Eyes popping with excitement, Dickie shot to his feet, startling the roan into snorting, head-tossing alertness. Once the sheriff saw those guys, he'd *know* he'd been telling the truth about bank robbers.

Already he could see himself, perched on those boxes at the back of Dincler's Barbershop, regaling the gathered crowd with the tale of how, single-handedly, he'd helped the sheriff bring down two terrible desperadoes.

He hoped they had guns. It'd be a whole lot better tale if there was a shoot-out in it.

Chapter Nine

Dickie Calhan burst into the jail like a tornado on the rampage.

"They're here! They're here! You gotta come see!" Panting and wide-eyed with excitement, the boy grabbed Witt's sleeve and tried to pull him out of his chair.

Startled, Witt tugged free, then clamped his hands on the boy's shoulders, pinning him in place. "Who's here? What do you want me to see?"

"The bank robbers!"

"There are no bank robbers. I checked, remember? No one's seen any would-be bank robbers except you."

"Yeah, but I *seen* 'em!" Dickie insisted, squirming to get free. "They're walkin' up the alley behind the bank right now. Come *on!* You can catch 'em if you hurry!"

Witt shut his eyes in a silent prayer. First the mother, now the son. All it needed was for Miss Bonnie to whirl in here for his day to be ruined completely.

His grip on the boy's shoulders tightened. "Son, there are no bank robbers," he said, clearly enunciating each word so there'd be no mistake. "Just because a man looks like he could be a bank robber doesn't mean he is one. And until he actually robs a bank, he isn't. Understand?''

Dickie's jaw set hard and obstinate. ''So? If they're *gonna* rob the bank, don't you gotta keep an eye on 'em an' make sure they don't?''

''All I've got to go on is your suspicions. That's not near good enough.''

''You wouldn't say that if I was a grown-up!'' Dickie retorted hotly. ''It's because I'm a kid that you think I don't know anything, but I do! Those guys are gonna rob the bank for sure, and when they do, you're gonna be sorry you didn't listen to me, but then it'll be too late!''

Witt sighed, let his hands drop. ''All right. Show me which men you mean.''

For the next half hour, Dickie dragged him up one side of Main Street and down the other, then through half the alleys in town, but without success. The boy's would-be bank robbers had vanished.

For the third time that morning, Molly tried toting up the costs for this new expansion she was planning, and for the third time, they refused to come out right. The numbers were being particularly perverse today. It had *nothing* to do with DeWitt Gavin because she refused even to *think* about him, and she did *not* care that he did not want her generosity, and she was *not* going to apologize or even talk to him again, *ever!*

She was just nervous about this next big step she was planning, Molly assured herself, scanning the lists and scribbled notes spread across the counter. If she could rent the back half of Doc Smither's office next door, she could knock out a door in the wall the two buildings shared and make that her storeroom. Then she'd knock down the wall that divided her store from the present storeroom and use all that space to expand into.

Doc was all for the idea. He was getting old and didn't see as many patients as he used to. The extra income from renting out the space he didn't use would come in handy for him, and she'd have the room she needed to grow. Someday she hoped to buy the rest of his shop, too, but that was for the future. This was for now.

She'd been thinking about it for some time, about how she'd like to divide up the displays a bit better so that the tools and hardware and whatnot had their own area, and the dry goods and household things had theirs. Nobody else she knew arranged their merchandise that way except for the really big stores in Denver, but she was convinced an expansion would pay for itself in no time, even in a town the size of Elk City. After all, men liked to linger over hardware, but they tended to run away if somebody right at their elbow was shopping for women's drawers and petticoats. And women would be a lot more willing to spend their money if they didn't have to deal with their menfolk pacing and fretting while they shopped.

She was convinced the plan would work, but the list of merchandise she wanted to add kept growing, which meant the costs kept mounting until her head swam just thinking of it. And then there was the loan to arrange, a process that had become considerably more unpleasant since Gordon Hancock had taken the reins of Elk City State.

Courage! she told herself firmly, and bent again to her task.

By the time Dickie finally trailed through the door

half an hour later, however, she hadn't made much progress and her head was starting to ache.

At the sight of him, she put down her pencil and forced a smile. "All done?"

He nodded warily and kept his distance. "Uh-huh."

Guilt smote her. "I'm sorry if I was curt with you earlier. I was annoyed about something else. It had nothing to do with you."

"Hmm," said Dickie, and poked at her carefully arranged display of scented soaps, throwing it out of whack.

"Please don't do that."

He hunched his shoulder resentfully, tried to straighten it, and made things worse.

Molly winced. He was still angry, and she couldn't blame him. She *had* been unreasonable. Worse, she'd taken her irritation with the sheriff out on him.

Abandoning her accounts, she came around the counter and gave him a hug. "I love you, Dickie Calhan."

He almost hugged her back, then remembered that he was eight and a big boy, and squirmed away. She laughed and tousled his hair before he could duck out of reach. He giggled and looked up at her, eyes sparkling.

Her laughter died. Something in his expression, in the way he tilted his head, plucked at her heart.

His smile faded. "What's the matter? Is something wrong?"

When she reached for him this time, she simply smoothed the thick, unruly hair away from his face. "Nothing's the matter. It's just…you look so much like your father."

He blinked, then abruptly turned away to stare at the

display of soaps. He picked up one of the paper-wrapped samples, turned it over in his hand, set it back down.

"I dream about him sometimes," he admitted. "Scarey things, about the cave-in and waiting to hear what happened and everybody cryin', but…"

"But…?" Molly prodded when he didn't continue.

He poked at one of the soaps, then another, then lifted one shoulder in an embarrassed shrug. "But I don't remember him very well. I look at the picture of him, there in the parlor, trying to remember. But I can't."

Molly's heart shredded. She wanted badly to gather him in her arms, but the stiff-backed way he was standing warned that he didn't want to be touched.

"You were only four. You couldn't be expected to remember." It was only as she said the words that she realized she *had* expected more, perhaps because she remembered so very, very much.

"But now I'm eight, goin' on nine. Almost grown-up!"

She smiled despite the sting of the tears starting in her eyes. "Yes. You're growing up fast."

Too fast, but she didn't say that.

"Your father would have been very proud of you, Dickie. Almost as proud as I am."

He blushed at the praise and tried not to look relieved. "Really?"

"Really." Though a man of almost nine might not like to be hugged, a mother of thirty-one couldn't resist.

He tried to squirm away. "Mother!"

She gave him one last squeeze, planted a quick kiss on his brow, then reluctantly let him go.

"The new issues of *Beadles* and *Brave and Bold*

came in today," she said, deliberately changing the topic. "You may choose one, if you like."

"*Beadles!*" His face lit up at a sudden thought. "An' now that I got my own money, I can buy the other!"

"No. One will be enough. In fact," she added before he could argue, "I was thinking that now you're earning such good money, we ought to open an account for you at the bank. You must have at least a dollar by now."

"Dollar-sixty." It was an automatic response. His thoughts were headed off in another direction entirely. "Does it have to be the bank? Can't I just keep it in a jar at home? Lots of folks do that."

"Of course they do, but that's not nearly as wise as keeping it in a bank."

"But banks get robbed. What would happen to my money then?"

"Nothing. The bank would still owe you your money, plus the interest you'd have earned. And you know about interest, remember? How your money can make money? Putting your savings in a secure, well-managed bank is much wiser than stashing it in a jar under your bed."

He didn't look convinced.

Molly put her son to work sorting through a box of yarn that had just come in and went back to her accounts. The numbers still refused to cooperate. Nothing added up, nothing made sense, and her thoughts were too much a jumble to sort it all out.

Dickie, the sheriff, Richard, memories and the lack of them, what she'd said, what he'd said, accounts due and bills payable—it all tumbled around in her brain until her head started to ache.

Wherever they started out, however, her thoughts always circled back to DeWitt Gavin. Her son liked the sheriff, and the sheriff seemed to like him. A boy needed a man around, someone he could look up to, someone who could teach him the things his mother could not. Regardless of what he thought of her, she knew Gavin would be good for Dickie.

And for herself?

She didn't want to answer that. Couldn't answer it. Not yet.

Maybe it was sheer foolishness to think the question even needed to be asked. She'd talked to him, what? Four, five times? Given him chocolates, sorted out his cleaning supplies, fed him dinner. Nothing important. And nothing he'd said or done indicated he'd thought of her in the same way she'd thought of him.

Too shy, something within her said. *Too soon.*

And then there was his divorce.

Which left her exactly...where?

Frustrated, Molly tossed her pencil aside, gathered up the slips and bits of papers and her account book, and stuffed them all into a drawer. She'd deal with it tomorrow.

Witt stood on the corner where he'd stood that first afternoon and stared at the words painted on the store's whitewashed siding: Calhan's General Store. Guaranteed Best Store in Town! If We Don't Have It, We'll Get It, No Extra Charge!

He'd read it over more times than he could count, trying to get up the nerve to go over there and apologize to Molly Calhan. A couple dozen paces to the other side of the street, maybe. Three steps up. Half a dozen more paces to the door. That's it. Cross the street, walk in the door, apologize, walk back out. How hard could that be for the man who'd felled Crazy Mike McCord with one blow?

Just the thought of it made him sweat.

It wasn't the apologizing that bothered him so much—he'd had plenty of practice on that with Clara since nothing he'd done had ever pleased her, no matter how hard he'd tried. No, it was the thought of *why* he was considering apologizing to Molly Calhan that had him twisted into knots.

The woman tempted him in a way no woman had since he'd been so besotted with Clara that he didn't know which way was up. Not that there was much chance of her paying any more mind to him than she did to any other man who waltzed in to buy a chew of tobacco, but he didn't want her thinking he was not only rude and crude, but a fool, as well. But how was he going to manage that without making an even greater fool of himself in the process? He'd never had much talent for talking to the ladies, and when it came to this one lady in particular it was pretty much a guaranteed sure thing he'd make a mess of it.

One thing for sure, he'd have to do something. Sooner or later someone was going to notice he'd been staring at Calhan's for the better part of the past half hour, and if that didn't start tongues wagging, he didn't know what would.

He sighed and shoved away from the wall he'd been propping up for so long. Best get it over, one way or the other. Nothing ever got easier by running away from it.

It took eighteen paces to cross the street, another seven to get from the top of the boardwalk steps to the front door of Calhan's. He counted every one. He was on the point of reaching for the handle on the screen door when Molly Calhan's voice stopped him dead in his tracks.

"I'll be back in a few minutes, Dickie. You keep an eye on things while I'm gone. And if Mrs. Thompson comes in, don't let her talk you down on the price of anything, all right? Just tell her she'll have to discuss it with me when I get back."

An instant later, the screen door slammed open and Molly Calhan walked straight into his arms.

"Oh!"

He grabbed her to keep her from stumbling. It was instinct that made him wrap his arms around her and draw her closer.

"Oh," she breathed, staring up at him wide-eyed.

He almost stopped breathing when she relaxed and swayed into his embrace. She fit as neatly as if she'd been made for him, and his body automatically responded. He could feel her breasts pressed against his chest, her hips against his. If he slid his hands farther down her back he could press them into the neat curve of her slender waist, or lower still to the firm, tempting swell of her hips beneath the flaring skirt.

He couldn't help noticing the bit of lace on her collar. The tiny pearl buttons at her throat made his mind go blank and his fingers twitch with the urge to unbutton them, one by one, all the way down until—

"Ma'am." It was all he could get out against the sudden constriction in his throat.

She braced her palms against his chest and pulled away. Witt sucked in air and tried to be grateful, but he'd swear her hands lingered longer than was absolutely necessary.

He gulped, backed up. "I was just coming—"

"I was going—"

They stopped, stared. Her cheeks were turning a pale rose-red.

Witt cleared his throat. If you couldn't get out of wrasslin' with a bull, it was always wiser to grab the horns straight off.

"I wanted to apologize for takin' so long to return your plate. I meant to bring it back but what with one thing and another…"

No, that was skirting a little too close to an outright lie. And there was no way he could tell the truth.

He swallowed, tried again. "See, I was sort of embarrassed. Here you'd been so kind to me and I hadn't hardly said thank you properly, let alone returned the favor. I sure didn't like to trespass on your generosity and what with all—"

"*Trespass* on my generosity? Is that what you said?" she demanded, suddenly intent. "You didn't want to *trespass?*"

He nodded, puzzled.

She threw back her head and laughed. "I should have known!"

"You should?"

"That's what we get for relying on an eight-year-old boy to carry a message. Dickie told me you didn't want my *generosity*. He didn't say anything about trespassing on it."

"Didn't want—? Oh!" Understanding dawned. His grin went lopsided with relief. "I could see where that wouldn't go down too well."

"It didn't go down at all. If you'd tried to hand me that dime yourself, I'd have flung it back in your face."

That he could easily believe. "And my filthy money that you didn't like? What was that all about?"

"Filthy money? I didn't say anything about— No!

Wait! I think I said something about not wanting your filthy lucre, and that if dinner wasn't enough…'' Her mouth curved in a wicked smile. ''Which explains why you sent more money.''

He nodded, relieved. ''Seemed mighty strange to me, but I figured maybe there was a sudden shortage of sour balls. Either that or you were mad about a lot more than me not bringin' that plate back pronto.''

''Oh, dear. I should have known. Well, I did! I kept telling myself you wouldn't be so rude, but then I thought—''

She stopped, blushed.

''You thought…?'' Witt prompted, fascinated by the mix of emotions that washed across her face.

She bit her lower lip, shook her head. The color in her cheeks was rapidly changing from rose to scarlet.

''Yes?'' There was less than a foot of empty air between them now. ''You thought…what?''

She had *very* kissable lips.

''I thought—''

He bent closer. He couldn't help himself. She drew him like a magnet drew iron. ''Yes?''

''I thought you thought I was too…forward. That I was…''

Closer still. *''Yes?''*

''Chasing you.'' The words escaped on a gasp.

Witt's head spun. Molly Calhan? Chasing him? *Him?* He liked the thought. A lot.

''I wouldn't ever have thought that.'' That was the honest-to-God truth.

She stared at his mouth. ''That's what I decided. Eventually.''

A couple of inches was all that separated them now.

All he had to do was lower his head just the tiniest little bit and—

"If you two'd quit spoonin' in the doorway, I could maybe get past." Mr. Fetzer's quavery voice brought Witt up with a snap.

He glanced around to find the old man staring at them, head cocked, pale old eyes bright with unabashed curiosity. Witt moved aside and, with more presence of mind than he usually showed in such circumstances, took Molly's arm and pulled her with him.

Mr. Fetzer snickered into his collar as he edged past them into the store.

"Would you care to go for a walk this evening?" Witt said, forcing the words out before he lost his nerve.

"A walk?" She stared at him. "You mean, as in a *walk?*"

Witt nodded and felt his throat go tight, choking off his air. Too late to back down now. If you were in for a penny, you were in for the whole damned pound.

"That's right. Just a…uh…" He groped for a word that might make it sound a little more tempting. None came. "A walk."

She blinked a couple of times, glanced into the store where Mr. Fetzer was rummaging around, then looked back at him. Her chin came up a defiant inch.

"Yes," she said.

"Yes?"

"Yes, thank you, I'd like to go for a walk. Say, seven o'clock? Would that suit?"

His head spun. "That'd suit just fine."

Silence, then, almost regretfully, she said, "I have to get back to work."

"Oh. Right. Of course you do. Sorry." He shook his head a little to clear the dizziness. "Seven, you said?"

She nodded, smiled, and pulled open the screen door. "Seven." And then she was gone.

Molly floated into the store. Neither Mr. Fetzer's avid glance as she walked in nor his dickering over his bill ten minutes later was enough to prick the heady feeling that had claimed her.

She didn't care what Mr. Fetzer thought. She didn't care what anyone thought. It was just a walk. She took them every night when the weather was good, only this time she'd have a man beside her when she did. A big, iron-jawed man who blushed and tripped over his tongue whenever she smiled at him. A man with laughter in his eyes.

It took Dickie emerging from the back room to bring her back to earth with a jolt. She was a mother, for heaven's sake, not a callow schoolgirl with nothing better to do than wallow in stupidly romantic daydreams. And as a mother, she had responsibilities that needed tending to.

Half an hour later, she'd closed up the store, hung a sign to say she'd be back by four, and escorted her mutinous son into the Elk City State Bank, right across the street.

"Good afternoon, Mr. Goff," she said to the pinch-faced little man sitting at his desk behind the railing.

"Mrs. Calhan." Hiram Goff didn't seem at all pleased to see her, but then, he never seemed pleased to see anyone. "What can I do for you?"

"My son would like to open an account."

"No, I wouldn't," Dickie muttered. He'd kept his fist balled around the coins in his pocket ever since she'd informed him that he didn't have any choice in the matter.

Molly nudged him forward, through the railing gate. "Yes, you would."

Hiram Goff eyed him disapprovingly. "Checking or passbook savings?"

Dickie glared right back at him, eyes narrowed with suspicion. The rigid set of his jaw gave warning of impending rebellion. "Neither. I don't wanna put my money in the bank."

"Dickie."

"There's bank robbers out there," he protested. "I got a whole dollar and sixty cents an' I don't want no robber gettin' it."

At the word *robber,* Goff's nostrils flared.

"Any robber," Molly corrected, distracted. "And I have, not I got."

"I don't want *any* robber gettin' it."

"Where," Mr. Goff demanded icily, "did you hear of robbers?"

"I seen 'em."

"You saw them," Molly said automatically, then realized what he'd said. "You did? What robbers? There are no robbers."

"Yes, there are," Dickie insisted. "I *saw* 'em. This morning."

"Did you tell the sheriff?"

For an instant, he looked as if he wasn't going to answer, then, reluctantly he replied, "Yes'm."

"And what did he say?"

"They were gone by the time he went lookin' for 'em," Dickie stated even more reluctantly.

"More likely they were never there at all," Goff said acidly. "Young people these days spend entirely too much time reading trashy novels and those appalling penny dreadfuls. Bank robbers! Ridiculous!"

It was Molly's turn to let her nostrils flare. "I believe we were talking about a new account?" she said coldly.

"You're opening a new account? Wonderful!"

Molly jumped, startled. She hadn't seen Gordon Hancock emerge from his office. Perfectly groomed, as always, he looked the epitome of the handsome, successful man of business. And as always, just the sight of him made her prickle like a porcupine.

He beamed at her, then at Dickie. "Mrs. Calhan. And you must be our newest depositor?"

"No," said Dickie.

"Yes," said Molly.

"He's afraid of bank robbers," Hiram Goff muttered.

Hancock stiffened, instantly wary. "Bank robbers? Wherever did you get the idea that there are bank robbers around?"

"I seen—*saw* 'em," said Dickie.

"Bank robbers! Hah, hah, hah! There's no bank robbers, boy. This bank is perfectly safe, isn't it, Mr. Goff?"

The clerk sniffed as if at a bad smell, then withdrew a printed form and a small bank passport from a drawer and pointedly put them down in front of Dickie.

"Fill this in and sign it. Here's a pen." He eyed Dickie disapprovingly. "You do know how to use a pen, don't you?"

Dickie squirmed, caught between resentment and embarrassment. "Mother doesn't let me use a pen. She says I make too many blotches."

And got ink on everything in sight, thought Molly, remembering. It had taken three soakings before she got all the ink out of his shirt the last time he'd tried.

Goff's mouth puckered. Without a word, he set the

pen aside and pulled out a pencil. "Use this, then. And make sure there are no mistakes."

If anything could have gotten Dickie's mind off the safety of his money, it was a challenge like that. Pencil firmly clutched in his fist, brow furrowed in concentration, he slowly worked his way through the form.

"It's a proud day for a mother when her son takes this first step into manhood," Hancock said.

He'd maneuvered around so that he was standing a bit too close, not enough to be obvious, but too close for her comfort. Molly edged to the side and hoped he'd think she was angling for a better look at her son's face.

Hancock sidled after her. "They make some fine coffee down at the Grand, Mrs. Calhan. Can I tempt you to join me for a cup?"

"Now?"

"This evening, if you like." He smiled, showing lots of straight, white teeth. "You can't keep turning me down forever, you know."

"There," Dickie said, saving her from the need to reply. "Done."

Hiram Goff scanned the form. He didn't seem to think much of Dickie's sprawling, ill-formed cursive, but there wasn't anything else he could object to.

"Now if you'll sign, Mrs. Calhan. There. Thank you. And now young man, the money you wish to deposit?"

Dickie dug out the coins and, after a moment's hesitation, laid them out on the desk.

"Twenty, twenty-five, seventy-five." Molly watched, amused, as the pinched expression on Hiram Goff's face smoothed out under the balm of counting money. "One dollar and sixty cents. Very good."

He fussily made out a deposit slip, then wrote down the amount in the savings book and slid the book across the desk to Dickie. "You've made a wise decision, young man. Watch your pennies and your pounds will look out for themselves."

"I don't got no pounds."

"You don't have," Molly chided. "It's a saying. It means your dollars will keep earning more dollars because you're being careful with your pennies."

"You *sure* it's safe?" Dickie demanded, suspiciously eyeing first Goff, then the bank president. He hadn't touched the book.

"Don't be a fool, boy."

"Of course it's safe, young man," Hancock assured him with a condescending heartiness that raised Dickie's hackles. "And even if by some wild chance bank robbers did actually steal our money, you can be sure the sheriff would stop them. That's why we hired him, you know. Because he's done it before."

"You mean he really is a gunfighter like Freddy Christian said he was?" Dickie demanded, suddenly eager.

"I don't know what Freddy Christian said, but Sheriff Gavin did, in fact, shoot two bank robbers back in Abilene a few years ago."

Dickie's eyes popped. *"Really?"*

Hancock nodded. "Shot them dead right there in the street. One shot each, straight to the heart."

"Wow!" Dickie said.

Hiram Goff look grimly pleased.

To Molly, it was as if the earth had fallen away from beneath her feet.

Chapter Ten

The minutes and hours crept past with excruciating slowness. By a quarter to seven, Molly had changed her mind at least two dozen times.

She would walk out with DeWitt Gavin. She absolutely wouldn't. She would, but she'd demand an explanation. She wouldn't say a word. What was past, was past, and the man had obviously only been doing his job, and it was none of her business, anyway.

When his knock sounded on the back door, she almost sent Dickie to tell him she was indisposed, but making her son lie for her was stooping a little low.

"Sheriff Gavin." She forced a smile. "You're very prompt."

"Ma'am." He'd swept his hat off the instant the door had swung open, and now he held it, two-fisted, in front of him like a shield. He looked, she thought, exactly like a man who wished he were somewhere else entirely.

"Let me just get my jacket and hat," she said, and remembered only after she'd shut the door in his face that she should have invited him in.

When she emerged five minutes later, DeWitt Gavin

was halfway down the long, narrow yard at the back of her house, bent over smelling the roses that edged her vegetable garden. She watched as he delicately cupped a blowsy red blossom, then buried his nose in its heart, and wondered what part of him was the man who'd shot and killed two people.

Slowly, thoughtfully, she picked her way down the narrow, wooden back steps. At the sound of her footsteps on the path, he straightened.

"Haven't seen such pretty roses in a long, long while." Gently, he ran the tip of his finger across one scarlet petal, then another.

Heat washed through her. She could so easily imagine that finger tracing a path across her naked skin. "My husband brought them from Denver when we first settled here. He knew how much I loved my roses."

"Can't be easy, having a garden this high in the mountains."

"It's not. Nothing's easy to grow here. Late frosts, early snows, cold nights. They all work against a gardener. Some things I don't even bother with anymore. Corn hardly even gets high enough to tassel before the first freeze gets it."

He glanced at the neat garden rows that marched down the length of her yard. "You seem to manage pretty well, in spite of it all."

"I try." Then, impulsively, "Do you have a pocketknife, sheriff?"

That brought his head up. "What?"

"A pocketknife. May I borrow it, please?" She shouldn't do this. She really shouldn't do this. But when, clearly bewildered, he handed her his bone-handled folding knife, she took it and neatly cut off a half-open bloom, then trimmed away the thorns.

"There you are," she said, extending the rose. Because she couldn't help it, she smiled. "You can keep it in your water glass at the jail. Add a little color to the place."

When he continued to stare at it, she stepped forward and shoved the stem into the top buttonhole on his lapel, tugging it into place. By the time she finished, her head was spinning and her chest felt tight, as though someone had suddenly yanked on the lacing strings of her stays.

She stepped back, away from him, fighting for breath.

"Never had a lady give me a rose before."

"Well, now you have."

To Molly, her voice sounded overbright and slightly strained, but Gavin never noticed. He had his chin tucked all the way back to his Adam's apple and his eyes half-crossed, trying to get a good look at the showy red rose that now adorned his lapel.

"Shall we?" she said to distract him. The last thing she wanted was for him to start wondering why she'd picked that rose.

In unspoken agreement, they headed west, away from the center of town and the streets where they'd be most likely to run into someone they knew. He didn't offer to take her arm, for which she was grateful. She'd swear she could still feel the heat of him beneath his jacket, the rock-solid wall of his chest.

Six blocks brought them to the edge of town. Elk City didn't so much as end as it petered out. The houses got smaller and farther apart, the weeds beside the streets taller and more obstreperous, until the raw dirt road they'd followed simply ran into a meadow and disappeared.

From here the land dropped away in a sweep of rocky soil and grass dotted with wildflowers. A boulder-strewn river that didn't carry enough water to warrant the name tumbled down the cut, its waters not yet muddied by the mines farther down. Beyond the river, the land swept up again, the grass eventually giving way to pines, then raw gray rock and the rugged peaks of the Elk mountains.

For a long while, they didn't speak, too engrossed at the wild beauty before them for words to matter. Despite her sharp awareness of the man beside her, Molly could feel the strains of the day slipping away, just as they always did whenever she walked out this way.

"This was a fine place to build a town," the sheriff said at last, softly.

Molly laughed. "You may not think so come winter, when the snow's up to your waist and the wind's howling and trying to freeze your bones. The only thing you'll want then is a nice warm fire to cozy up to."

And someone to cozy up with, she thought, and felt a longing so intense it startled her.

She glanced up to find him watching her. A shadow flickered across his face, then was gone. He deliberately looked away, to the peaks and the lowering sun that was casting long shadows in its wake.

"Reckon a man gets used to the cold, just like most everything else," was all he said.

He feels lost, too, Molly realized suddenly. Divorce was just another kind of loss. Maybe not so wounding, but a loss nonetheless.

"Let's walk down to the river, shall we?" she said, as impulsively as she'd plucked that rose in his lapel. "To that clump of aspens, see? There's a trail from there that will take us back up to the far end of town."

The grove of aspens and young pines seemed a world unto itself. This late in the day, the sun shot through

the trees in bars and ribbons of gold, deepening the
shadows, making it a place of secrets. The air was heavy
with the smell of grass and damp earth and water. Elk
City seemed a thousand miles away.

Gavin halted at the river's edge, just where a huge
gray boulder thrust up out of the frothing river and the
trees parted, framing a breathtaking view of the peaks
to the west.

"Pretty place" was all he said.

"It's one of my favorite spots, and a great place for
a picnic on a Sunday afternoon." As she often did,
Molly clambered up the side of that upthrust rock and
claimed a seat at the top, too late remembering she was
supposed to be a lady and tugging her skirts decently
around her ankles.

He perched on the fallen trunk of an old pine that
was the only available footbridge across the torrent for
a mile in either direction. It gave him a good view of
the peaks...and of her. Molly chided herself for the
thought, but couldn't help checking to make sure her
hair was neatly in place.

She had to admit, he was a rather breathtaking sight
himself with the dying sun gilding the rough-hewn
planes of his face and the strong, long lines of his body.
The rose in his lapel provided an incongruous splash of
color in this place where there were a hundred shades
of green and brown, and not one dab of red.

It took an effort of will not to look at the gun that
hung at his side, readily visible now that his jacket had
fallen open. If he was aware of the weapon, he gave no
sign of it, too used to it, perhaps, to notice except when
it wasn't there.

She'd swear there was a tension in him to match the
tension that thrummed through her.

"Thing I can't get used to," he said, breaking the silence, "is how quick it gets dark here once the sun goes down. Back in Kansas, seems the evening lasts longer."

Kansas.

"Mr. Hancock said you'd been sheriff in Abilene."

He went still, suddenly, and his eyes took on the dull, dark gray of a brewing storm.

"Undersheriff," he said. He took a breath, slowly let it out.

"Hancock told you about the men I killed." It wasn't a question.

Her throat felt tight, as though his hand had fastened on it. "Yes. I shouldn't ask, but there's Dickie, you see. He looks up to you and I—I have to know."

For a moment, she didn't think he'd answer. His gaze had turned inward, and judging from the shift of shadows across his face, he didn't much like what he saw. Abruptly, he shoved to his feet. Three long strides took him to the river's edge. For a long while he simply stood there, staring across the rushing water to the stark and distant peaks beyond.

"They were coming out of the bank," he said at last. "I wasn't even on duty, but there'd been shots, screams. They were carrying money bags with the bank's name stamped all over them and they were so panicked they were shooting at anything they thought was in their way. When they almost shot a child, then kept on shooting…"

He turned to face her. His gaze pinned her to the rock.

"I had to stop them before an innocent bystander got hurt." His voice was rough with passion and remembered pain. "Contrary to what you might read in those

dime novels your son likes so much, it's not that easy
to shoot a gun out of a man's hand, even when he's
standing still. But I would have tried. I swear to God I
would have tried if it hadn't been for that child.''

She saw the instant the fight drained out of him, replaced by the regret of a man who'd done what he'd
had to do, yet never learned to accept it.

''They were boys,'' he said softly, sadly. ''Just boys
who thought it'd be easy to rob a bank, then found out
it wasn't and panicked.'' He turned back to stare at the
uncaring peaks that were fast swallowing the sun. ''The
oldest was nine days shy of his twenty-first birthday.''

Molly shivered, then scrambled off the rock and
crossed to him. At her light touch on his arm, he jumped
as though he'd forgotten she was there.

''Thank you for telling me.''

He looked as if he wished he hadn't, but all he said
was, ''We'd best head back. I wouldn't want to be
stumbling up that hill in the dark.''

When he turned to lead her back, she stood her
ground.

''No,'' she said. She laid her hand upon his chest to
stop him, and wondered if he could hear her heart hammering in her chest. ''Not yet.''

She rose on tiptoe, slid her other hand around his
neck and pulled him down to her. And then she kissed
him.

Night had fallen and a million stars had claimed the
heavens by the time Witt had walked her all the way to
her back steps. They hadn't spoken a word since she'd
retreated from that single kiss, there on the riverbank—
he because he had no words and she, perhaps, because
he'd left her nothing to say.

He made no move to follow her into the house, just stood there at the bottom of the steps and waited while she opened the door and stepped inside. She paused in the doorway for a moment, head cocked, her expression unreadable while the lamplight spilled out around her.

"Good night," she said at last. "And...thank you."

A moment later she had closed the door behind her, leaving him speechless in the dark.

Dimly he could hear her footsteps moving away through the house, then her muffled voice calling out to the children. He caught Dickie's answering call, though he couldn't make out the words. He didn't hear Bonnie's voice at all.

He would have liked to linger, to just stand there and watch as the lights went out in her house, one by one. Town this size, though, there was bound to be somebody around who'd notice. All it would take is one sharp-eyed old biddy putting the cat out for the night and by morning half the town would know he'd been out in Molly Calhan's back yard making a damned fool of himself.

He only got as far as the garden's edge. The scent of roses and of green, growing things hung on the night air, heady and rich with promise, tempting him to tarry. Even without the moon there was enough light to make out the neat rows of vegetables and the unruly masses of flowers that marked the borders.

It would have taken a lot of hard work and patience to make this rocky Colorado mountain soil produce like this. Late frosts and early snows and cool nights, she'd said, yet still she'd planted and worked and dreamed of the harvest to come, despite the risks.

A faint breeze curled past, rustling the leaves on the pole beans and whispering of settled things, of homes and kitchen gardens and the warmth of a place where a man could walk in the door and know that he belonged.

Witt listened, and then he settled his hat more firmly on his head and slowly walked away.

Dickie had demanded to know if the sheriff had told her anything about his adventures. Bonnie had been silently disapproving.

Molly had neatly sidestepped her son's questions and ignored her daughter's sulking, but when she had seen them both safely tucked into bed and been free to seek her own, she'd found that sleep eluded her. Her mind and body were still too roused by that one quick kiss for her to settle down just yet.

As often as she'd blushed because of DeWitt Gavin, you'd think she'd be blushing now, remembering. But she wasn't. She hadn't when she'd pulled him down and pressed her lips to his, either.

DeWitt. What a stiff, formal name for a man who was anything but. From what she'd heard, he went by Witt, which wasn't such an awkward mouthful.

She tried it out, whispering it to herself. *Witt.*

The name slid easily over her tongue. She liked the taste of it.

Restless, she threw back the covers, then propped a pillow against the painted iron headboard and sat up, drawing her knees up and tucking her gown neatly around her feet, frowning into the dark.

It hadn't really been much of a kiss. She'd put a little more into it than she might have if she'd been seventeen, but not that much. There hadn't been any tongues or heavy breathing—it didn't count that she'd had a hard time catching her breath afterward. He hadn't touched her, hadn't leaned into her, hadn't demanded more. He certainly hadn't swept her up in his arms and tried to devour her. Unfortunately.

If she'd been younger and known less of men, she'd have thought his silence afterward to be from disapproval. But she was thirty-one and had been married to a man she loved and she didn't make that mistake— he'd been as shaken by that simple kiss as she was.

What puzzled her was why he hadn't tried to claim more. She'd have sworn he wanted to. And while she'd give the man due credit for being a gentleman despite his conversational failings, she didn't think it was mere good manners that had kept him from taking advantage of what she'd offered. Call it vanity, but she knew when a man was aroused, and DeWitt Gavin had definitely been aroused.

She squirmed a little at the thought.

All right, she *had* taken him by surprise. That kiss had taken her by surprise, as well. It wasn't until she'd come close and seen that hollow yearning in his eyes, not until she'd touched him, that she'd even thought of trying. She'd made the leap from thought to action in a blink. He certainly hadn't resisted.

He hadn't participated, either, she reminded herself with a little snort of amusement. But oh, he'd wanted to!

Her fingers curled at the remembered feel of his skin and the way his hair had brushed the back of her hand.

He'd *wanted* to. She was sure of it. He'd wanted far more than just a simple kiss; more, even, than the tumble in the grass that any other man might have expected. A woman didn't need such things spelled out for her. She'd sensed it in the way he'd gone still and taut when her lips had pressed against his, heard it in the aching quiet when she'd withdrawn an endless moment later.

But what did *she* want?

The question seemed to echo in the dark.

What *did* she want? A week ago she'd have known. She could have listed it if someone had ever asked. She wanted her children to be healthy and happy and to grow up into strong, kind, happy adults. She wanted Calhan's to expand and become more profitable, and she wanted to plow those profits back into the store and the investments that would provide for her children's future. She wanted a new linen tablecloth, some new wallpaper for the parlor, and for Dickie to quit dragging his toes through the dirt so that his shoes wore out faster even than he could outgrow them. That was it, really.

But now?

Molly sighed and slumped back against her pillows, then slowly drew the covers up to her chin. She had to face it, all that wasn't enough. Not any longer.

Calhan's wasn't enough. The satisfying, sometimes harried routine of her life wasn't enough. Even her children, as much as she loved them, weren't enough to fill the empty places in her soul, the places she hadn't even admitted were there until DeWitt Gavin had walked into her store and made her remember that she was a woman long before she was a storekeep and a mother.

Chapter Eleven

Molly was late opening the store the next morning. With the exception of the days following Richard's death, she had never been late, and she had no doubt about whom to blame. DeWitt Gavin had robbed her of her sleep last night, wandering through her waking thoughts and her sleeping dreams with equal arrogance. He hadn't been one whit more communicative in her dreams than he was in person, either.

The thought made her laugh. She was still laughing when she came around the corner of Calhan's. Despite the lack of sleep, there was a bounce to her step this morning that had her skipping up the boardwalk steps as lightly as if she were a girl again. The bounce vanished at the sight of the three ladies standing on the walk in front of the store's locked front door.

"You're certainly chipper this morning," Emmy Lou Trainer said, frowning a little to show she didn't much approve of chipper.

"We were starting to get worried," Coreyanne Campbell added. "It's not like you to be late."

"But then, it isn't every evening that she walks out with our good-looking sheriff, now is it, ladies?" Elizabeth Andersen added, beaming and giving her a knowing wink.

Molly couldn't stop the flush seeping up her throat and across her cheeks. "I'm sorry. I didn't know you ladies would be here so bright and early or I'd have made a point to be on time."

"If you'd been at the Ladies' Society meeting last night, as expected, you would have known," Emmy Lou said, laying the stress on the word *would*.

"The meeting!" Molly fumbled with the lock, grateful for the distraction. Any one of the three of them was sharp enough to see her secrets clearly written on her face. With them all together, she hadn't a hope unless she could get out of the morning sun and into the shadowy depths of Calhan's. "I completely forgot about the meeting. These days, seems like I'm behind on everything. Orders, bookkeeping—"

"But not so much behind you won't go out for an evening's stroll," said Emmy Lou disapprovingly.

"Now, Emmy," Elizabeth chided gently.

"He really *is* good-looking," Coreyanne added. "And he seems awfully nice, too. We're all very happy for you, Molly."

Molly's heart sank. If Coreyanne was sharing in the gossip, there wasn't a hope in heaven that the rest of them would keep their noses in their own business and leave her to tend to hers.

As long as they didn't scare him off.

At the thought of DeWitt Gavin being scared off by a passel of ladies half his size, Molly giggled. She covered it with a cough and swung the door open. "I suppose you want to order the bunting and whatnot for the Founders' Day festivities, just like last year. That's what the meeting was about, wasn't it?"

"That's right," Elizabeth said, sweeping in past her. "We can't seem to find the records from last year, but we were sure you'd be able to tell us what we got."

"Of course," Molly murmured, turning the sign on the door to Open.

"And you'll sell them to us at cost, just like last year?" Emmy Lou demanded, sailing in on Elizabeth's heels.

"Yes, of course I will." Molly rolled up the shade on the window on the right.

Coreyanne paused in the doorway just long enough to lean close and whisper, "Don't you worry, Molly. We all approve of him. Even Emmy Lou. All except for his being the sheriff, you know."

Molly almost jerked the second shade right out of its mountings.

Because he couldn't trust himself to keep away from Calhan's, Witt saddled the big, heavy-muscled bay he'd bought from Nickerson's stable shortly after he'd arrived and rode out to visit the various mines that surrounded Elk City. They weren't really in his jurisdiction, but it never hurt to make yourself known, just in case.

To his embarrassment, the tale of his encounter with Crazy Mike McCord had spread. Every place he stopped, sooner or later someone brought it up. And just as soon as they did, there'd be someone offering him a drink on the strength of it.

"Mike's a good man," said one manager, topping up the glass of whiskey he hadn't let Witt refuse. "Wish I had a dozen like him. Used to be there wasn't a steadier man in all of Colorado. Damn shame about the woman. Once he gets to thinkin' of that Jezebel who ran off on him, he gets to drinkin', and then he's as useless as a three-legged mule for days after.''

"Good job, that," said another cheerfully, cracking open a new bottle of whiskey in honor of the occasion. "I hear you gave the fellow a good talkin' to. Hope he paid attention. Although I don't mind admittin'," he added with a wink, "it'd be a good thing for my fellows if Mike wasn't quite up to snuff come Founders' Day. There's always a few competitions got up between the mines. Mike's a hard man to beat when he's in top shape."

"I don't suppose you box?" another foreman inquired, sizing up Witt through narrowed, speculative eyes.

"Nope," said Witt. He didn't feel up to saying much more than that. This was the seventh mine he'd visited, and the hospitality had been a great deal more generous than he was accustomed to.

Right now, the level of whiskey in the bottle on the desk was considerably lower than it had been a half hour before, and though he had insisted on adding water to his glass—a practice the foreman hadn't hesitated to castigate as downright indecent and an insult to any thinking man—he was still having trouble focusing.

"Pity," said the foreman sadly. "You're damn near big as Mike, and if you could flatten him, drunk or no…" He shook his head, then heaved a sigh of resignation. "We don't find somebody bigger'n Mike purty quick, he's bound to take top prize, just like the last few years."

"That right?" said Witt. If he squinted just so, he could make the edge of the desk stop wavering, but it was taking a lot more energy than it ought.

"Yup. Foreman over at the Gradie Rose, where Mike

works, he's got a standin' bet that nobody can take old Mike. Bastard's won near a hunnert dollars off me over the past couple'a years. I'd purely love to get a little of my own back. Purely love it.''

By the time he rode up to the Gradie Rose Mine that afternoon, Witt was having a hard time keeping upright in the saddle. It wasn't that he was drunk, exactly, but all those glasses of whiskey and bottles of beer when he hadn't had much of anything to eat were beginning to have an effect. If it weren't for the fact that the Gradie Rose was his last stop and that he didn't want to create any ill will by ignoring one mine after he'd visited all the rest, he would have pointed the bay toward town and trusted the beast's instincts to get them both back where they belonged.

To his relief, neither the manager nor the foreman of the Gradie Rose was available. He was about to leave word that he'd come back some other time when the office clerk interrupted him.

"There's Mike," he said, pointing to a great, black-faced bear of a man coming out of a long shed. "His shift ain't due to change for another half hour yet. Musta had to come up for something."

Mike spotted them at the same moment. He stopped midstride, frowned, then abruptly changed direction and came their way.

"I'll just leave you two to discuss old times, shall I?" said the clerk a little too heartily. He was gone before Witt could draw breath.

Witt sighed and said a silent prayer that Crazy Mike wasn't the kind to hold grudges.

The miner came to a wary halt a couple feet away. "Sheriff."

"Mr. McCord." Impossible to read the expression on

the other man's face. Coal dust coated every visible inch of him. Only his teeth and the whites of his eyes were not covered with dust. Under the coating of coal dust, his nose was still a little swollen.

"You lookin' for me?"

Witt shook his head, then wished he hadn't. "Nope. Just visiting the mines."

Mike squinted up at him doubtfully. "You look a mite pie-eyed t'me. Hope you don't mind my sayin' so?"

"Nope." Witt couldn't help chuckling, though it made his head ache. "Talked to damn near every mine foreman in the county today, and every one of 'em wanted to drink a toast in your honor. Or maybe I should say, in mine."

The big man blinked, then threw back his head and roared. "That's a good'un, that is! Wait'll I tell the boys!"

Witt winced. "You go right ahead. Me, I'm headed back to town for a thick steak and about a gallon of coffee."

"Not a bad idea. You wait a bit for me t'wash up, I'll go back with you. Not that you *need* to wait." The grin on Crazy Mike's face was making the coal dust crack. "Way you look, you won't move faster'n a slow crawl, anyway."

Witt didn't really want the company, but he couldn't argue with the logic. Besides, there wasn't any sense in making an enemy of the man. And Mike was right—if he tried to move any faster than a walk, the jouncing would likely jar the top of his head right off.

In the end, since Mike didn't own a horse, they ended up walking with Witt leading his mount. It wasn't the sort of exercise he favored, but looking down at the big miner had made him dizzy and the last thing he wanted was to make a damn fool of himself by falling off.

Sober, Mike McCord proved to be intelligent, well-informed, and ambitious. It was the ambitious that surprised Witt.

"I was on my way to foreman," Mike admitted. "I was workin' hard and savin' every penny I could. Wanted to offer my girl—"

"Clementine," said Witt, and blinked. The drink had loosened his tongue more than he'd realized.

Mike nodded. "That's right. Clementine." He looked a little wistful. "Prettiest little thing you ever saw. Golden curls and the biggest, bluest eyes…"

His voice died away. For a moment, he seemed a thousand miles away, remembering, then he grimaced and shook his head regretfully. "Guess the more she thought about it, the less she liked the idea of bein' married to an ugly old buffalo like me."

He held out his hands, fingers spread. "No matter how much I scrub, I can't get rid of the black. Coal gets into a man's skin, see, just burrows right in and won't come out no matter what. Pretty woman, now, she don't much like that. Leastwise, Clementine didn't. One evenin' I come for a visit and her ma, she told me Clementine had just upped and left with some good-lookin' feller from back East. You know, the kind that bathes regular an' dresses nice an' wears that good smellin' stuff the ladies like."

Witt's mouth twisted. "Samuel Kroshack, to a tee."

"What?" said Mike, startled.

"Fellow my wife ran off with," Witt explained. The admission caught him by surprise. He'd never talked about Clara with anyone. "She wanted a fancy dressin' man, too. One who didn't look like a damned fool drinking from a teacup and who knew all the right things to say in public.''

''That so?'' Mike eyed him thoughtfully. ''Way I heard it, she was the one divorced you.''

Witt shrugged, uncomfortable with the direction of the conversation. ''Didn't see any sense in dragging her through the courts.''

The big miner mulled that over, then nodded. ''I can see that. Man looks a damn fool when his wife runs out on him like that.''

''That, too.''

They walked on a ways in silence before Mike spoke again. ''Heard you was walkin' out with Missus Calhan.''

Witt choked.

''My landlady was talkin' with the cook this mornin','' Mike explained. ''Place like this, word gets around.''

''We went for a walk.''

''Uh-huh. That's what I heard.''

''It's not the same as walkin' out,'' Witt insisted, cursing the whiskey fumes that had loosened his tongue and made his head feel two sizes too big for his shoulders.

Mike shrugged. ''Maybe so, but folks around here, they don't see much difference between the two.''

His eyes narrowed slightly, just enough to be menacing without being an outright threat. ''She's a fine lady. You treat her right, you hear? You don't…'' Mike flexed his meaty hand, then closed it into a fist the size of a boulder.

Witt eyed him right back. Damned if he wouldn't take the fellow, drunk or not. ''You got any interests that way?''

"Me?" Mike looked surprised. "Heck, no. The lady's above my touch. But she's always been nice to me. I wouldn't like to hear anyone's been messin' with her."

"Me, neither," said Witt thickly.

"Good," said Mike. "That's good." He grinned, suddenly, and gave him a friendly slap on the back that almost dislodged a lung. "I like you, Gavin. Darned if I don't."

Witt staggered, sucked in air, and was, for the moment, devoutly grateful that he did.

Molly crumpled yet another scribbled sheet of figures and angrily tossed it at the already overflowing trash can under the counter. No matter how she added things up, this expansion she'd been planning was going to be expensive. A thousand dollars worth of expensive.

The sum was enough to take her breath away. A thousand dollars! Why, she and Richard hadn't had much more than that when they'd first taken the notion to run a store over twelve years ago!

Not that she didn't have the money—she had more than that invested in gilt-edged stocks and bonds, with a bit put away in the bank, but she didn't like dipping into Bonnie and Dickie's future like that. She'd taken out loans in the past when she'd wanted to expand and always managed to pay them off early, and she was convinced she could pay off another. But she'd never asked for anywhere near this much before.

The only thing good she could say about it was that it had distracted her from other, more troubling matters. Her first three customers hadn't been the only ones to have heard of her evening stroll with the sheriff—around here, a woman couldn't get dust on her petticoats without somebody hearing about it and telling half a dozen others—but that wasn't the problem.

The problem was her own too active imagination building castles on some very shaky foundations. If any of her customers guessed just how often she'd thought of that kiss she'd so boldly claimed last night, they'd have tied knots in their tongues from all the flapping. Let them suspect how easily that hungry heat washed through her at the thought of his physical response and they'd probably choke on all the words that would come tumbling out.

The only way she'd managed to get through the day was to concentrate on this last, careful review of her plans.

Molly scanned her notes and figures, and reviewed the list of new merchandise she'd order. It was all there. Anything less than a thousand and she wouldn't have the cash to do it right. And if she didn't do it right, she might as well not do it at all.

Nothing for it but to grab her courage in both hands and *do* it. She'd been scared before and it had all worked out. It would work out this time. She'd make sure it did. The only really hard part of it all was asking Gordon Hancock for the loan in the first place, and she could handle him as long as things stayed on a strictly business basis.

With Hancock in mind, she took extra time to tidy her hair and clothes, then carefully pinned on her hat so the narrow brim with its edging of silk roses sat just so. When she caught herself wondering if DeWitt Gavin would like the hat and the way she looked wearing it, she wrenched herself away from the mirror.

After one last check to be sure she had everything, she gathered up the folder with her notes and calculations, flipped the sign to Closed, added the smaller sign that said, Back in Half an Hour, and locked the door behind her.

Hiram Goff was his usual disapproving self, but he grudgingly admitted that Mr. Hancock was in. After a moment's consultation with the great man himself, he even more grudgingly ushered her into his office.

"Mrs. Calhan! What a pleasant surprise!" Hancock smiled that wide, white-toothed smile that she so disliked and came around the desk to welcome her.

Molly took the chair he indicated, then watched with scarcely concealed disgust as he claimed the chair beside her.

"To what do I owe the pleasure?" He leaned closer. His voice became softer, slightly more intimate. "Not that you have to have an excuse. You know you're welcome anytime."

Molly shifted her chair to face him, which meant her knees would conveniently be in the way if he tried to move closer. "I'm interested in taking out another loan, Mr. Hancock."

"Another!" He laughed. "You've been busy, I see. Always planning and scheming, eh, Mrs. Calhan? Work, work, work!"

"Just like any other serious businessperson, Mr. Hancock." She extended the folder. "I've worked up my notes and calculations, made a list of what it would be spent for. It's all right there."

"You're always so…organized," he murmured, taking the folder. He didn't bother to open it. "And how much are you thinking of this time? Three hundred? Four? I believe the last loan was for four hundred, wasn't it?"

"Four-fifty, and paid in full three months early. But I need a thousand this time."

That brought him up short. "A thousand!"

"And not a penny less." The words came out boldly enough, but her stomach squeezed at the thought of so large a debt.

He frowned at the folder, then at her. "That's quite a bit of money for a small store like yours, Mrs. Calhan."

Molly's grip on her purse tightened. "I'm aware of that. But if you will look at my notes, you'll see that I've considered everything. Expenses, interest, return based on increased sales. The bank won't lose its money any more than it did with the other loans I've had."

"Yes, but a thousand!" He stared a her a moment, his eyes hooded and unrevealing, then flipped the folder open.

"All very orderly, I see. A note from Dr. Smithers confirming his intention to rent to you. Construction costs, repayment schedule, new merchandise. Shoes, housewares, roofing supplies, wallpaper, toilet paper. Yes. Hmm. Plumbing." His head came up. *"Plumbing?"*

"Plumbing," said Molly firmly. "Elk City's growing. When the city puts in those sewer and water lines like the town council's been discussing, people here will want better indoor plumbing. Water closets, bathtubs. Even water heaters."

"Water heaters!"

"I take it you don't heat and haul your own bath water, Mr. Hancock?" said Molly dryly.

"My— Of course not!"

"Trust me. The ladies in town will figure out a way to buy water heaters for their homes. They've heard about the plumbing system in the Grand Hotel, and a number of them have personally inspected the facilities at the homes of several of our leading citizens. Don't forget, the Elk City Ladies' Society meets in our members' homes in rotation.''

Hancock squirmed in his seat.

Molly found herself relishing his discomfort. "The new water closet in Mayor Andersen's house was quite a sensation, I assure you!"

Gordon Hancock, president of the Elk City State Bank, distinguished member of the town council, chairman of the board of the Elk City Miners' Benevolent Fund, member in good standing of his men's club, and respected advisor to the annual Sunday school charity drive, boggled at the thought.

He snapped his mouth shut and tried to regroup. "And if the city doesn't put in those water lines?"

"I imagine the voters will have something to say about that, Mr. Hancock." She gave him a demure, dangerous little smile. "Their wives won't give them any peace until they do, I assure you. The members of the Ladies' Society have studied the matter very carefully and would be glad to discuss the public health issues of private wells versus city water and cesspits versus public sewers, if you like."

"Sewers!" said Gordon Hancock. He grimaced in distaste. "That's not the sort of thing a lady should be thinking about."

"We ladies have been emptying chamberpots for years. I assure you, we know a great deal about latrines and cesspits."

"Cesspits! My God!" He almost shoved the folder at her.

The satisfaction turned to triumph. She'd wanted to

get the best of Gordon Hancock for a long time, but never thought she'd do it in the guise of a business conversation.

She couldn't help adding one more item, though.

"That's why toilet paper's on my list along with the plumbing supplies. I don't sell very much of it right now, but once folks start putting in their own water closets, I expect sales of toilet paper to increase at least three hundred per cent, and probably a whole lot more."

"Really, Mrs. Calhan!"

"I didn't want you to think I hadn't considered this expansion very carefully, Mr. Hancock. I have! Right down to the last box of bolts and the last roll of—"

"Yes. Yes, of course," he interjected hastily. "I wouldn't expect anything less from an intelligent businesswoman like you, but cesspits...!"

He cleared his throat, tugged on his tie, and squared his shoulders. He eyed her, then the folder she now held.

"A thousand dollars, you said?"

Molly nodded. "That's right. Under the same terms as the last loan, but with a longer repayment period, of course."

With talk of dollars and terms, Gordon Hancock was back on familiar ground. "I'm afraid that's not possible. Interest rates have gone up—"

"The same terms except for the repayment period," Molly repeated firmly.

His expression turned as pinched and disapproving as his clerk's. "We don't do business that way, Mrs. Calhan."

"You do if it's with a business*man,* Mr. Hancock."

For an instant, she thought he would snap her head off, but she'd misjudged him. Gordon Hancock was nothing if not flexible. After a moment's thought, he tried another tack.

"You know, I worry about you, Mrs. Calhan," he said.

He edged his chair around beside hers, propped his elbow on the arm, and leaned toward her confidingly.

"All those responsibilities. Two children, a store and a house to run."

His voice dropped a little to carry a faint, but unmistakable note of intimacy. He leaned a couple of inches closer and smiled.

"It can't be easy."

"It isn't." She had to fight against the urge to shrink back in her chair, away from him.

"Having to plan and scheme and try to make ends meet. Most women couldn't do it."

"Most women," Molly said flatly, "manage just fine."

He smiled, a very gentle, sympathetic, *understanding* smile. His voice dropped lower still, until it was just this side of an intimate whisper.

"You know, there are ways to make things easier."

"*Are* there?" Her skin crawled just at the thought of what he was suggesting.

"Yes. Yes, there are." His smile widened as he leaned even closer, then gently placed his hand on her knee. "I could show you, if you liked."

Molly drew a deep breath, smiled and looked him straight in the eye. "Mr. Hancock, if you don't remove your hand from my knee this instant, I will personally break every one of your beautifully manicured fingers until you do."

Chapter Twelve

Elk City was beginning to stir with the comfortable, end-of-the-work-day relief that promised supper and maybe a quick visit to Jackson's, if a man could sneak past his wife, or a long session with the Denver and Gunnison papers that would have come in on the late train if he couldn't. The only part that interested Witt was the supper.

"Steak," he said. "At Mrs. Jensen's. I'll buy."

McCord nodded agreeably, swinging wide to miss a large pile of horse droppings adorning the street. "Don't mind if I do. Better'n the grub where I board, and that's a fact."

They were half a block from Nickerson's stables and almost to the broad steps that led up to Elk City State Bank's front door, but Witt's attention was on the front of Calhan's across the street. The sign on the door said Closed. The candy display was long gone, and he was grateful for it.

The sour balls Molly had given him were tucked at the back of the bottom drawer of his desk at the jail. Yesterday afternoon he'd bought some lemon drops in George Goodnight's little store at the other end of town.

He'd told himself it was good politics to spread his visits among all the stores, and known that he was lying. It hadn't helped that they weren't half as mouth-puckering sweet as the ones Molly sold.

"You tried the steaks at Mrs. Jensen's?"

Mike's cheerful query dragged Witt back to Main Street and the thought of supper. "Not yet. Heard she makes a good cup of coffee."

"Darned good apple pie, too."

He winced, remembering Molly's pie and the plate and her laughter at the confusion and what it had all led to last night, down there by the river. He'd tried to put it out of his thoughts and for a while, with the whiskey dulling everything, he had. Now, with just a few casual words, McCord had brought it all back.

"I'd rather have a steak," he said, just as the sound of hurrying footsteps brought his head around with a snap.

Molly damn near knocked him down, she was going so fast.

He put out his hand to steady her. His horse jerked backward, startled, so that he ended up grabbing her arm more roughly than he'd intended. She yanked free and spun aside, furious.

"Keep your hands off me!"

And then she was gone, storming across the street like a black and very angry cloud. Witt just stood there openmouthed, staring after her. They could hear the front door of Calhan's slamming shut from clear across the street.

"The lady seems a mite upset," Mike said mildly after a moment. Too mildly.

Witt turned to study the front door of Elk City State bank, and frowned.

* * *

Molly didn't bother changing the Closed sign to Open when she slammed the front door of Calhan's shut behind her.

The cad! The scheming, unprincipled, oily cad! If she were a man, she would have hit him in that pretty face of his. Pow! Square on that perfect nose.

For a moment, Molly stared into nothing, blissfully contemplating the prospect of Gordon Hancock, Esquire, with his nose bloodied and twisted askew.

The bliss changed to a scowl. The one whose nose she should have smashed was that arrogant animal who'd grabbed her arm there in the street. One quick blow and—

The scowl gave way to a dawning horror.

The *sheriff* had grabbed her arm. She'd run smack into him, rude as could be, then snarled like a she-cat and stomped away without so much as a word of apology.

Her cheeks flamed at the memory.

Too bad she couldn't tell him the reason for her temper—he could flatten Hancock's nose for her. In fact, she'd bet he'd enjoy rearranging the banker's features. The one time she'd seen the two of them together, right here in the store, they'd been as wary as two dogs, hackles up and circling for a fight.

Molly tossed her folder under the counter, then thoughtfully drew out one of the long, pearl-headed pins that kept her hat in place. What she couldn't figure out was why Hancock had thought his advances would be welcome. Without saying a word, he'd long ago made it clear that he was more than willing to "keep her company" so long as there was no commitment involved, but until now, he'd never dared step over the line into an outright advance. What had tempted him to do so now?

The answer came in a flash of certainty so disconcerting that she pricked herself with the second hat pin. *The sheriff.*

Thoughts spinning, Molly stuck her finger in her mouth and sucked at the welling blood.

Hancock had heard the same gossip as everyone else—that she'd walked out with the sheriff last night and hadn't come back until long after dark. His perverse little mind had made the leap from speculation to conviction and decided that he might as well get in on the fun. From his perspective, her need of a loan was the perfect lever to ensure he got what he wanted. Presumptuous toad!

She ripped off her hat, then shoved the hat pins back in so savagely that the roses on the brim quivered. Next time Hancock tried to put a hand on her knee, she'd yank out a pin and stab him. And then she'd ask the sheriff to do what she couldn't and flatten Hancock's nose.

She could picture it now—the sheriff standing tall and fierce, triumphant, her vanquished enemy groveling in the dirt at his feet. He'd be glorious, a knight in shining armour clad, not in steel, but in a rumpled work shirt and worn wool pants, with a dusty Stetson on his head and dusty boots on his feet and a gleam in his eyes that would be all for her. And then he'd turn to her and he'd smile and open his arms—

Had she gone mad? What in the world was she thinking?

Shaken, she pressed her hands to her face. Her cheeks burned her palms; the tip of her finger throbbed where she'd pricked it. She scarcely noticed. All day she'd fought against the temptation to think of him, yet still he'd slipped past her defenses.

Gavin. *Witt*

Why did he attract her so? What was it that gave him the power to rule her dreams and torment her waking thoughts? The way she was behaving lately, she might as well be a giddy girl of sixteen as a grown woman of thirty-one with children and more responsibilities than she cared to count.

If she closed her eyes, she could see him standing there by the riverbank, dark hair tossed by the breeze, that strong, hard face shadowed with remembered grief. She could feel his lips, firm and warm beneath hers, sense the almost imperceptible trembling in his limbs as she'd regretfully pulled away.

She smiled, remembering the plate.

She'd have to apologize for running him down, of course. Poor man was probably wondering what he'd done to merit such rudeness.

There was always kiss and make up.

The thought made her laugh.

The rose looked fine in the water glass, a flash of scarlet in the gray drabness of his room. In the space of twenty-four hours it had gone from a half-opened bud to a full-blown blossom. By this time tomorrow, Witt knew, it would be shedding its petals one by one until the lightest touch would scatter them all, leaving only the stem.

Witt stared at it, remembering the way she'd teetered on tiptoe to hook it through his buttonhole, the way her hands had pressed against his chest. He'd swear his flesh burned just at the memory, right where her hand had rested for a moment, just there, over his heart. He rubbed the spot thoughtfully, troubled.

Not a week in town and already things had gone too far. And that kiss last night...

He wished he'd kissed her back.

He'd wanted to. Badly. So badly that a day later he still ached from the wanting.

The hell of it was, he'd swear she wanted him, too. There she'd been, breathing hard, just like him, with her lower lip trembling and her hand trembling and that heat on her skin that sure as hell wasn't from the exercise. If he'd been another man, a man with a little more skill and a lot less size, maybe they could have made something of that wanting, there in the tall grass with the stars looking down. Maybe.

And maybe not. She hadn't looked any too pleased when she'd run him down in the street this afternoon.

Without any evidence whatsoever, Witt was more than willing to lay the blame for that square on Gordon Hancock's well-tailored shoulders. That low-down snake in the grass was just the type to try to take advantage of a fine woman like Molly, who had no man to protect her.

Not that she really needed one, he admitted with a sigh. Molly Calhan managed just fine on her own.

With an effort, Witt pushed aside the thought of her and concentrated on the mundane details of undressing for bed, instead. But as he bent to turn down the lamp, he spotted the small, crumpled brown bag that had sat there ever since that first day he'd met her. There was one chocolate cream left. He'd been saving it, telling himself he didn't need it even though his mouth had watered at the thought of it.

Truth was, he'd been afraid to eat it, knowing that the taste of it would make him think of her.

Slowly, frowning, he opened the bag and shook its treasure out onto his open palm. It made him think of the first one she'd given him, and how she'd looked, smiling at him over the top of that glass case.

It tasted as good as the first, too. For a moment, he simply let it lie on his tongue while the flavor filled his mouth. God, he loved chocolates! But what in the hell was he going to do if just the taste of them was enough to make him think of her?

At the thought, he bit down, crushing the chocolate shell so that the sweeter cream filling spilled out. Better and better.

Witt closed his eyes, savoring the taste, only to see her as she'd been that first day, with strands of hair spilling along her cheeks and throat and that smudge on her cheek and that smile that made him think of sunshine.

With a groan, he turned down the lamp, suddenly grateful for the enclosing dark. The rough sheet and rougher blanket were solid and utterly normal. The bedsprings creaked as he tried to find a comfortable position on the too short bed. The lumpy excuse for a pillow seemed more lumps and empty ticking than ever, and as he pounded it into a ball, he realized he could buy a good one from Molly. She'd be bound to have one in her store somewhere.

Just the thought of Molly and pillows was enough to make him sweat. With a curse, he rolled over onto his back—to hell with having to hang his feet over the foot of the bed. It wasn't any help.

The taste of chocolate was sweet and heavy on his tongue, the scent of roses on every breath he took as he lay there staring into the dark, aching for what he knew he could never have.

Morning brought cold good sense: Apologies, yes; kiss and make up, no. Absurd to feel so disappointed.

Since it was Friday and Dickie's day to sweep up, Molly accompanied her son to the jail. Witt was tilted back in his chair, feet casually propped on the desk, glaring at a sheaf of papers in his hand. Stacks of papers and folders and battered ledgers littered the desk. If he was making any progress with them, whatever they were, she could see no sign of it.

At the sight of them, he tossed aside the papers and brought his feet to the floor with a thump. A sudden tightness squeezed Molly's throat.

He studied her warily, as if he expected her to bite him. "Ma'am."

"Sheriff Gavin." She'd almost said, Witt.

He winked at Dickie. "Mornin', boy. Still game, are you?"

Dickie beamed back. "You betcha!"

Molly gave him a little nudge.

"Uh, I mean, yes, sir, I sure am."

"That's good. Broom's right where you left it last time. You can start with my room, there at the back. I already got my laundry bundled up in a sheet off my bed."

Dickie vanished, leaving Molly tangled in dangerous thoughts.

"I wanted to apologize for my rudeness yesterday," she said, stumbling a little over the words. "I was…distracted."

"Looked to me like it was more upset than distracted.'' He cocked his head, studying her. That calm, direct gaze was unnerving.

"That, too," she reluctantly admitted.

"Hancock?"

She bit her lower lip, remembering how she had imagined him standing over the defeated banker, remembering a kiss.

"A...business matter."

He didn't believe her—she could see it in his eyes and the way he stood, so still and poised, as if he could extract the truth simply by waiting. He was too polite to call her a liar, though. When she remained silent, he stepped back.

"Anyone bothers you, you tell me. I'll take care of them."

"I...ah...thank you."

"Mmm," he said.

Since there really wasn't anything else to say, she took her leave. He walked her the whole five steps to the jail door and stopped, but she'd swear he watched her until she'd unlocked the front door of Calhan's and slipped inside. She didn't have the courage to look back and see for sure.

The familiar routine of opening the store didn't go quite as smoothly as it usually did. She jammed the right window shade when she tried to roll it up, forgot to change the Closed sign to Open until the first customer banged on the door, wanting in, knocked over the display of soap, then forgot to get the day's cash for the cash register out of her small safe until she had to make change.

From thoughts of kisses to thoughts of sheets. It wasn't, Molly decided, an improvement.

Chapter Thirteen

Molly Calhan was avoiding him.

Witt was no expert on women, but even he could figure out that much. It had been two weeks, going on three, since she'd last come by the jail. In all that time, all he'd had from her was, "Good morning, Sheriff. What can I get for you today?" followed by a "Will that be all?" and then the total for his purchases and a "Here's your change." And that was it, except for the occasional comment about "Nice day today, isn't it?" which really didn't count for much of anything.

He wouldn't have had that much if he hadn't resorted to some pretty desperate measures. Gradually, ounce by ounce, he'd bought up every sweet treat and candy she had in the store—so much that she'd had to send a special order into Denver for more before he'd emptied that glass-fronted case entirely.

He bought licorice whips and peppermint drops, horehound squares and lemon drops and sour balls. He bought gumdrops and roasted peanuts and malt balls and toffees and chocolate drops and red-hot cinnamons, taffy and lady kisses and seven different flavors of chewing gum. He bought them by the pack and the bag and the box and the half dozen, but he only bought them one kind at a time, and never more than he absolutely had to.

The only thing he hadn't bought was a chocolate cream, but that wasn't from not wanting to.

Most of what he bought he ended up sharing with the children of Elk City. There'd been a lot to share. So much, in fact, that he couldn't hardly turn around these days without tripping over one or another of 'em, coming and going. He'd had to make a rule of never giving them anything outside of Calhan's or he'd have been tethered to that store as tight as any horse hitched to the rail out front.

Worse, folks were beginning to notice.

"Been to Mrs. Calhan's, have you, Sheriff?" they'd say with a grin and a wink when they'd find him doling out the sweets. Or, "Got a lemon drop, sheriff? I swear, my mouth just puckers up at the very thought of one." Or, "I'm considerin' buyin' up stock in a candy factory, Sheriff. What d'you think? Will this run on the market hold?" And then they'd snicker and walk away and he'd be left standing there, looking like a damned fool and feeling even worse.

They hadn't yet noticed that his nightly rounds were taking him by the Calhan house more often than any other place in town. He'd never have survived the ribbing if they had.

He hadn't started out this way. In fact, he'd been relieved when three whole days had gone by without seeing her. But then that Friday when she'd apologized for running into him on the street had swung round to Monday and there was Dickie on his doorstep, so to speak, chattering like a magpie and sweeping up more dust clouds than he was sweeping dirt into the street, and Witt had been forced to admit he hadn't forgotten her at all.

That's when he'd left Dickie to his dust and wandered over to the store. He was out of shaving soap and candy, so it wasn't, or so he'd told himself, as if he were trying to find an excuse to see her. No, he was just a fellow who needed soap and Calhan's was the closest.

She'd been cold as frost in January. Not rude, of course, but not warm and friendly like she'd been. What smiles she'd had were reserved for other customers, not for him, and there were no free samples of chocolates to be had. He'd eventually wandered back out feeling strangely out of sorts.

The first pack of kids he'd come to, he'd given them the gumdrops he'd bought. That had cheered him up a little, so he'd gone back for more. Molly had been even frostier than before. *That* had made him mad, and the more he'd thought about it, the more his mad had festered.

It wasn't as if there was anything between them— just dinner and a kiss and a chocolate cream, and he doubted she even remembered the chocolate cream. It wasn't as if he expected anything to come of their relationship, either, despite the way his knees went weak whenever he thought of her, which was far too frequently for comfort. No, it was the principle of the thing. A man had a right to a little respect, after all, especially when he'd hired her son and offered to help with any piddling little troubles she might have with ungentlemanly bankers.

When he'd walked into Calhan's the first thing the next morning, he'd told himself it was just to prove she couldn't drive him away so easily. But he'd caught her by surprise, and when she'd spun around to face him, he'd seen that little start of eagerness that she wasn't quite quick enough to hide.

Oh, she'd tried to hide it under a sudden bustle to dust this and straighten that, but he could tell the difference.

He had to admit, he'd rather enjoyed seeing her all flustered like that. Usually it was he who got confused when there were ladies involved, not the other way around, and he found he liked the feeling of coming out on top for once.

It hadn't done him any good, though. She'd just gotten frostier and more formal than ever. He hadn't had a good "Nice day, isn't it?" for over a week. In fact, she was so cool, it was a wonder he hadn't gotten chilblains from the cold.

Which might not have been so bad if she hadn't started a fire way down deep inside of him that refused to die out, no matter what.

"So we're agreed. Elizabeth will coordinate the cakewalk and the punch stand, MayBeth will choose the music for the town band to play, and Coreyanne will speak to Reverend Brighton about the invocation. The decorations committee—of which I am in charge—will see to rounding up the men to make sure the job gets done right and on time."

Emmy Lou frowned at her notes, then peered over the tops of her reading glasses at Molly. "I'm assuming the decorations will be here on time?"

"They'll be here." Molly had to grit her teeth to keep from snapping.

She'd been ordering the decorations every year since Calhan's first opened for business, and every year

Emmy Lou, who'd long ago staked out the decorations committee as her personal fiefdom, had pestered and fretted and fussed over those decorations until they all wanted to scream.

This year the desire to scream had been replaced by open talk of armed mutiny. Through some stratagem no one quite understood—there was much dark muttering of bribes and blackmail, though Molly doubted it had gone quite that far—Emmy Lou had not only maintained control of the decorations committee, she'd managed to be named head of the entire Founders' Day celebration.

She was the first woman in the history of Elk City to be granted that distinction, and Molly privately thought they'd be lucky if the Society members didn't come to blows before this was over. Word was going round that Mayor Andersen was paying more frequent and extended visits to Jackson's saloon than even he was accustomed to, and that Zacharius Trainer had taken to joining him.

"You're *sure* they'll be here?" said Emmy Lou. "I can't stress enough how important it is that the decorations arrive in time."

Molly nodded. Emmy Lou eyed her doubtfully, and for a moment, Molly feared she'd launch into a long-winded lecture on the subject. There was a collective, muffled sigh of relief when, after a moment's hesitation, Emmy Lou turned back to her notes instead. The evening's meeting had already gone two hours longer than normal, and since they were meeting at Emmy Lou's house, Emmy Lou was sitting in the only comfortable chair in sight. Molly's backside had gone from stiff to sore, then moved straight into numb more than an hour ago.

"Cakewalk, punch stand, music, invocation, decorations," Emmy Lou muttered to herself, one by one ticking the items off her list with a stubby pencil. She raised her head. "Is there anything I've missed?"

"What about the treats for the children?" said Louisa Merton. "Nobody's mentioned those, but you know we always have something to hand out afterward."

The room went dead silent. No one moved a muscle; no one so much as breathed. Molly could swear her collar had suddenly gotten tighter. Trust Louisa not to have heard the gossip and gone blundering right in.

"Treats?" Emmy Lou said in awful tones.

Louisa blenched, clearly uncertain where she'd stumbled, but quite certain that she'd not only roused Emmy Lou's wrath, but the resentment of everyone present who'd finally begun to believe there might be an ending to the meeting after all.

"Treats," said Louisa in a small voice. "Little bags of candy? The ones we give to all the children after the speeches and before the fireworks? You know, treats?"

"Hah!" said Emmy Lou. She deliberately put aside her list and pencil, an awful gleam in her eye. "We won't be having any treats this year."

"But...why?" Louisa glanced around the room, puzzled. "Nobody told me anything about it."

No one offered to explain. Few even dared to meet her troubled gaze. Someone coughed and shifted uncomfortably, but when Louisa glanced that way, the room went quiet again.

Molly stared at her hands, knowing what was coming. Her fingers kept wanting to curl into a fist. Deliberately, she folded them in her lap, then raised her gaze to meet Emmy Lou's wrathful one.

"Why?" Emmy Lou snapped. "Because there's not

a child in town who'll have any teeth left to be eating
sweets come Founders' Day. Not after our good sheriff
gets through stuffing them with every gumdrop and
penny candy that Calhan's has to offer. Isn't that right,
Molly?''

''It's true the sheriff has been quite generous with the
children,'' Molly said with forced calm, ''but I seriously
doubt he's been so generous that their teeth are in any
danger.''

''Much you know about it!'' Emmy Lou was almost
quivering with indignation. All the satisfaction of having taken command of her Founders' Day army had
vanished beneath the reminder that her husband was not
sheriff, and that she was the only one in town who was
sorry for it.

*She's heard the rumors about her husband and the
mayor.* Molly stared into Emmy Lou's hostile, angry
eyes, shaken by the unmasked truth she saw there.
She'd always understood the woman's anger and resentment that life hadn't granted her the power and
status she aspired to. Until now, she'd never sensed the
pain that lay beneath the anger.

''So long as you make your profit,'' Emmy Lou said
bitterly, ''I suppose it doesn't matter, but someone
needs to tell you—''

''Goodness!'' said MayBeth Johnson, peering at the
watch pinned to her breast. ''Look at the time! Emmy
Lou, I hate to break up the meeting, but if I don't get
back right now Mr. Johnson will call out the army,
looking for me!''

She jumped to her feet. The rest of them eagerly followed suit, nervously chattering about how late it was
and my! how time had flown and hadn't it been a fine
meeting but so much to do, you know, really best get

home. The chatter was half-drowned in the scraping of chairs and the clatter of teacups and saucers being rounded up. More than one, under the pretext of straightening her skirts, rubbed her backside and grimaced.

In the midst of it all was Emmy Lou, hiding her feelings behind a spate of orders and sharp reminders that simply served to drive everyone out the door all that much faster.

Molly carefully didn't look her way, afraid her own feelings might show too clearly. The last thing Emmy Lou would want was pity.

Once out the front gate, Molly gratefully drank in the cool night air. Bonnie and Dickie were probably beginning to wonder where she'd gotten to, but she didn't much feel like rushing home. Not yet. She'd take the long way round, she decided. Stretch out the kinks from so many hours of sitting on that hard, straight-backed chair.

Most of the other ladies seemed to feel the same about not rushing home. Once safely out of sight of the Trainer house, they clustered in the street, eager to talk.

Coreyanne Campbell, usually the most even-tempered of them all, was the first to speak. "Much more of this and I swear I'll resign from the Society."

"We'll *all* resign," said MayBeth fervently. She glanced around to see who was still present, then added, "Someone needs to have a long, hard talk with the mayor. Whatever was he thinking, naming her head of the whole thing?"

"She must have caught him at something," another added. "She's wanted the job for years, but no one was crazy enough to let her have it until now."

Quietly, Molly edged away. She was tired and the

last thing she wanted right now was to listen to her friends work out their anger in this kind of talk.

Louisa Merton stopped her before she'd gone five feet.

"I'm really sorry, Molly," she said earnestly, laying her hand on Molly's arm. "I didn't mean to get you in trouble, but I didn't know about the candy. Honest, I really didn't."

"You didn't get me in trouble." Molly patted Louisa's hand. "It would have come up sooner or later, anyway."

"Really?"

"Really." Molly smiled. Louisa was often silly, but she was young and she had a kind heart. "I'm going to take the long way home, so I'll be going by your place. Do you want to walk with me?"

Louisa glanced at the cluster of women behind them.

"They'll be breaking up in a minute," Molly assured her. "There really isn't much to say, after all."

"But that won't stop them from saying it, will it?"

Molly laughed. "No, I don't suppose it will."

They covered the first block in thoughtful silence. Louisa wasn't one who could keep silent long, however.

"What I don't understand," she said slowly, as if picking her words with care, "is why Mrs. Trainer is so upset about the sheriff giving out all that candy. It's just a little bit, you know, and he mostly gives it to kids who wouldn't get much, otherwise."

"You've seen him?" Molly had to fight to keep the eagerness from her voice.

"He gave me some." The dark hid the blush Molly knew glowed on Louisa's cheeks. "A lady's kiss."

Louisa giggled. "I don't think he realized how it looked—him giving me the lady's kiss, I mean—until

I said something, and then he turned red as those red bandannas in your store.''

''Did he?'' Molly said, sternly ignoring the envy pricking at her.

''It's a shame he's so old. He's not really bad looking once you get used to him being so big and all.''

He's not old! she wanted to shout.

''No, he's not bad looking,'' she said instead.

And she should know. She'd been studying every line and curve and shadow on his face these past three weeks. Every time he'd stepped inside her store, she'd found herself searching for each familiar detail—that spot on his jaw that he often missed shaving, the way his eyelids drooped when he wanted to hide what he was thinking, that one dark, curly hair at the corner of his brow that always wanted to go a different direction from the others.

Even as she'd fought to maintain her dignity while she'd counted out chocolate kisses and weighed up gumdrops, every nerve in her body had been attuned to his slightest move and word and gesture. She couldn't help herself. After a while, she'd given up trying and settled for maintaining that safe, prim facade of hers, instead.

This sudden, aching need she'd discovered within herself was frightening and exhilarating, all at the same time. After so many years of marriage and raising children, after four years of widowhood, she no longer knew how to control it, and wasn't sure she cared to try.

Witt Gavin had become so much a part of her life, whether he'd intended to or not, that she worried when he was late or distracted or too quiet, even for him.

In three short weeks she'd learned his little tricks and

habits. He frowned when he was trying to decide between the licorice and the red-hot cinnamons. He kept his change in his left-hand trouser pocket on the side away from his gun, and when he pulled it out to pay for his purchases, he also pulled out the scraps of paper and odd little bits and pieces that seemed to accumulate in a man's pockets. His lower lip pooched out a little when he sorted through the junk to find the coins he wanted, as if it helped him concentrate on the task at hand.

It had been all she could do to keep from offering him another chocolate cream, just because she wanted to watch him while he ate it.

She thought of the way that crooked smile would creep across his face, and the laughter that could light up those changeable eyes of his. She thought of the way that dark lock of hair would fall across his brow sometimes, and the way he'd blink whenever she said something that caught him by surprise, of those broad shoulders and chest, and the strong arms that seemed made to hold a woman close.

No, Witt Gavin definitely was not bad looking.

She thought of that slow, deep voice, and shivered.

With a few casual words, Louisa had undone three weeks' effort of trying to pretend that this attraction to him wasn't serious and didn't matter.

"In fact," Louisa added confidingly, "a big man like that sort of makes you feel…safe, don't you think? Makes you feel like more of a woman."

Molly made a little strangled noise deep in her throat. She turned the corner on Hanson Street, ducking slightly to avoid the branches of a big pine that stretched out into the path, and ran right into DeWitt Gavin. Even in the dark, she knew him.

"What the hell?"

Molly gasped as his hand clamped down on her arm.

Louisa gave a frightened little squawk and grabbed her other arm. "Go away! Leave us alone or I'll scream!"

"It's all right, Louisa," Molly said, tugging free of both of them. Annoyed, she hitched her shawl back into place. "It's only Sheriff Gavin and his friends."

In the darker shadows cast by the pine, the other two men with Witt were little more than large, bulky shapes in the dark. The man in the middle looked like he'd collapse if the other two hadn't been propping him up.

Molly stepped closer, trying to make out details. "Mr. Trainer?"

The man in the middle shook off his supports. His head wobbled on his shoulders.

"We home, are we?" Zacharius Trainer blearily demanded.

"Almost," said the third man.

"Mr. McCord?"

"The same, ma'am." She could hear the grin in Crazy Mike's voice even if she couldn't see it.

"This one'uv Josiah's girlfriends?" Zacharius squinted, trying to get his eyes to focus. "My, ain't you a purty one! Pleashed t'meet yuh."

He tried to sweep her a bow. His burly escorts grabbed him just before he fell flat on his face.

"Oh, dear, oh, dear," said Louisa, wringing her hands. "Mrs. Trainer is going to be so upset. Do you really think you ought to take him home when he's like this?"

"We've been walking him around, trying to sober him up," Witt said, disgusted.

"You obviously haven't walked him enough," Molly

observed dryly. Zacharius was trying to sing. His words weren't slurred quite enough to disguise the vulgar lyrics.

"Keep telling you we ought to let him sleep it off in the jail." Mike was clearly enjoying himself. "Bed's not bad, and from what I've heard, his missus is almighty anxious to see him there."

"I'm not puttin' him in the jail."

"You didn't mind puttin me there."

"He didn't shoot the damned piano!"

"Watch your language, man," Mike chided, fighting not to laugh. "There's ladies present."

Balked, Witt turned his frustration on her, instead.

"What are you doing out this late, anyway?" he demanded, aggrieved. "I figured your meeting'd be over hours ago."

"Mrs. Trainer had a lot of things to discuss," Louisa said. "We've only just left."

"And the others may be right behind us," Molly added. "If you don't want them to see you dragging Mr. Trainer home, you'd better find a good alley to hide him in until they've all gone by."

"Jus' left?" said Mr. Trainer, weaving slightly. He thumped Witt's shoulder weakly. "Toldja coulda shtayed another hour. Women get to talkin', can't hardly *ever* shut 'em up. I *know*. I'm *married* t'one of 'em."

"Don't remind me," muttered Witt. "I should've left you to sleep it off at Jackson's. All right, then, we'll— Dammit!"

Voices, and footsteps coming their way.

Without another word, Witt dragged both her and Zacharius Trainer into the deepest shadows, back under the spreading branches of the old pine. Mike pushed through the bushes on their right, taking Louisa with him.

Heart hammering, Molly held her breath. Zacharius giggled weakly. Witt clamped his hand over the older man's mouth.

The women came closer, then, to Molly's infinite relief, went on. Only blind men would have missed them, even in the dark, if they'd come on round the corner.

Just when Molly was sure they could relax, another cluster of women went past.

Witt shifted, put his mouth close to her ear. "Any more?"

"Probably not," she whispered back. She had to fight against the urge to press her hand to her ear. The faint, warm brush of his breath against her cheek and throat had set her nerve ends burning.

"*Probably?* You mean, you don't *know?*"

"You want me to run after them to check?"

If it weren't for the smell of whiskey emanating from Zacharius Trainer, she could almost forget the older man existed. Witt was so close she could reach out and touch him if she'd had the nerve.

There in the dark, with the massive trunk at their backs and the broad pine boughs wrapped around them like a sheltering tent, the world had shrunk until he filled all the empty spaces. He wasn't touching her, yet she could feel him up and down the length of her body and all the way down her arms to her fingertips. She'd swear the very air was part of him, like blood and breath, warm and alive.

"Let's go." He hitched his arm more firmly around Zacharius Trainer's back.

"What if—"

"That's Zach's problem, not mine," he said gruffly. "Move."

Louisa and Mike stepped out of the bushes right behind them.

"Got us an idea," Mike said.

"A very good idea!" chimed in Louisa happily.

"Miss Merton an' me, we'll take Mr. Trainer home. Missus Trainer don't have a grudge against me, and she can't hardly abide the sight of you."

"You're welcome to him," Witt growled. "Old goat weighs a ton and I swear he's fallen asleep."

"Shleep," said Zacharius, and giggled.

Witt shifted to get a better grip. "You want to explain why Miss Merton should be involved?"

"Mike, that is, Mr. McCord—" Louisa glanced up at the big miner beside her, and smiled.

Even in the moonlight, Molly could see him smiling back.

"Mr. McCord?" she prompted, knowing what was coming.

"He said it would help if I knocked on the door since he'll have his hands full with Mr. Trainer," Louisa earnestly explained. "We agreed I could duck down behind the porch railing after so she doesn't know I'm there."

"I don't think—" said Molly.

"Fine," Witt agreed. "He's all yours."

Mike grunted at the dead weight, then shifted to drape the now unconscious Zacharius over his shoulders. "And here I thought he was heavy when there was two of us."

"Took six men to haul you out of Jackson's," Witt said with satisfaction.

"Come on," he added, taking Molly's arm. "I'll walk you home."

He didn't bother turning around. The last thing Molly saw when she glanced back was Louisa, looking up at Crazy Mike McCord and laughing.

Chapter Fourteen

"I'm not sure it's right for the two of them—"

"You're the one told me he was a good man," Witt interrupted. "You were right. There's no one Miss Merton would be safer with than Crazy Mike, and that's includin' the preacher."

He hadn't glanced at her since he'd dragged her away from that tree, and he hadn't slowed down. He also hadn't taken his hand off her arm.

Molly hadn't tried to pull free. It wasn't that she wanted him touching her, she silently assured herself, it was just too much trouble to argue. It had *nothing* to do with the warmth from his hand that had seeped clear through to her skin and was now spreading through her blood like heady wine.

"I can find my way home perfectly well," she said.

"I know."

"You really don't have to bother."

"No."

"You're hurting my arm."

He stopped so suddenly she staggered. Instead of letting her go, he dragged her around and grabbed her other arm, then pulled her to him and kissed her, right there in the middle of State Street and Pearl where all the world could see if they bothered to look out their bedroom windows.

Molly didn't know if anyone had bothered, and didn't really care. This was not the quick kiss she'd given him, there by the river. This kiss was hot, demanding, mouth crushing down on mouth with heat and hunger and a world of promise in it.

When he pulled back an eon later, gasping for breath, she gasped, too, and sagged against him. His broad chest was as safe and comforting as she had imagined it would be. She could hear his heart thundering inside it, just beneath her ear.

"You're still hurting my arm," she murmured, fighting against the dizzying need he'd so easily roused within her.

He swore and let her go. He would have shoved her away if she hadn't wrapped her newly liberated arms around his neck and dragged him down for another kiss.

He wouldn't have been half as staggered if she'd just shot him, instead.

She could feel the breath hitch in his lungs, then the sudden leap of his heart as it started beating again. His hands still held her, one cradling her head, the other pressed tight against her waist, pinioning her to him. Tongues met, tangled, probed, devoured.

They shared the same air, pressed so close against each other that they seemed as one, driven by the same furious passion. Molly knew they shared the same hunger. She could feel it in him, as sharp and demanding as the hunger that raged through her.

A quiver shot through his body like the quiver of a hound straining at the leash. It was the mate of the shudder that shook her down to her very bones as his mouth left hers to press against the soft, vulnerable flesh just beneath the angle of her jaw, then lower, where her starched collar began.

He was the first to come to his senses, not her. With a groan, he lifted his head. His eyes were black hollows in the darkness, full of secrets.

"I'm sorry. I shouldn't— That wasn't right." He let her go and backed away. "I'm really sorry."

Molly fought against the urge to laugh out loud and run dancing through the streets. She ought to be appalled by her behavior, but she wasn't. All the confusion and doubts and questions of the last few days seemed to be sorting themselves out somehow. She wasn't sure what it would all add up to in the end, but for the first time, she wasn't worried by the answer, whatever it turned out to be.

If she spread her shawl like wings she thought she might even fly.

"If you won't kiss me, will you walk me home?"

"Walkin' you home was what got us into trouble in the first place."

Inch by inch, he was edging farther away from her. He hadn't, Molly thought with amusement, quite worked up the courage to run.

"It wasn't the walking that was the problem," she teased. "And I don't consider what we just shared a problem, anyway."

"Still wasn't right."

"I'm sure Mrs. Trainer would agree."

The bite in her tone got his attention, as she'd hoped it would.

"She'd also think it quite proper to see a lady home when she'd got caught out late like this. Just to be sure she's safe, you know."

There were a dozen other things she wanted to say—rash, dangerous things—but she shoved the words aside. Tomorrow, when she had time to think, she'd pick the right ones. For now, she was too giddy, so excited by the emotions tumbling through her that she might go too far, too fast, and end up ruining it all.

Witt didn't say anything at all.

"I usually go that way." Molly pointed down Pearl. "Four blocks over, three blocks up."

He didn't move.

She made a quarter turn and gestured. "Or we can go three blocks up State, then four blocks over on Granite."

Nothing.

"Some people," she said thoughtfully, as if giving the matter careful consideration, "think it's better to turn on Gold Street. I suspect that's because Mrs. Jacobson always has such a lovely garden this time of year, but it may be because the trees there provide so much shade.

"That would be two blocks up State, four blocks over, then one more up on Delaford," she added helpfully. "Not counting the jog over to reach the alley."

Silence...with a dangerous rumble underneath, like a mountain just before an explosion.

Molly smiled, a small, secret smile all for herself. "Of course we can always walk one block up, four—"

He made a strangled sound somewhere deep in his throat. Gravel grated under his heel as he turned to face down Pearl.

"This way," he growled, and stalked off without her.

Her secret smile turned to a triumphant grin. Heart pounding happily, she set off after him.

They covered the blocks in silence save for the

sounds of their shoes on the hard-packed dirt streets and the sleepy barking of an occasional dog. The moon was higher now—not full, but enough to see their way. She wondered if he'd chosen Pearl in order to avoid that tree-shadowed section of Gold, but didn't ask.

They saw no one. Here and there a lamp glowed behind a curtain, but most of the houses were dark beneath their moon-silvered roofs. Elk City was in bed and asleep.

Unlike that one evening when they'd gone out walking, he made no effort to match his stride to hers. For each of his long steps, she had to take two. By the time they reached Delaford, the last street before hers, she was almost running to keep up.

They turned down the alley and his pace suddenly slowed, his stride shortened. It wasn't the lack of light because the broad alley was no darker than the unlit street behind them. It wasn't because he was worn-out with the exercise, even if he was breathing harder than he should have after that little walk. And the closer they got to her back door, the slower he walked.

The scent of roses and damp earth and garden greenery wrapped around them as they walked up the path leading to her back step.

He waited at the foot of the steps as she checked to be sure Bonnie had left the screen unlatched and the door unlocked. Rather than going in, however, she came back down, stopping on the last step but one.

From that vantage point, she was almost an inch taller than he was. His head was tilted up slightly, but his hat shaded his eyes so that all she could see was a faint glint in their depths. In the moonlight, his mouth looked uncompromisingly stern, his jaw an unyielding rock.

"I liked it, you know," she said. "I liked you kissing me very much."

And then she leaned down and kissed him on that stern mouth, which was much warmer and more welcoming than it looked.

"Good night, Sheriff." It was hard to get the words out past the sudden tightness in her throat.

"Ma'am," he said in a strangled sort of voice.

She swung the back door open. The lamp she'd left burning on the kitchen table had long since burned out. The house, like all the houses around her, was dark and silent, its occupants soundly asleep.

Witt was backing up the path. He got all the way to the roses before he spun around.

"Good night," she called, not caring if the neighbors heard.

The only sound out of the darkness was that of footsteps, hurrying away.

"Toldja!"

"Shh!" Bonnie glared down at her brother. They were kneeling on his bed, trying to see what was happening in the yard below, and the last thing she wanted was to be caught at it.

Dickie had rushed into her room not two minutes before to inform her that their mother was returning and that it looked as if the sheriff was with her. Bonnie had started to argue, but the barking of old Mr. Schroeder's dog across the alley, followed by the muffled sounds of footsteps out back, had brought them on a run to Dickie's window. Unfortunately the combination of darkness and window screen made it impossible to see what was going on on their own back steps.

"I toldja they was gettin' sweet on each other," Dickie insisted in a whisper.

"He just walked her home," Bonnie whispered back. "Any gentleman would see a lady got home safe, this time of night. It doesn't *mean* anything."

"Oh, yeah? Well, Tom Seiffert says they're takin' bets up at Jackson's about it."

"Are not."

"Are, too. Ask Tom."

Bonnie gave a ladylike snort. "I wouldn't believe a word *he* says. He exaggerates."

"Does not," said Dickie, though he didn't sound perfectly convinced. "Anyways, the sheriff's brought Mama back tonight. An' she's late. Must be 'leven o'clock. She's *never* this late."

He smooshed the side of his face against the screen, trying to get a better view.

"Stop that. You'll make the screen bag out, just like the last one. You know what mother said. How you'd have to pay for a new one if you did it again."

"Who cares," said Dickie, removing his face from the screen just long enough to argue. "I got money, even if you don't."

Bonnie thought of arguing, then decided it wasn't worth the effort and pressed her face against the screen, instead. She caught her mother's voice, too low to make out the words, then the sheriff's "ma'am." And then he was walking backward up their garden path. Backward!

The only time she'd seen a man do that was when Jimmy Jacobs was courting Mary Sue Mandelbaum. Jimmy had been seventeen, near a man full-grown, and he'd been pretty much gone on Mary Sue. Every time he'd left her house he'd walked backward until he ran into their front gate. The whole town had been laughing about it and how moony he was over Mary Sue, but it must have been all right in the end since Jimmy and Mary Sue had been married going on for two years now and already had their first baby, with another on the way.

But her mother? And the sheriff?

"Good night," her mother called. Pretty loud for so late at night. If she wasn't careful, she'd wake the neighbors and then Mrs. Fein would talk and everyone in town would know that the sheriff had walked her home tonight.

The sheriff didn't say a word, leastwise not that she could hear. She didn't find that particularly encouraging, somehow.

Dickie slowly sank back on his bed. "It's sorta like that story about Tim Toller. His mother was sweet on the sheriff, see, but there was this bad guy who—"

"Oh, be quiet. I don't want to hear about any of your silly stories. Not right now."

Troubled, Bonnie gave her brother a poke, just on general principles, then slid off his bed and out the door, taking especial care to avoid that spot in the floor that always creaked.

It seemed like forever before her mother finally picked her way up the stairs, still in the dark.

The man had courage, she'd give him that.

Molly watched as Witt Gavin, after only a moment's hesitation and at least fourteen trips past the front of Calhan's—she might have missed a couple, coming and going—walked into the store at eleven o'clock the next morning. That was only an hour later than he usually dropped in for the day's quota of candy. Not bad, considering.

Just as it had for every working day of the last three weeks, her heart gave a little leap at the sight of him. This time, however, she didn't try to hide her reaction behind a wall of ice and good manners. Useless to pretend she didn't care, or that last night's kiss hadn't mattered.

"Good morning." She smiled. "Sleep well?"

It seemed a fair question, since she hadn't slept at all.

He blushed and dragged off his hat. The shadows under his eyes were answer enough.

"Mrs. Calhan." He started to say something, swallowed it back, and scraped his hand over his hair, instead. "Ma'am."

"What will you have this morning, Sheriff?" she said brightly. "More gumdrops? You haven't had those in a while. Or," she added, suddenly bold, "how about the lady's kisses? As I recall, you're rather fond of *those.*"

If any of the ladies in the Society heard her talking that way—if they even *guessed* at what had happened last night—she'd be Elk City's main topic of conversation for a month. The thought wasn't enough to tie her tongue.

After a sleepless night spent trying to sift through the jumble of emotions his kisses had stirred, she was sure of one thing, and one thing only—that she wanted him to kiss her again. Only longer this time, and with no distractions, like wondering who was watching them and going to tell the tale.

"About that kiss—"

"If you're going to apologize or tell me it was a mistake, I'll be very offended."

His eyebrows knit together worriedly. "Offended?"

"That's right. Offended."

There was something about him that reminded her of a wild horse when it realized it had run into a trap, something a little white-eyed and sweaty.

Getting another kiss might prove a little more difficult than she'd thought. The thought made her blush. She hadn't been this brash even when Richard had courted her all those years ago.

She hadn't known what could follow a kiss, either, all those years ago.

Her blush deepened. Blame it on a night spent tossing in bed until she'd pulled out the edges of the sheets and had to get up and tuck them in again—twice.

Both times she'd thought of sheets and kisses, and that had made it worse.

And while she tossed and turned, her emotions had tumbled and skittered around inside her. Like those tiny balls in the children's game, the one where there's a picture full of little, ball-sized holes inside a glass-topped box. You tilt the box this way, then that, trying to get all the balls into the little holes where they belong. But the balls don't want to settle in a hole and stay there, so every time one slips into place, another pops out and, often as not, it knocks another out, as well, and round they go again and again and again. Her emotions had been like that, refusing to sort themselves out so they made a proper picture.

Better to concentrate on business. She slid back the glass door of the candy case. "So, what can I get for you today? Red-hots? Pralines?"

He stared at the collection of sweets as if his life depended on his choice.

She picked up a paper-wrapped square. "Butterscotch?"

He shook his head.

"Chocolate creams?"

"No!"

Startled, she dropped the cream atop a mound of lemon drops.

"Those." He pointed, and made sure to keep a safe distance.

"But you don't like jawbreakers."

"Kids," he said, like a man being strangled. "The kids like 'em."

He bought ten pennies' worth, then fidgeted the whole time she weighed and bagged them. She didn't hand him the bag, however, despite the outstretched hand.

"Tell me, Sheriff," she said, suddenly serious. "Were you going to take Mr. Trainer home, or were you going to let Mr. McCord do it? The truth now!" she added when he shifted nervously.

He stared longingly at the open door and freedom.

"You were, weren't you? To save Mrs. Trainer's feelings." Molly tasted triumph. She'd been sure of it, there in the 2:00 a.m. darkness.

Emmy Lou had to hate that her husband had gotten stinking drunk in Jackson's. It would have been much worse for her, though, if DeWitt Gavin had been the man to bring Zacharius home, not Crazy Mike. It would have been like rubbing salt into a wound. Witt had known that, and been kind.

He couldn't meet her stare. His gaze dropped to his

hands. He frowned, then picked at a hangnail on his right thumb.

''Doesn't pay to rub folks' noses in the dirt,'' was all he said.

She thought of all the grief Emmy Lou had given him, and was quite sure she wouldn't have been so generous.

''No, I guess it doesn't,'' she said gently, and handed him his jawbreakers.

Bonnie was dragging up the front steps to Calhan's when the sheriff burst out of the store. At the sight of him, she stopped dead, mortally embarrassed. She'd spied on him and her mother last night, but she hadn't counted on running into him this morning. Not right here, where there was no place for her to run to.

He didn't see her until the last second. She tried to get out of the way, but her foot caught on the edge of a board. If he hadn't grabbed her, she would have fallen and made a fool of herself.

Instead of being grateful, she swung at him. ''Let me go!''

Her fury carried weeks of pent-up resentment and confusion. A flailing fist caught the paper bag he carried, sending it and its contents flying. Jawbreakers rained down, a multicolored hail that clattered on the boardwalk, then went careening off in all directions.

''Damn!'' he said, then, '''Scuse me,'' and stooped to pick up a jawbreaker that had rolled to a stop against his toe.

Bonnie kicked a yellow jawbreaker, sending it bouncing past him, across the walk, down the steps, and into the dirt.

"Sorry," she said, though she wasn't really sorry at all.

His eyes narrowed with suspicion. "Yeah?"

Squatting on his heels like that, he was her height, and his pale eyes were on a level with hers. They saw far too much for her comfort.

Too late, Bonnie remembered her grown-up dignity. She tugged on her pinafore, then raised her chin. "You ran into me. When I run into someone, Mama always makes me apologize."

His left eyebrow cocked. "And you think I owe you an apology."

She nodded. It wasn't easy with him studying her like that. Didn't he ever blink?

"Well, I suppose you're right about the running into you, so, I'm sorry about that, Miss Bonnie. I apologize. I certainly didn't mean to do it."

The small bubble of triumph popped. It wasn't going to be that easy, after all. She stiffened her spine, determined not to give in, and suddenly felt very young.

"So," he said, "how about an apology from you for all those jawbreakers. If you hadn't hit at me, I wouldn't have dropped the bag and lost 'em."

Under that calm, unblinking stare that saw far more than she would have liked, her spine wilted; her chin dropped. Bonnie stared at the toes of his boots.

"I'm sorry. I didn't mean to make you drop the bag."

He didn't say a thing. She looked up, surprised, and saw the corner of his mouth twitch, as if he were trying not to smile.

"Didn't mean to make me drop the bag, but you did mean to hit me?" he said.

"I'll pick 'em up." No way was she going to admit to wanting to hit him. Mother'd make her do the dishes for a month, all by herself, if she ever found out about it.

Without looking at him, she retrieved the bag, then collected the jawbreakers and tossed them in it, heedless of any dust and dirt they might have acquired in the interim. When she finished, she found him, still squatting on his heels, with three jawbreakers in his outstretched palm. He had an awfully big hand.

Gingerly, Bonnie took the jawbreakers and dumped them in the sack. When the sheriff rose to his feet, it was like having a mountain sprout up right next to you. He smiled down at her, rousing a funny little warm glow somewhere inside her.

"You're pretty good at pickin' things up," he said. "If your brother doesn't work out at the jail, maybe your ma'll let me hire you, instead."

Bonnie's answering smile died as she suddenly remembered why she'd gotten mad at him in the first place. Deliberately, mouth set in an unyieldingly grim line, she turned the bag upside down and dropped the jawbreakers into the dust of the street.

His mouth fell open. For an instant he just stared at his jawbreakers. Then he stared at her. Then he threw up his hands.

"Women!" said Sheriff Gavin, and stalked away.

She wondered what he meant.

From the shadows at the edges of Calhan's front door, Molly watched Witt stride down the street. She'd send Bonnie with an apology and a replacement bag of jawbreakers…later.

Watching the two of them, listening to their spat, had sent her jumbled thoughts rolling again. But this time, the box had tilted just right. This time, all the little balls had landed in the right holes and stayed there, every one. Her emotions had finally sorted themselves out, leaving her dazed and delighted and wanting to dance.

She was in love with DeWitt Gavin. And she was going to marry him, no matter what he said.

Assuming, she thought, her smile widening, that he managed to say anything at all.

Chapter Fifteen

"So then Nick, he tackles the bandit, see, and Robert, his friend—"

"The one who went bad," said Witt.

"No, that's Jim," said Dickie impatiently. "Robert's his friend from school. You know, the one with the dog."

Dickie had been recounting his favorite hero's adventures in the latest issue of *Nick Carter,* but they'd strolled over half the length of town and Witt still hadn't managed to get the details straight.

"Dog. Right." Witt couldn't remember any mention of a dog, but he wasn't fool enough to ask for clarification.

"So then," Dickie continued, "Robert, he grabs the other bandit an' they start rollin' around on the ground, fightin', see, and then his friend—"

"Robert's?"

"No, the bandit's friend."

"Ah."

"Yeah. Anyways, he comes in right then an' Pow! he hits Nick. But Nick's quick, see, an' he rolls away."

With fierce grimaces, a little vicious boxing at thin

air, and many theatrical grunts for effect, Dickie managed to work his way through the story's big fight scene without further interruption.

However good the fight, the end of the story was clearly a letdown.

"An' then the girl kissed him." Dickie made a face, as if he'd just sucked on a sour lemon. "To thank him for savin' her an' all."

He looked up at Witt. "Do girls always do that? Kiss you, I mean?"

Witt thought of Molly. Just the thought of her was enough to rouse that by now familiar ache of longing.

"Do girls kiss you? Not often," he said. "Not in my experience."

Not anywhere near as much as I'd like.

Dickie heaved a sigh of relief. "That's good. When I grow up, I wanna be a detective, just like Nick Carter, but all that kissin', it worried me some."

"Give it a few years and the kissing part won't bother you near as much," Witt said mildly. It would, he knew, be easier to convince the boy that cows could fly.

Even though the jawbreakers Bonnie had reluctantly brought him were long gone and no one else in town had anywhere near the selection of sweets, he hadn't been in Calhan's since last week, when he'd tucked his tail between his legs and run.

He'd walked past the store a hundred times since then and down the alley behind Molly's house a hundred more—always at night, when he was making his rounds and nobody was likely to see him. These days, he was smelling roses and tasting chocolate in his sleep, yet he still hadn't worked up the courage to walk up that path and knock on her kitchen door.

Or maybe it was just that his good sense hadn't com-

pletely gone, after all. Just because there'd been a lot
more fire in her kiss than any of Clara's had ever had
didn't mean he was the kind of man a woman wanted
cluttering up her parlor for the rest of her life. Didn't
matter that Molly wasn't the kind of woman who'd go
around kissing a man for the hell of it, either. She might
be a whole lot more willing than Clara ever was, but
he wasn't any less big and clumsy when it came to
pleasing a woman and keeping her happy, and he tried
to remember that whenever he got to dreaming of what
wasn't going to be.

"Mother, she likes the Frank Meriwell books the
best," said Dickie, dragging him back to the present.

"And you don't."

Dickie shrugged. "He's awful good. Always doin'
what he's sp'osed to and never cussin' or gettin' in
trouble."

"Says yes, ma'am and no, ma'am and that sort of
thing?"

"Yeah. Pretty dull stuff, you ask me. Oh, he has
some good adventures, too, but not like Nick. Now
Nick—"

A dog's shrill yip of pain cut through his words, then
another, coming from the weed-choked alley behind the
blacksmith's shop. Three boys were huddled at the far
end, kicking and poking at the scrawny mutt cowering
at their feet, too intent on their own entertainment to
notice anything else.

"Here, now!" Even without shouting, Witt's voice
carried clearly. "What do you think you're doing?"

The boys jumped back, startled. The tallest and
scrawniest of the three eyed him resentfully. "Weren't
doin' nuthin'."

"It's a dog." The pimply-faced boy—a miner's

child, if Witt remembered right—who'd been the most enthusiastic in the kicking wiped his nose on his sleeve and glowered. "A stray that's always stealin' scraps. Jim's father, he wanted him driven off."

Jim, who Witt now recognized as the son of one of the town's butchers, swung his foot at the cringing lump of dirty fur cowering on the ground at his feet. "Pa tried to shoot him last week, but that mutt run away with a chop, anyway."

Witt glanced down at the dog.

"Poor doggie," said Dickie, darting forward before Witt could stop him. He knelt beside the dog, which flinched, but held its ground.

Too starved and battered to run from the looks of him, Witt thought. It might have been better for the beast if the butcher had shot him a week ago. It would have saved the poor creature a week of misery.

Dickie cautiously stretched out his hand. The dog sniffed, threw a wary glance at his abusers, then craned closer and sniffed again.

"Good doggie," Dickie said softly. The dog weakly thumped its tail on the ground and crept a couple inches nearer.

"Oughta shoot it," Pimple-face said with a sneer.

"Putting a beast out of its misery is one thing," Witt said sternly. "Abusing it is another. I catch you mistreating another animal, I'll have a talk with your folks. Understood?"

"It's just a damn dog."

"Understood?"

Pimple-face wiped his nose on his sleeve again, then shrugged and led his friends away. Their swaggering didn't quite cover their resentment, or the shame of having been lectured by the sheriff as if they were small boys.

Witt watched them until they'd slunk out of sight, then looked back at the dog. He'd never seen an uglier mutt. Bones stuck out beneath the matted brown-and-black hide. One black ear drooped. The other, mostly brown, looked as if it had been set on crookedly. The curly tail was too long for the stubby body and short legs, its long, matted white-and-brown hair dragging in the dust.

Dickie scratched behind its flyaway ear, crooning admiring words.

"Best not get too close to that mutt," Witt warned. "No telling what kind of disease and vermin it's got. Your ma'll never forgive me if you go home infested with fleas."

"She won't mind. She likes dogs, too."

"I doubt she likes fleas." He also doubted she'd be too impressed with a mangy mutt like this, but he didn't say so.

"I'm gonna call him Pete," Dickie said, bringing his face down to dog level. "How do you like the sound of that? Pete."

The dog licked his face and thumped his tail again, a little more enthusiastically this time.

"Here, boy. I'll take care of the dog while you—"

"No!" Dickie hugged the dog so hard the poor beast whined. "You'll shoot 'im. Nobody's shootin' Pete."

"That dog's half-dead from hunger and abuse. It'd be a kindness—"

"*No*. He's not all the way dead, and he's mine."

Witt sighed. He had an awful feeling that his first confrontation with Molly Calhan in a week was going to be over the top of one determined boy and one very ratty dog. It didn't bode well for the outcome.

"You'll never believe! Such good news! You'll be so pleased when you hear!"

Emmy Lou Trainer had swept into Calhan's, flags flying, and brought all conversation to a halt by picking up Molly's heavy brass paperweight and rapping it on the counter. One or two hardy souls had tried to continue their private discussions only to be quelled with a look that would have frozen hell itself.

Louisa Merton, who'd meekly entered in Emmy Lou's wake, looked just a little breathless. Her eyes, however, were sparking with excitement, putting Molly on full alert.

"First," said Emmy Lou, loudly enough for all to hear, "we've found a tuba player to round out Elk City's band so they can play for the Founders' Day festivities."

The crowd managed to control its enthusiasm.

"Second," she said, even more expansively, "the mayor has agreed to open the festivities with a speech."

Since the mayor always opened the festivities with a speech, that roused no enthusiasm whatsoever.

"And third, Miss Merton tells me that Mr. Mike McCord from the Gradie Rose Mine has rounded up a dozen of the unmarried miners to help hang the decorations. Isn't that wonderful!"

There were some vague murmurs and not a few curious glances at Louisa.

Molly just plain stared. Louisa smiled back, then blushed and ducked her head. The rest no doubt thought she was too modest to accept such public praise, but Molly knew better.

Louisa and Crazy Mike McCord, hmm? Molly smiled, pleased.

She wondered if Witt Gavin knew, and felt a stab of irritation that she couldn't ask. It had been over a week, yet the big lunk hadn't yet dredged up the nerve to face her. If he didn't show up soon, she was going to have to resort to drastic measures just to talk to him.

But talk to him she would. A week of thinking and trying to shake some sense into her head had only made her more determined to marry DeWitt Gavin, no matter what it took to do it.

"Huh!" said Thelma Thompson, unimpressed. "Those miners will come in handy, but one tuba player more or less won't make a difference to anybody. And if there's a way to stop Josiah Andersen from talking, I've yet to see it. That man loves to talk almost as much as he loves to break the seventh Commandment."

Molly could see a few of her customers frowning— one was even counting on his fingers—trying to figure out what that particular Commandment forbade.

"You may not have anything to say worth mentioning, but *I* do," Thelma continued, grimly determined. "I've been telling them there's something funny going on, over at the bank."

"The bank!" Emmy Lou exclaimed, indignant. "What does the bank have to do with Founders' Day?"

"Nothing. That's what I'm trying to tell you. This is *important*. Missing deposits, bad math. Not the sort of thing that should happen at a well-run bank. I wanted to take a look at the books, but that uppity Gordon Hancock wouldn't let me. Imagine! Me! One of their very first depositors!"

"But you said you got the money you're s'posed to," someone objected.

"Of course I did!" Thelma snapped. "I'm not about to leave my money in the hands of thieves and scoundrels and incompetents. What do you take me for? A fool?"

Wisely, no one answered that particular question.

"But it's not just my money that's at risk, here, and so I told that Hiram Goff. Man looked liked he'd swallowed poison, just at the thought. But I'm telling you all now, there's dirty doings over at Elk State. You'd be wise to draw your money out while you still can."

Molly decided it was time she stepped into the fray.

"Thelma, this is pretty serious talk, you know. Especially if you don't have proof. Now I'm not saying you didn't find a couple of errors," she said, holding up a warning hand when Thelma started to object. "Mistakes happen, even to the best of us. But your accusations are exactly the sort of talk that can start a run on a bank, and if that were to happen, we really *would* have problems."

"I'm not trying to start a run," Thelma insisted, pointy chin stubbornly set.

"I know you're not, but you can't go around saying—"

"Mother? Mother!" Her son burst into the store like a firecracker, making everyone jump.

"Dickie! How many times have I told you—"

"You gotta come." He tugged on her hand. *"Please?"*

No blood, no ripped clothing, no signs of disaster. If it weren't for the tension in him she would have scolded him for interrupting business.

"All right, then. But make it quick."

She murmured an excuse to Thelma and her other customers, tugged off her apron and hung it on its peg, then followed her son out the door and around the side of Calhan's to the alleyway behind.

At the sight of Witt, she stopped short. "Sheriff?"

He looked, she thought, exactly like a little boy caught stealing apples. Every nerve ending in her body tingled at the sight of him.

"Ma'am." He cleared his throat and squared his shoulders. "I want you to know, this wasn't my idea."

Only then did she notice the sorry mongrel crouched at his feet. "What in the world…?"

"It's a dog, Mama. Me and the sheriff found 'im."

"The sheriff and I," Molly murmured automatically, distracted. She'd never seen a more pathetic specimen of dogdom in her life.

"Jim Perkins and his friends were kickin' him, Mama. Real hard, so he cried. Can I keep 'im? Can I? Huh? Can I?"

"Dickie…" How was she going to find the words to explain that the poor creature was already half-dead? Or that the last thing she wanted was to add a flea-bitten mongrel like this to her household?

The animal watched her warily, then gently wagged its tail.

"Please? The sheriff'll shoot 'im if you don't say yes."

Molly angrily looked up. Any man who'd say such a thing in front of an impressionable boy like Dickie ought to be shot himself.

He raised his hands, palms up, shrugging an apology. "I didn't say I'd shoot him, just that he maybe ought to be put out of his misery."

"Please?" Dickie was almost writhing in his agony.

At that moment a handful of her customers burst round the corner of Calhan's.

"Thought you might need some help," huffed one old gentleman, eyes alight at the possibility of disaster.

"You all right, Molly?" Emmy Lou demanded. "We were so worried about you and the boy—"

"Hah! Speak for yourself," said Thelma, elbowing the old man aside so she could get a better look. "I just wanted to see what was going on."

"My son has found a dog—" Molly began.

"That's a *dog?*" Thelma sniffed. "I've seen better-looking rats. Cleaner, too."

"For once," said Emmy Lou, "I agree with you completely. You can't possibly let that creature in your house, Molly. Think of the diseases it must be carrying."

"And the fleas," said Thelma.

"It's probably vicious."

"Maybe even rabid."

The dog crouched, then crept to Molly's feet and stuck out his paw, gently brushing the toe of her shoe where it poked out from beneath her skirt. The flyaway brown ear drooped pathetically.

Without thinking, Molly stooped to scratch behind the ear. The dog wagged its tail once, then grew still, as if waiting for the verdict.

"Pete ain't vicious!" Dickie protested hotly.

"Isn't," Molly said. "Pete *isn't* vicious."

"And he ain't rabid, neither," said Dickie, missing the point entirely.

"He's smart, though," Witt said helpfully. It didn't quite have the ring of conviction, but he was trying. "*Real* smart."

Dead silence. They all stared at Witt. Then they stared at Pete.

Tongue lolling, Pete stared back.

He had beautiful eyes, Molly thought, and knew she'd lost the battle. She might withstand Dickie's pleading, but she couldn't withstand those big, sad brown eyes. She sighed. Pete was joining the family—dirt, fleas, mange and all.

As if sensing victory, Pete barked and painfully scrambled to his feet, tail wagging.

"Hey, boy," Dickie said, falling to his knees and wrapping his arms around the mutt. "You're mine now, all mine."

And that, thought Molly wryly, watching him, was that.

"You'll be sorry," Thelma gloomily volunteered, pleased at the prospect.

Emmy Lou tsk-tsked, then turned away, clearly washing her hands of the whole insanity.

"Carbolic in the bath," she called over her shoulder. "It's the only way to get rid of the fleas. Lots of carbolic."

"Dalmation Insect Powder," Thelma advised.

"Carbolic!"

"Hah!"

With the rest of the crowd reluctantly trailing after them, the two women walked away, still arguing.

"Take the dog home, Dickie," Molly ordered. "But stop off at Tommy McLaren's butcher shop and get some scraps for him first. From the looks of him, he needs food more than he needs even a bath."

Dickie whooped and jumped to his feet. "Come on, boy. Let's go home." After a moment's hesitation, Pete limped after him.

Molly, resigned, watched them go. "Thelma's right. I'm going to be sorry."

"Maybe not," Witt said. He didn't sound optimistic.

"There's some crusts in the bread box," Molly called after her son. "And eggs in the cupboard. Mix them with the scraps.

"But not too much or he'll get sick!" she added more loudly an instant before Dickie and his dog disappeared from sight. She wasn't at all sure he'd heard her, or that he'd pay attention to her warning if he had.

"I'll deal with the bath when I get home," she muttered to no one in particular.

Witt made a small, encouraging little sound and started to edge away.

"And *you*," she added, scowling fiercely and stabbing a finger into his chest before he could escape. "You, I'll deal with just as soon as I've dealt with that darned dog you've foisted on me."

Chapter Sixteen

It was half past seven when Witt walked up the Calhan garden path and knocked on their back door.

Bonnie opened the door. For a second she just stared at him, then at what he carried. Then she swung the door wide.

"Come in," she said, and smiled. "I'm sure Mother will be glad to see you."

Her smile struck terror in his heart. She looked as if she was waiting to enjoy a hanging, and he was the chosen hangee.

Witt stepped into a room transformed. The kitchen table and its chairs had been pushed back against the far wall and a battered tarp spread on the floor in their place. In the center of the tarp stood a large tin washtub half-filled with water. Four large kettles on the stove steamed gently, waiting to be poured out. A pot of soap and a large bottle of carbolic stood on the floor beside the tub. A pile of what looked like old towels and sheets had been tossed at the edge of the tarp, safely out of the reach of any splashing.

On the far side of the tub and as far as possible from the cupboards and cooking area, Dickie and his dog sat in the middle of another old cloth. Dickie was covered with bits and clumps of dirty brown fur. Pete was covered with not much of anything—all his fur except the long hair on his ears and tail had been cut off, leaving him looking like a misbegotten and badly shorn brown sheep. Without the fur to hide them, his bones seemed ready to poke through the scruffy hide. His belly, however, looked comfortably rounded.

Impossible as it seemed, the dog was even uglier with its fur off than it was with it on, Witt decided.

At the sight of him, Pete's ears perked. He gave a welcoming bark, then turned and gave Dickie's ear a friendly lick. Dickie giggled.

"Hi, Sheriff." He waved the pair of shears he held. "I'm trimmin' Pete up for his bath."

"He needs lots more than a bath," Bonnie huffed. The huff might have been more convincing if she'd hadn't gone out of her way to give the dog a pat before she walked out of the kitchen.

"Mother!" Witt heard her call. "Water's boiling."

A moment later, Molly walked into the kitchen. She wore a fraying work dress under the biggest apron Witt had ever seen, and had covered her hair with a large and extraordinarily ugly head shawl. His blood raced, just at the sight of her.

He forced down dangerous thoughts and held up his gifts, instead. "Figured since you're holdin' me partly responsible for all this, I ought to contribute somethin' to the cause. The harnessmakers did up a proper collar and braided leash for him." He grinned. "Doesn't look like you're going to need the comb tonight, though. I've seen rocks with more hair than that dog has left."

Dickie grabbed for the collar. "Hey, Pete! It's got your name and everything! See?"

Pete sniffed, ears perked. When it proved inedible, his ears flattened. He whined and looked pitiful. Dickie slipped him a bite of bread when Molly wasn't looking.

Witt took a step backward, toward the door. "Guess I'll let you get on with—"

"Oh, no you don't!" Molly grabbed his sleeve before he'd gone a foot. "You're not getting out of it that easily. Here," she added, slapping a thick pot holder into his hand. "You pour the hot water, I'll add the soap."

He thought of protesting. The dangerous gleam in her eye convinced him not to try.

"Decided to go for the carbolic instead of the flea powder, I see," he said, tipping out the first of the big kettles. Steam and the harsh smell of carbolic filled the air, making them both blink.

"I decided to go for both," Molly said, setting the half-emptied bottle aside. "There's two boxes of powder on the table for as soon as he's dry and brushed."

"Better safe than sorry."

"If I'd thought that, I'd have sent the dog home with you instead of letting Dickie keep him," she replied tartly.

Witt glanced at the boy, then leaned close, lowering his voice conspiratorially. "If it were up to me, I'd have shot 'im."

Molly grinned and lowered her voice to match. "Actually, so would I."

Witt's heart skipped a beat. Another couple of inches and he'd be kissing her.

He jerked back, breathed deep, and choked on the carbolic fumes. When he returned with the second kettle, she'd moved around to the far side of the tub.

She eyed the tub, then the dog, then him. Then, jaw

set in unyielding determination, she unbuttoned her cuffs and rolled up her sleeves. "Ready?"

His last hope of escape died. Reluctantly, Witt removed his vest and gun belt and set them aside, then even more reluctantly rolled up his sleeves. He flexed his muscles, stretched his fingers. "Ready."

Pete might have been starving, but there was plenty of strength left in that scrawny body. It took both of them to get him in the tub—Witt lifting, Molly sticking first one leg back in, then another, as Pete struggled to get free.

"I'll hold, you scrub," Witt gasped, blinking at the stinging faceful of carbolic-laced water he'd just been hit with. He grabbed for a leg before Pete scrambled back out of the tub. "And make sure you scrub *fast*."

On her knees on the opposite side of the tub, Molly started scrubbing. The first run through barely cut through the worst of the dirt. Her head shawl kept slipping down, dirt and soapsuds streaked one cheek, and water dripped from her chin. Her apron was so wet, it clung to her in sodden wrinkles.

Twice they bumped heads. Witt swore, apologized, then swore again as Pete almost got away from him.

"I've known full-grown steers weren't as hard to wrestle as this sorry lump of wolf bait," he panted.

He wrapped his left arm more securely around the mutt, then risked freeing his right to wipe his face. Instantly, Pete wriggled away and lunged for freedom.

"Damn!"

A gout of dirty water splashed over the side and into Molly's lap. She squealed and rocked back on her heels.

"*Hold* him, drat it!" she snapped. "Don't let him jump around like that!"

"I'm *tryin'*."

"Don't hurt 'im!" Dickie pleaded, anxiously dancing around the lake spreading over the tarp-covered floor.

Witt wrapped both arms around the dog until he was half in, half out of the tub. His knees ached. His pants and shirt were drenched and water was creeping into his boots. He glared at Molly, only inches away.

"Would you please just finish with it?"

She shoved her head shawl away from her face and glared right back. "I can't. Not with you wrapped around him like that."

"And I can't hold him any other way." When she just kept on glaring at him, he added, low and menacing, "I can always let him go as is, clean or not. You choose."

She thought about it for a second, snarled and dug into the pot of soap once more.

He should have been more reasonable, Witt decided two minutes later. Scrubbing the dog meant her hands sliding along his chest and ribs. It meant leaning so close that he could smell the scent of her, even with the carbolic filling his nose. It meant her shoulder brushing against him, and her warm breath on his bare, wet arm, and the edge of her head shawl tickling his nose so that he ached to rip it off her.

It meant coming dangerously close to making a fool of himself by closing that small gap that separated them and kissing her right there in her kitchen in front of God and Dickie Calhan. Pete, he decided, didn't count.

It got so bad, he loosened his grip on the still-squirming dog so that when she leaned back and said, "There. All done. You can let him go," he let Pete go, just like that.

In one great sucking swoosh of water, Pete vaulted out of the tub, drenching them both. Molly barely had time to put up her hands and turn her head when the mutt got all four feet under him and shook.

Water sprayed everywhere—on the sodden floor, the walls, the chairs and them. Whatever hit the stove hissed and turned to steam.

"Stupid dog," Molly said, and got sprayed again as Pete gave one last, good shake to his dripping tail.

Witt laughed, and got a sodden washrag in the face for it.

"Atta boy, Pete!" Dickie pounced on him, towel at the ready.

Half-buried in the towel, the dog wriggled and squirmed and shook some more, then lavished anxious wet kisses on a delighted Dickie.

"Make sure you get him *dry* before you take him out again," Molly warned. "It may be summer, but this time of night it's too cold for him to be out there, wet like that and without a thick coat of fur to protect him."

If Dickie heard, he gave no sign. He was too busy scrubbing at the dog and crooning outright lies about how handsome he was and what a good, brave dog he'd been.

Witt was too busy drinking in the sight of Molly to pay any heed.

She caught him staring, and frowned.

"What?" she demanded crossly. "I can't possibly look any worse than you do."

He couldn't help but smile. "You look absolutely beautiful."

Since she'd already thrown the washrag at him, she had to settle for splashing him, instead. He laughed, but didn't bother to dodge.

"You'd have a hard time making me any wetter."

Her eyes gleamed. "Oh, I don't know. I'll bet your socks aren't as wet as mine."

He wiggled his toes experimentally. "You'd lose."

"Want to bet?"

"I'll show you mine if you'll show me yours."

She laughed, then, and the sound of it washed through him like sunlight.

"Next time, Mr. Gavin. Next time." She rose, still laughing, then shook out her sodden apron.

"I don't know about you," she said, "but I need some dry clothes and a hot cup of coffee. But *only* after we've cleaned up this mess in here. I swear, you could drown a cat with what the darned dog slopped out on my floor."

Witt started to get to his feet when it hit him, just like that—he was in love with Molly.

The revelation shook him so, he damn near fell head-first into the tub.

It took them a good half hour to empty out the tub, carry out the tarp and mop the floor. The mound of dirty dog hair Molly bundled up in the old sheet she'd spread on the floor and put in the shed to empty when she burned the rest of the week's trash.

By the time the kitchen was restored to its usual tidy state and she'd put a pot of coffee on to brew, Dickie had gotten Pete dried off, taken him out on the new leash and collar for one last walk, then wearily but happily led him up to bed. Molly was willing to bet her son hadn't heard one word of her reminder that the dog could sleep on the rag rug in his room, but was *not* to be allowed up on the bed.

Pete might be dry, she thought, plucking at the still

damp front of her dress, but she was getting chilled in her wet clothes. Witt didn't look any drier.

He was slouched in a chair, playing with the braided leather leash he'd given Dickie, and frowning. His hair stood up in spikes and there was a streak of dirt across his chin. His clothes were still dark from the soaking he'd gotten.

He looked as if he belonged right here in the quiet, lamp-lit kitchen. As if he belonged with her.

"You know," she said, and wondered if he could hear the hungry tightness in her voice, "I think there's a shirt and a pair of my husband's trousers that might fit you. Well enough so we can dry your things off by the stove while we have that coffee, anyway."

She picked up the smallest lamp and hurried out of the kitchen before he could object—and before she could lose her nerve. There'd been a couple times when they were bent over that tub that she'd been tempted to lean a little closer and claim a kiss. She was absolutely sure there'd been more than a couple times when he'd had the same idea.

It wasn't just the thought of kisses that troubled her, however. She could remember every hard curve and angle and line where the back of her hand had rubbed against him while she'd scrubbed Pete. The memory was enough to start a little fire burning, deep in her belly, and another, hotter one, lower still, there, between her legs. It had been a long time since she'd felt such hungry need, and that frightened her as much as it stirred her blood.

As she knelt beside the trunk where she'd put Richard's clothes away four years before, she hesitated. Four years wasn't so long, after all. Not to mourn a kind and decent man like Richard, a man she'd loved with all her heart and soul.

But Richard is dead, she told herself, *and I am alive and in love again. Richard, of anyone, would be the first to understand and wish me well.*

With deliberate care, she lifted the heavy lid. She pulled out a woolen shirt, then burrowed deeper for the corduroy trousers that had been too big for her husband.

"Here they are," she said, bustling into the kitchen a few minutes later. "They'll probably be a little snug, but they'll do while your things dry. You can change down here," she added when he looked doubtfully around.

"I don't think I should—"

She didn't give him a chance to finish. "I'm going up to change my dress. I won't be long. I don't know about you, but I *need* that coffee."

He laughed despite his embarrassment and took the clothes she offered. She hurried out again before he had a chance to say more.

It wasn't coffee she'd been thinking about, but him and how it would be to unbutton his shirt, button by button, then slide it off over those broad shoulders. The thought made her blush and fumble with the fastenings of her dress. She didn't want to take too long changing because he might well slip away in spite of his wet clothes.

Before she went down, she stopped to check on her children. Bonnie was neatly bundled under the covers, fast asleep. Dickie was sprawled across his bed, with blankets and sheet rucked up on one side and trailing off the bed on the other. Pete, as Molly had known he would be, was on the bed, curled into a ball tight against

Dickie's stomach. She couldn't tell whether it was the dog or the boy who was snoring.

Witt should see this.

Molly blinked, startled by the thought.

Yet, why not? There wasn't a man in five counties who liked children more than DeWitt Gavin. It had gotten so he could hardly walk a block without picking up one small admirer or another. And he'd been kind to Dickie.

Besides, he was responsible for the dog.

Moving quietly so as not to wake the sleepers, she crossed to the stairs. Halfway down, she stopped and leaned over the railing.

"Sheriff? Witt!" she called, keeping her voice low. It would be easier simply to get him from the kitchen, but she didn't dare go that far for fear she'd loose her nerve. She wanted him to see what having a family meant, wanted to share this one small moment, knowing that he would understand.

"Ma'am?" At her beckon, he came up the stairs, treading cautiously. Despite his care, the steps creaked beneath his weight. "Is something wrong?"

She smiled and shook her head, ignoring the high-water pants and the too tight shirt straining across his chest, then pressed a finger to her lips in a gesture of silence. When she turned, he followed.

At the door to Dickie's room she stopped. "I thought you ought to see what you're responsible for," she whispered, and raised the small lamp high so its light filled the room.

He glanced at her in surprise, then crossed to the bed. Molly silently trailed after him.

She'd thought he'd smile, maybe give a little chuckle.

She hadn't expected to see such sudden, intense yearning.

For a moment he just stood there, staring. Then, without a word, he bent to throw back the covers and gently shifted Dickie to a more comfortable position. Pete raised his head, ears pricked, tail thumping.

"Stupid dog," Witt murmured, then shifted the dog as gently as he had the boy, and tugged the covers back into place.

Dickie muttered something in his sleep, snuggling deeper under the blankets, and wrapped his arm around his dog. Pete licked his nose, glanced at them as if to make sure they wouldn't bother his boy further, then settled back, tucking his nose into his belly with a contented sigh.

And still Witt lingered, hungrily watching them.

If she'd had any last doubts about the wisdom of loving DeWitt Gavin, they died right there, unmourned. When he crept out of the room at last, she followed, shaken by the unexpected insight into the man.

He didn't pause on the stairs, didn't even make much effort to be quiet. By the time she walked into the kitchen, he had already wadded his wet clothes into a bundle and retrieved his hat and gun belt.

"Best be going," he said. His hand was on the doorknob, his expression distant and expressionless. "I'll bring the clothes back tomorrow. Will that be all right?"

"Of course, but—"

"Thanks for the offer of the coffee."

And then he was gone, leaving her standing alone in the middle of the kitchen, still holding the lamp.

Eventually she roused to lock the door and bank the fire in the stove. She set the coffeepot aside and returned the cups and sugar pot and spoons to their places on the shelf. Witt had set it all out on the table, but arranged it so the width of the table would be between them.

Molly smiled, thinking of how it would have been with him across the table from her, tugging on shirt sleeves that were a good two inches too short, trying not to spill his coffee or meet her gaze. He'd probably have been thinking about the kisses they'd shared, there in the middle of Pearl and State. It was only fair, since she'd thought of them so often since.

As she did every night, she turned down all the lamps except the one she carried, then checked the windows and doors to be sure they were closed and locked. In the parlor, she paused in front of Richard's photographic portrait.

The protective glass reflected the light when she raised the lamp, blinding her and hiding her husband's face. She blinked, and lowered the lamp, and found him smiling at her. Gently, and with understanding.

Tears started in her eyes.

"You were a good man, Richard Calhan," she whispered, brushing her fingers over the glass. "A good, good man."

When she went up the stairs this time, there was peace in her heart. Richard would have understood, and been glad for her.

Chapter Seventeen

DeWitt Gavin was a no-good, no-account, low-down, miserable coward.

Molly glared at the Acme Patented Washing Machine—None Better! calendar hanging on her storeroom wall. Eleven days had passed since he'd fled her kitchen, ten since she'd returned home from Calhan's to find the shirt and trousers she'd loaned him sitting on her back step, neatly folded, without so much as a note of thanks attached. She hadn't had a word from him since. Hadn't so much as seen him walking past the store in all that time. Not even once.

"He's a coward and a fool," she informed Pete, who was sitting on the floor at her feet hoping for a handout.

Pete pricked his ears and tried to look sympathetic.

"And don't try to tell me he's not interested because I won't believe a word of it. *He's* the one who kissed *me,* after all!" Molly abandoned the calendar in disgust.

Pete barked and jumped to his feet, tongue lolling, tail furiously wagging.

"And *you,*" she sternly informed the dog, "are wasting your time. I know all about the stew meat that idiot sheriff bought for you. *And* the chops. *And* the ribs and the bits of liver and the chicken gizzards he cadged off Mrs. Boulton. And if you think I've forgotten about those biscuits or the fried egg, you have another think coming.''

Pete's head drooped. The wagging tail stopped wagging. With a sigh of long suffering, he slumped to the floor, then laid his head on his paws, pointedly not looking at her.

Eleven days of good food had put a sheen on his coat and plumped him up so his bones no longer stuck through his coat. Eleven days of being spoiled and cosseted and fawned over by Dickie and Bonnie had also given him an inflated sense of his own importance. He slept on Dickie's bed at night and sat under the table during meals, and lately, whenever Dickie left him at the store, he'd taken to begging from every customer who walked into Calhan's.

It hadn't helped that Witt kept slipping him treats, Molly thought sourly. Not that Witt had bothered to tell *her* anything about it! Oh, no! These days the sheriff was cowering in his jail and ducking down alleys to avoid running into her. But Dickie had told her, and that had only added to her irritation with the man.

Spoil the dog and ignore her, would he? Well, they'd just see about that!

''Come on, Pete,'' she said, slipping off her apron. ''We've got an errand to run.''

Witt wasn't in the jail or the barbershop or the post office. He wasn't at Mrs. Jensen's having a late lunch or poking through Jenkins Hardware or talking with the old-timers on the bench outside of Potter's Pharmacy. She stopped by the other general stores, the newspaper, the Chinese laundry and even the Women's Christian

Temperance Union reading room, to no avail. She didn't try any of the three saloons.

Everywhere she went, Molly left word that she was looking for the sheriff and would be much obliged if they'd just send him over to Calhan's when they saw him. "Founders' Day, you know," she'd say, and everyone would nod and at least try to look as if they believed her.

Pete finally ran Witt to earth in Nickerson's stables. They were walking past the open stable doors when Pete perked up, nose twitching, then gave an excited bark and dashed into the stables. Molly found him dancing around Witt's feet, trying to get his attention. No one else was in sight.

"No, no food," said Witt sternly, glancing down.

He was grooming his horse and his back was to her, which gave Molly a moment to get her heart rate under control. Absurd that even the back view of him could set her every sense on alert.

"Where's Dickie?" At Witt's query, Pete barked and tried to dance on his back legs. "Don't beg. No self-respecting man ever begs."

"He wouldn't beg if you wouldn't keep feeding him when he did."

The horse brush fell from Witt's hands, making the horse toss its head and sidle away. Slowly, Witt turned to face her. From the quick rise and fall of his broad chest, it seemed he was having difficulty breathing.

"Good afternoon, Sheriff," said Molly sweetly, pleased with her effect on him.

Witt swallowed nervously. "Ma'am."

"Ma'am?" She frowned, considering that, then moved closer. Eleven days of frustration were making her feel bolder, and just a little bit mean. "After foisting that disreputable mutt on me, I think you ought to call me something besides ma'am, don't you?''

"Mrs. Calhan?"

"How about just plain Molly?"

He licked his lips, then stooped to retrieve the horse brush. When he straightened, his face was redder, but he seemed a little more in control of himself. Looks could be deceiving, though. He was holding the brush so tightly that the bristles were mashed into his palm. That had to hurt, but he didn't seem to notice.

"That wouldn't be very—" he groped for a word "—respectful."

She moved closer still. He took a step back. He would have taken another if the horse hadn't been in the way.

Her own heart was pounding so hard she could hardly hear herself think, yet seeing him, seeing the proof that he wasn't indifferent to her, made her dizzy and breathless herself.

Eleven days! a little voice in her head screeched.

She lowered her voice so that only he would hear. "It wasn't very respectful for you to kiss me right there in the middle of Pearl and State, but I don't recall objecting."

For a moment, she wasn't sure if he was even breathing at all. Then he gasped and sucked in air. Satisfied, she backed up a bit.

"Anyway," she continued in a more normal voice, "that's not really why I came."

"No?"

"No." She tugged on the edge of his vest to straighten it. "I need some help with the decorations for Founders' Day."

"Decorations."

"Your voice sounds a bit…tight. Does your throat hurt?"

He shook his head. The whites of his eyes gleamed in the shadowy stable.

"That's good. As I was saying— I'll just take this brush, shall I? You keep squeezing it that way, you'll ruin the bristles. I'll set it right here so it doesn't get lost. There. Now, where were we? Ah, yes! Decorations!"

She smiled. She was beginning to enjoy this, after all.

"You know Mr. McCord and some men from the community have volunteered to put up the public decorations? You heard that? Good! Anyway, they're going to be decorating the streets and town hall and places like that, but they're not going to decorate businesses like mine."

He made a strangled sound at the back of his throat.

"Did you say something? No? I could have sworn you started to say something." Actually, he'd sounded like a duck whose neck was being wrung. "Well, as *I* was saying, Mr. McCord and his friends aren't going to hang decorations for me, but I thought you might. Just a little bunting, you know, looped from the roof."

"Roof?" said Witt.

Molly's smile widened. She wouldn't have let her children torment a housefly like this. She couldn't think of anyone who deserved it more.

"That's right. A half hour's work maybe. I have the ladder and a hammer. Would ten o'clock be good for you? It would?" He hadn't moved or made a sound. "Excellent! I'll have everything ready, I promise. Well, I won't take up any more of your time. I'm sure you must be very busy these days since I never seem to see you anymore. Ten o'clock, then. Let's go, Pete. Bye!''

She couldn't remember when she'd last had so much fun, Molly decided, grinning, as she headed back to Calhan's.

If he'd realized how good it could feel to pound on something, Witt grimly admitted the next morning, he would have turned to carpentering long ago. He leaned back a bit to study the nail he'd just driven, decided it could go a little deeper, and picked up the hammer again. *Bam! Bam! Bam!*

Damned satisfying, this pounding on things.

He dug another nail out of the rusting tin can Molly had given him and pinned the next big loop of red, white and blue cloth to the front of Calhan's General Store. *Bam! Bam! Bam! Bam!*

Molly had had the bunting, the step ladder, the hammer and the can full of nails waiting for him when he'd walked in the door at ten. He'd checked but hadn't seen any gloat at the edges of her smile, but even that hadn't done much to relieve the tension in him. In one fast flanking maneuver she'd gotten past every last one of his defenses yesterday—all without breathing hard or working up a sweat. If it weren't for his razor-sharp memories of Clara and her scornful comments on his abilities as a man and a husband, he'd have surrendered long ago.

At the thought, Witt ground his teeth together and clobbered another nail. *Bam! Bam! Bam!*

''If you keep that up, we'll have to take down the whole storefront to get the bunting off.''

The laughter in Molly's voice shook him so, he almost dropped the hammer. Witt glared at her from over the top of the ladder. Glaring was safest since what he really wanted was to leap off the ladder and on top of her.

She was staring up at him, one hand on her hip, the other raised to shade her eyes against the sun. A breeze had teased some of her hair free of her bun so that it blew across her face, making his fingers itch to tuck it back. The teasing smile on her face was so bright it seemed to have swallowed part of the sun itself.

He wrenched his gaze away and blindly fixed it on the whitewashed clapboard storefront. The front could use a little paint here and there.

"Are you sure you're going to have enough nails?" she asked.

That innocent tone didn't fool him one bit. He scowled at his handiwork, then tugged at a loop of the bunting. The thing was hung *firm,* that's all.

"Why can't I help?" Dickie demanded for what must be the tenth time in as many minutes. "I'm good at hammerin'."

"You're good at falling off ladders, too," his mother told him. "Besides, there's only one ladder, and Sheriff Gavin's on it."

"But I—"

"No."

"Why don't you come help me, boy?" The booming voice brought them all around. "I could use a handy fellow like you on my crew," Mike McCord added, giving Dickie's head a friendly rub.

Witt cursed under his breath and laid his hammer down. Being this close to Molly was addling his wits— he hadn't noticed Mike or his crew coming down the street. It took a lot of addling to miss a man Mike's size, especially when he was carrying a six-foot ladder hooked over his shoulder and was accompanied by some of Elk City's finest toting ropes and banners and flags and leading a pony and cart loaded with bunting.

"*Can* I? *Really?*" Dickie was almost jumping at the prospect.

"Sure, now, that'd be a fine thing!" Mike grinned. "What do you say, Missus Calhan? Since you've put our sheriff t'work, would you mind if I put that lad of yours t'good use? Saints know we've work and to spare!"

"I'll watch out for him, Molly. That is, Mr. McCord and I will," Louisa Merton added, blushing.

The normally well-dressed Miss Merton was standing at Mike's side, hat in hand and with her hair undone so that it spilled over her shoulders and down her back in a shining, pulse-stirring fall of silken black hair. She'd always been a pretty woman, but right now, like this and with her face aglow in the sunshine, she was downright breathtaking.

Witt couldn't help noticing that there was a proud, rather proprietary look about Crazy Mike every time he glanced at the lady, which was pretty much every other second.

Molly must have noticed it, too. She glanced from Mike to Miss Merton, then back again, then scanned Mike's crew, all of whom seemed determined to enjoy themselves even if they had been roped into the job.

"Surely you'll be too busy—" she began, while Dickie danced at her side in an agony of hope.

"The boy can fetch and carry and maybe hammer a thing or two," Mike said, earning a look of undying gratitude from Dickie.

"Well…" said Molly. Her son was dying a thousand deaths, but Witt could tell she was going to say yes.

"All right," she said, making Dickie whoop with delight. "But only if you'll tell me what happened to Louisa's...er, hat."

Louisa giggled, then tossed her head, making all that black silk dance.

"Mike—that is, Mr. McCord—knocked it off with his ladder." She looked up at the big miner, face alight with teasing laughter and something else, something a little softer and a lot more dangerous.

Witt gave a silent whistle and grabbed another nail. One thing good—from his perch atop Molly's ladder, he'd have a front-row seat.

To his relief, Molly retreated into her store with a teasing reminder to let her know how many more pounds of nails he'd need, that she could always go begging at Jenkins Hardware. Dickie was put to work helping unload the pony cart. They'd be hanging bunting from the hitching racks on either side of the street and flags on the telegraph poles that lined the other side. The banners would be suspended from ropes strung across the street and anchored on the roofs of the taller buildings.

It was the latter that brought Hiram Goff out of his lair. He picked his way across the street like a fussy old lady, mindful of the dirt, and demanded to know who was in charge of this circus that was disrupting business and obstructing traffic.

"No one told me about this," he huffed, tilting his head back to glare at Crazy Mike. Even without his glasses, he looked like he was peering disapprovingly over them. "You have to have permission from Mr. Hancock before you can do something like this. Ropes and banners and flags on the bank indeed!"

Mike shrugged, irritated, but clearly determined to

keep a rein on his temper. "I'm just the labor and do as I'm told. It's Mrs. Trainer you'll be wantin' t'talk to, not me."

"This is most irregular," Goff fussed. "All this noise. All this dust you're kicking up. It wasn't like this last year. I'm sure it wasn't like this."

"Perhaps I'd better go find Mrs. Trainer," Louisa said.

Even from his perch on the ladder, Witt could see the clerk's mouth thin with distaste. "Mrs. Trainer does *not* run the bank!"

Witt debated whether to work faster so he could finish and be gone before Mrs. Trainer appeared, or slower so that he'd be sure to have a front-row seat. Mrs. Trainer and Gordon Hancock butting heads, he finally decided, was simply too good to miss.

He'd only had to move the ladder once before Mrs. Trainer came striding down the street like a ship sailing into battle, cannons primed and ready. Louisa trotted along behind her, the laughter in her face replaced by a brow-crinkling, worried frown.

Hiram Goff had been surreptitiously keeping watch— Witt had seen his face pop up at the bank windows every now and then, then as quickly disappear. As soon as the enemy hove into sight, he flung open the bank doors, then stood aside to let his champion take the field.

Mike's people dropped whatever they were doing and strolled over, clearly primed for fun.

From long experience at waging war, Mrs. Trainer had the sense to pick her own ground. She claimed Molly's second step, not so far up that Hancock would be obliged to shove onto the boardwalk, but high enough to force the bank president to look up at her while he himself remained standing in the dirt.

Hancock was not pleased. "Mrs. Trainer?"

Ever the dutiful second in command, Hiram Goff dug in a foot to the rear, pinched face alight at the prospect of battle.

Mrs. Trainer clasped her hands beneath her bosom and frowned down at him. "*Mr.* Hancock?"

"I understand there's some misunderstan—"

"Not on my part, I assure you! I clearly remember informing you that we would be hanging banners over the street."

"Yes, but—"

"To do that, we must string ropes from buildings on one side of the street to buildings on the other."

"Of course, but—"

"We can't do that from short buildings, Mr. Hancock."

"No, but—"

"Elk City State is one of the tallest buildings in town, Mr. Hancock."

Hancock kept his mouth shut and glared.

"Therefore, anyone of intelligence would realize that we planned to attach ropes to your bank. *Especially* since it is also located on one of the major intersections in town."

Stubborn silence.

"I always thought you were an intelligent man, Mr. Hancock."

Tittering from the crowd. Hancock's face reddened. His mouth thinned.

"Just how badly do you want to hang those banners of yours, Mrs. Trainer?" he silkily inquired.

Mrs. Trainer opened her mouth, then shut it without saying a word.

The banker was too much the politician to want to antagonize one of Elk City's leading citizens, however, no matter how rude and overbearing she might be.

"Of course, Elk City State is always a good citizen, and we are happy to support important events such as Founders' Day. Had we been *properly* notified of your plans, we could have arranged to have some men on hand to assist you. As it is—"

"But, Mr. Hancock!" Hiram Goff's interruption got everyone's attention. The clerk glanced nervously at the crowd, then stood on tiptoe to whisper into his employer's ear.

Hancock's frown deepened. "Well, yes, there is that... Hmm...perhaps the sheriff—"

"He's right there." Goff pointed an accusing finger at Witt.

"Gavin?" Hancock squinted, shading his eyes against the sun. "May I ask what you're doing up there?"

"Hammerin'" said Witt shortly. He dropped his hammer into the bucket of nails, then climbed down the ladder. "There somethin' I ought to know?"

Now it was Hancock's turn to study their assembled audience unhappily. "A word in private, Sheriff."

"Calhan's good enough for you?"

To his surprise, Hancock hesitated. He was about to suggest the bank when Hancock squared his shoulders, adjusted his starched shirt collar, and nervously checked his cuffs. "Calhan's will be fine."

"What about the decorations?" Mrs. Trainer demanded, temper rising.

Hancock ignored her and walked into Calhan's. Witt followed warily.

The screen door banging shut drew Molly from the storeroom at the back. "Can I—"

At the sight of Hancock, she stopped dead. Her smile vanished.

"Mr. Hancock. What a surprise." Frost coated every word.

"Mrs. Calhan. Sorry to intrude. I just needed a private word with the sheriff, here."

The man sounded as if he were trying to dance on hot coals in bare feet. Witt's right hand automatically curled into a fist. He shoved it into his pocket. What in hell had Hancock been up to? Not that he couldn't guess.

Molly just stared at Hancock, outwardly polite but with a gleam deep in her eyes that made the banker squirm. "Don't let me interrupt."

Even coldly angry like this, she was beautiful, Witt thought, and felt his blood stir at the thought of the fire beneath the frost. When more than his blood started stirring, he wrenched his hand out of his pocket and forced his fingers to flex.

He couldn't decipher the expression on Hancock's face as the man watched her walk away, but he was damn sure he didn't like it.

"So, Hancock, what's this about?"

Hancock shook himself like a man coming out of a trance, then glanced out the door to be sure no one was listening. Everyone was gathered in the street, chattering and laughing. Still, he moved closer and lowered his voice.

"You have to keep an eye on the bank, Gavin. I don't care if they are just hanging decorations for tomorrow.

There are four mines' payrolls in the safe in my bank right now, and I don't like the idea of anyone hanging around the bank, no matter what the reason.''

"Payday's more'n a week off, still. What are you doin' with the payrolls this early?''

"A special arrangement that needn't concern you,'' Hancock replied testily. "What *does* concern you is that the money *stays* in that bank until payday. Understood?''

A muscle in Witt's jaw jumped. "I know my job, Hancock.''

Hancock's hostile gaze locked with his. "Then see that you do it, Gavin. Remember those men in Kansas? I expect you to be as efficient in dealing with any problem that might arise here as you were in dealing with that one.''

If the banker hadn't abruptly turned away, Witt would have punched him. Witt stood there, flexing fingers that still wanted to curl into a fist, and listened to Hancock's cheery apology to the people waiting outside. The man sure could turn on the charm when he wanted to. Within minutes he had Mrs. Trainer giggling like a schoolgirl as she accepted his invitation for a little coffee before she once again, as Hancock put it, took up the burden of her responsibilities.

"Is he gone?''

Molly was standing by the table with the stacks of soap and cans of who knew what. Her hand was wrapped around the top of a solid-looking tin big enough to do some damage if it was swung just right.

Witt nodded. "He's takin' Mrs. Trainer for some coffee.''

"Good. How's Dickie doing?'' Her fingers slowly uncurled.

He watched her flex them, just like he'd flexed his, and grinned. He'd have to stay on his toes or Molly was likely to flatten Hancock first.

"Dickie's doin' fine, and Pete hasn't been more'n half a pest, so far."

She laughed. "Need more nails?"

Witt could have sworn the air in Calhan's suddenly got a little thin. How was a man supposed to keep his distance when just listening to her laugh was enough to make him dizzy?

"Won't need any nails if I don't get back and finish," he mumbled, and fled.

Hancock and Mrs. Trainer were nowhere in sight. Mike's crew had returned to whatever they'd been working on before. Mike was burying Dickie under a pile of folded banners.

"Don't drop 'em, boy," he warned as Dickie tried to shift the load so he could scratch his nose. "Missus Trainer'll string you an' me both up, you get 'em dirty."

Louisa Merton giggled, her expression radiant again.

"Everything all right?" Witt asked.

Mike nodded. "Just fine. Hancock's gone off to sweet-talk Missus Trainer, an' Hiram's over in the bank, waitin' to show us where to put things."

"And none too pleased about it, I imagine."

Mike just grinned and winked at Louisa. "Miss Louisa'll sweet-talk him out of it purty quick."

"Not Mr. Goff!" she said, blushing. "He was born a sourpuss."

"Come on, boy," said Mike, stacking one last banner atop Dickie's pile. "I hear you got your eye on that bank, anyways. Whaddya think? That flagpole there at the top be a good place to tie the rope?"

Witt eyed the bunting he'd hung so far, then reluctantly headed back up his ladder. He picked up his hammer and fished another nail out of the can. This one was big and shiny, but bent enough so that it would never go in straight. Hancock, to a tee, he thought, and grabbed the next bit of bunting.

Bam! Bam! Bam! Bam! BAM!

Chapter Eighteen

Lamplight and the silent house around her—Molly raised her head, then laid down her pen and rubbed her eyes. She really ought to go to bed. She'd spent the last three hours sorting through her notes and figures for the expansion to Calhan's, yet still come to no firm decision.

After that first unpleasant encounter with Gordon Hancock, she'd put her plans aside, knowing she was too angry to make a wise decision. She'd returned to it tonight as distraction against thoughts of Witt, only to find herself once more caught by the possibilities of her plan.

And the risks, she reminded herself.

But there were always risks, in life as well as in business, and this expansion…

Frowning, she picked up a sheet covered with scribbled figures. Even using worst-case estimates of sales, the expansion would pay for itself in a little over two years. Two years wasn't bad, and she'd never once come close to worst-case. But there was always a first time and now, because of Hancock, the money would have to come out of the investments she'd put aside for the future, for her children's education and a good start in life.

The *click-click* of toenails on the stairs dragged her out of her thoughts. Pete clipped into the kitchen and over to the back door, then sat and looked at her over his shoulder.

"You've already gone out for the night," Molly told him sternly.

Pete grinned and scratched at the door.

Molly hesitated. Until now, she'd insisted that Dickie go out with the dog to make sure the mutt didn't wander off, but she wasn't in the mood to dog-sit tonight. Pete had an annoying habit of sniffing every bush and fence post in sight, thereby turning his little trips out into expeditions.

"Promise you won't run away?"

Pete gave a low, encouraging growl and wagged his tail, then dashed down the steps the instant she opened the door. Since he went straight to the closest bush, Molly left him to his business and went back to hers.

She picked up the folder she'd prepared for Hancock, then tossed it down again, unopened. She knew what she wanted. The question was, was she willing to accept the risks involved to get it?

Decide, she told herself. Yes or no.

Sometimes you have to take a chance.

She thought of Witt and drew in her breath, then slowly let it out and sat back down at the table.

Five minutes later she sealed the envelope containing her letter to the Denver broker who handled her investments, authorizing the sale of enough stocks and bonds to raise one thousand dollars. A few more pen strokes for the address, then she set it aside, turned down the lamp and slowly went up to bed.

* * *

Witt couldn't remember the last time he'd had a good night's sleep. Not since he'd kissed Molly, for sure. After several nights spent tossing and turning, he'd eventually given up the battle and taken to patrolling Elk City's streets, instead. The townsfolk thought he was being conscientious. He didn't intend to tell them otherwise.

Not that the walking helped much, though. Alone in the streets like this it was too easy to let his thoughts run off in dangerous directions. Waking or sleeping, his mind churned with images of Molly Calhan, laughing. Of Molly, smiling. Of Molly touching him.

His blood burned just at the thought of her touching him.

If he could just stop thinking, it would be a whole lot easier, all the way around.

He heard the dog before he saw it, a small, defiant, annoyingly familiar bark, then the sound of toenails scrabbling on wood. He peered into the shadows. "Pete?"

He almost didn't catch the beast. Pete was quick and clever and enjoying his freedom, but Witt was quicker. He grabbed the dog as he shot past. "Oh, no, you don't!"

Pete squirmed and wriggled, to no avail. Witt tucked him securely under his arm.

"I'd be doing Molly a favor if I let you run off."

Pete wagged his tail, then licked Witt's hand as if to reassure him that he'd never have gone *that* far. Just out for a stroll, he seemed to say. Really. *Trust* me!

"You're a damned ungrateful hound and you ought to be ashamed of yourself."

Pete gave a little bark, then relaxed in Witt's hold, panting softly.

He'd take the mutt home, Witt decided. Just knock on the back door, hand him over when Molly answered, then walk away. What could be simpler?

This time of night, she'd probably have let her hair down. She'd come to the door and her hair would be a fall of silk and shadow around her shoulders. The lamplight would be behind her, soft and welcoming, and she'd thank him and invite him in for a cup of coffee if there was any left in the pot. He didn't dare let his imagination go any further than that.

Unfortunately, there were no lights on in the Calhan household. Witt walked around the place twice, just to be sure.

"Snuck out without 'em knowing, huh?"

Pete whined, then wriggled to get free.

"Oh, no, you don't. She'll string me up if she finds out I had you, then let you get away." He frowned, considering, then headed back the way he'd come. "There's only one place to put you where neither one of us can get in trouble," he informed the dog, "and that's the city jail."

Molly had let down her hair, hung up her dress and unfastened the hooks and laces of her corset when she remembered Pete.

Irritated, she tossed the corset aside, grabbed her wrapper, and clumped back downstairs. The mutt was nowhere in sight. She called his name, then gave a low whistle. Not a sound—no bark, no eager whine. Nothing.

For a moment, she considered leaving him to his fate, but the thought of explaining it to Dickie should anything happen to his dog drove her back upstairs to dress. She didn't bother about her hair. There'd be no one to see her. She wouldn't be lucky enough to run into Witt every time she was out too late.

Bonnie and Dickie were sound asleep, but since there was no telling how long it would take her to find Pete in the dark, she reluctantly woke Bonnie and explained the situation. Bonnie muttered something about a stupid dog, rolled over and went back to sleep.

Half an hour later, Molly had searched every alley and street between home and Calhan's, without success. Her lantern had gone out for lack of oil—she would have to have a talk with her son about tending to his chores—and she was tired and chilled and very, very cross. She was about to give up and go home when a shadow loomed in the dark.

"Sheriff Gavin?"

"Mrs. Calhan? Thought that was you. You're looking for your dog." It wasn't a question.

"You've seen him?"

"Got him in the jail. He was sniffin' round the back door of Tommy McLaren's butcher shop. I'm thinkin' of charging him with attempted breaking and entering." Laughter rumbled in the words.

She stifled a snort of disgust. "That dog has a bottomless pit for a stomach."

For a moment, she didn't think he would answer, then, without the laughter he said, "A fellow gets that way sometimes, so hungry for somethin' that nothin' else quite fills him up."

As it always did, his soft voice sent shivers down her spine, starting a small, warm fire inside her. It was only her imagination that there was an intimate roughness in it, and more beneath his words than there seemed.

"I'll take you back to the jail," he said curtly, as if he were sorry for already having said so much.

He didn't offer to take her arm, but he was close enough that the heat from his body seemed to wrap around her, driving out the lingering chill.

The jail was dark, the shades pulled. When Witt shut the door, the air suddenly seemed to compress around her, making it harder to breathe.

"Wait here while I light a lamp," he said gruffly.

From the back of the building came an eager whine, immediately followed by a sharp, imperative bark.

Lamp in hand, Witt opened the door at the back that Molly knew led to the jail cell. He quickly stepped through and drew another door shut, but not quickly enough. She caught a glimpse of a window with an old blanket tacked over it and a narrow, rumpled bed. The pillow still had a hollow where his head had pressed.

"Dog's in here," he said—unnecessarily, since Pete was scrabbling at the iron bars of the cell, whining and demanding to be let out. "Figured he couldn't get out if I locked him up."

"I've half a mind to leave him right where he's at," Molly said.

She stared at Pete, but what she saw was a narrow iron bed, tumbled sheets, and a crushed pillow in its wrinkled case. The scent of him would be on the pillow and the sheets. Almost she could feel the rasp of the coarse muslin against her skin.

"I'll let him out," Witt said.

She could hear the strain in his voice, and thought how strange it was that she always heard so much in it when he said so very little.

"No, wait." She swallowed, trying to force her heart back out of her throat. "Not yet."

Sometimes you have to take a chance. She'd told herself that only a few hours earlier. The envelope with her letter lay on her kitchen table, proof of her choice.

But all she risked with that letter was money. She wasn't sure she could tally what she risked now, and wasn't sure she cared to try.

Of one thing she was certain, however—if she waited for Witt to make the first move, she'd be waiting a long, long time.

"Here, let me take the lamp," she said.

He breathed out, huffing a bit, like a man who'd held his breath too long. A small, secret smile tugged at her lips. Poor man thought she was being helpful.

She set the lamp on the floor, safely out of reach where there was no risk of tripping over it. Then, calmly, despite her pounding heart, she rose on tiptoe and wrapped her arms around his neck and kissed him.

He staggered, groaning like a man in pain, then wrapped his arms around her and kissed her back, deep and hot and hungry. And as he kissed her, he dragged her down until they were half seated, half sprawled on the floor. He held her so tightly she could scarcely breathe, but she could kiss him and that was more than enough.

It was Pete's anxious whining that dragged them back from the madness. Witt slumped against the wall, eyes closed, and let his head drop back.

"Damn dog."

Molly collapsed in giggles on his chest.

Gently, he shifted her so that she was in his lap, cradling her against him. She could feel his fingers playing with her hair, his palm drifting down her side, then up again.

Still safe and close against him, she tilted her head

back and looked into his face. It was such a strong, compelling face.

Fascinated, she brushed a finger across one brow, then down the side of his face and along that granite jaw.

His eyes opened, locked with hers. In their depths she read his longing and all the truth she would ever need.

"I love you, Witt Gavin," she said softly. "Will you marry me?"

A right to the jaw wouldn't have stopped him as easily. He stared at her. And then he sucked in air, taking deep breaths, fighting for control. She could feel his hand fisting in her hair. He didn't seem aware of it.

"No," he said. It was more an exhalation of air than a word.

She pushed away and sat up, still on his lap. "Why not?"

His brow furrowed, as if he were struggling for an answer. "Because."

"That's not good enough. I don't go around kissing men I'm not serious about, and I don't think you go around kissing women just because you happen to run into them on the street. I'm in love with you, and I want to marry you. It's as simple as that.

"Besides," she added, teasing, "if I waited for you to get around to asking, I'd be too old to care."

"Don't be a fool," he said, and tried to shove her away.

She grabbed the front of his shirt and hung on. "Don't try and tell me you don't love me because I won't believe you."

Before he could throw her off, she shifted so that she was straddling his lap, pinning him down.

That's when she knew she'd won, no matter what he said. The proof of it was pressing hard against her center, unmistakable even through the layers of clothing between them.

She grinned. "You want me, Witt Gavin, just as much as I want you."

"Wanting's not loving," he said harshly.

"No, wanting's not loving, but it's part of it. A wonderful and very important part of it." She leaned close and stared straight into his eyes. "I love you, DeWitt Gavin, and I want you. And I know damned well you love me and want me, no matter what you say."

He blinked at the curse.

She kissed him, and this time she blatantly rubbed herself against him, wanton as any fallen woman.

With a roar, he threw her off, slamming her into the bars of the cell and startling Pete into a frantic barking. Neither one of them paid the dog any heed.

"You think it's as easy as that?" he shouted. "That all it takes is love to make a marriage work? Well you're wrong. *Wrong,* dammit! I know! I loved my wife and it wasn't enough to keep her with me. Not near enough!"

He was half on his feet, looming over her.

"There's some with a talent for building a marriage. There's more that get by because they don't know any other way. And there's some—" he leaned closer, so close she could feel the anger and a deeper, darker pain coming off him in waves "—who can't ever make it work, no matter how hard they try. Love? Hell!"

He surged to his feet.

Molly leapt to hers, darting in front of him to stop him storming out of the jail, away from her.

"Is this what happened to your marriage?" she demanded, bracing her hands against the doorjamb on either side as if that would stop him. "You ran away?"

"Me?" For a moment he just stared at her, then, to her surprise, he threw back his head and laughed. The scorn in the laughter was like acid, burning her even though she knew it was meant for him, and him alone.

"I didn't run away," he said. "It was my wife who ran, straight into the arms of a fine, well-dressed gentleman who knew what she needed and could give it to her." The words came tumbling out like water over a floodgate, driven by his fury and his pain. "He could talk pretty and dress pretty, and he knew all the right things to say and the right places to go and the right way to do things once he got there. I'll bet he did all the right things in bed, too, since I sure as hell never managed to please her there, either."

Understanding hit Molly with near blinding force. He had loved his wife, but she had flung that love in his face—and he blamed himself for all of it.

"There's all kinds of whores," she said softly, "and some of them wear wedding rings and wouldn't so much as glance at a brothel."

That stopped him.

"You're a good man, Witt Gavin, no matter what went wrong in your first marriage. Do you think I can't see that?"

"I'm a *divorced* man." He darned near spat the words at her. "I wasn't able to make Clara happy. What makes you think I can do any better now?"

Anger exploded within her. She slammed the heel of her hand against his chest, making him take a stumbling step backward.

"Who said I expected you to make me happy?"

She punched him again, harder this time. "Didn't

anyone ever tell you it takes two to make a marriage work?''

He grabbed her hand before she could hit him a third time.

''That's pretty darned arrogant, Mr. Gavin, thinking that everything depends on you.''

''If I'd been a better man…'' He shook his head, then let her go. His shoulders slumped as he turned away, defeated.

Molly hoped she never met Clara Gavin because she'd be tempted to claw out the woman's eyes.

Nothing she could say would make Witt change his mind, certainly not right now. But then, words weren't always the best solution.

She had the first six buttons of her dress undone when she threw open the door to Witt's room and walked in. She'd freed the rest of the buttons by the time he realized where she was.

''What the hell do you think you're doing?''

''Me?'' She smiled at him and let the dress slide to the floor. ''I'm undressing.''

''You—you can't do that.''

''No?'' she said sweetly.

He shook his head, wild-eyed as a bull being pestered by a very determined gnat. ''No.''

The last lacing strings on her petticoats came free. Yards of starched muslin and lace slid to the floor in a billow of wedding-cake white.

''Oh,'' she said, and tugged at the ties at the top of the chemise.

He'd stopped breathing, but he hadn't stopped looking—his eyes were getting bigger by the minute. His gaze fixed on her breasts. Freed of their normal boned support, they swayed a little with her movement, the nipples pricking to hard points beneath the delicate fabric of her chemise.

She wondered how long it would take before he exploded from lack of oxygen.

"Would you care to help me with the last of it?" she asked, and held her arms open wide.

He gulped, stunned, then took another look and charged.

It was lucky she hadn't bothered to put her corset back on because he probably would have snapped the laces and torn the hooks right out of the fabric if she had. As it was, her chemise and bloomers were all going to need some mending. She heard the fabric tear as he ripped them off her, and almost laughed out loud for the sheer joy of it.

Madness drove him. Witt knew it, yet he couldn't stop himself. All these weeks of thinking of her, dreaming of her, *wanting* her, and now here she was half-naked in his room with the bed only a foot away.

She bent as he tugged on that simple white top she wore, letting him pull it up and over her head. He flung it away, not caring where it landed, and reached for the waistband of those funny pantaloons she wore. The fabric ripped when he yanked on the strings at the waist, but he didn't care. He just pulled harder, dragging it down, almost toppling her in his frantic haste to get it off.

And then she was naked, smooth, bare flesh gold in the light from the lamp they'd left outside the door. Her hair tumbled around her like something out of his dreams, covering one shoulder, baring the other, teasing at the curve of a breast, the swell of her hips. Caressing the tops of her thighs.

He stopped breathing and drank her in. Need consumed him, yet pinned him where he stood, unable to move or think.

She watched him staring, and smiled, unashamed and sure.

The smile dragged a groan from somewhere deep in his gut. This was madness. *He* was mad—drunk, perhaps, or dreaming. All he knew was that if he was drunk, he wanted more; if he was dreaming, he prayed he'd never wake up.

Clara had never granted him such a gift. Always she wore a chemise or a gown, hiding her body from him. Their lovemaking, what little there had been of it, had always been committed in the dark, as if it were a crime.

Never, until now, had he realized what a crime the darkness itself had been to have hidden such wonders from him.

Molly laughed and held her arms out from her body as if offering him...everything.

"Looking's fine," she said. "But making love is better."

She reached to undo the first button on his shirt.

He never let her get to the second. Crazed with wanting, he laid her on the bed and freed himself from his trousers. And then he was driving into her, his self-control shattered, his hunger a thing with claws that threatened to rip him apart, so hot and fierce was it.

Instead of screaming or trying to push him away, she laughed and clung tighter, moving with him rather than against him, demanding more rather than passively waiting for him to be done, crying out in what, in his madness, he would swear was pleasure and not pain.

When his climax came, it damn near killed him.

It was her tongue in his ear that eventually, ages later, brought him back to life.

"What—?" He swatted at the distraction, then groggily shoved up on his elbow.

Tried to, anyway. He didn't get very far before she wrapped her arms around his neck and her legs around his waist and dragged him back against her.

"Don't move," she murmured. "Not yet."

"I'm crushing you."

"Mm-hmm. I like it."

That's when he realized that there was something going on down there between them. He was dead as a drowned rat, but she—

"You're squeezing me!" He gaped at her, stunned.

"Clever man." She pulled his head down even as her hips shoved up against him.

He would have sworn it wasn't possible, but she was bringing him back to life, too. Yet when she cried out and arched against him, eyes shut, face tight with ecstasy as her own climax claimed her, he simply held her, too awed by the wonder of it to do anything else.

"I didn't know…" he whispered when she roused at last, blinking up at him and smiling like the cat that got the cream.

"Now you do." Her fingers were playing in his hair, distracting him. She ran her tongue across her lower lip as her hands dragged down his back, then up again, and over to the buttons of his shirt.

When he reluctantly stood to remove his trousers and

his boots, he turned away and wished he'd thought to put out the lamp, first. He should have known she'd laugh and tug on his arm, demanding he turn around, instead of turning away in disgust.

"You're a fine-looking man, Mr. Gavin," she said, tracing the line of his ribs with the tip of one fingernail. "All the ladies say so."

He'd been about to toss his pants aside, but at her words, he instinctively wadded them in front of himself, instead. "They do?"

She laughed and nodded. The light rippled across her hair with every move.

"They do," she said with satisfaction. "Despite the fact that you're so very big."

He had the sudden, disconcerting notion that she wasn't just talking about his height and weight. He didn't have much chance to worry about it, though, because a moment later she boldly pulled his trousers out of his hands and tossed them aside, giving him something else entirely to think about.

"I *told* you. It'd be wrong to take advantage, to marry you just because of…this," Witt protested.

Molly looked up at him and smiled. He'd been arguing for the past ten minutes, caught between love and pride as only a man could be.

"You wouldn't be marrying me because we've made love, but because you love me as much as I love you. Where's the taking advantage in that?"

He set his jaw in a stubborn, mulish look she was coming to know all too well.

"Go ahead," she added, openly challenging. "Tell

me you don't love me. All you have to do is tell me
that and I'll never say another word about marriage."

With typical male bullheadedness, he retreated behind yet another useless argument. "I've nothing to offer you, no money, no land. Only a job, and that's not
all that secure."

"And not very well paid, either," Molly said, calmly
fastening the last of the buttons on her dress.

"And not very well paid." He didn't look as if he
appreciated her help on the subject.

"It doesn't matter because I have the shop."

"I'd make a damned poor shopkeeper."

She smiled and stood on tiptoe to kiss his cheek. "I
agree. You're much too large. You'd never fit behind
the counter."

"Molly, would you please listen?" he demanded, ex-
asperated.

"No. I'm not listening to another word until you say,
Yes, thank you, Molly Calhan. I'd be delighted to marry
you."

He crossed his arms over his chest and scowled, instead.

This morning, his stubborn refusal might have dismayed her, but not now. Witt Gavin loved her—her
body still ached and throbbed with the satisfying knowl-
edge of just how very, very much he loved her. She'd
bring him round to the rest of it in spite of him.

"In that case, would you please release my dog? Or
do I have to post bail to get him out?"

She laughed when Witt just growled and stomped
out. While he unlocked the cell door, she turned out the
lamp they'd left on the floor, then cautiously made her
way across the now dark office to the front door. Behind

her, she caught Pete's happy bark, then the click of his toenails as he trotted across the floor after her, clearly pleased to be free.

"Shhh," she said, moving to block the door so he wouldn't dart out the instant she opened it. An instant later, she eased the door closed and sagged against it, heart pounding.

"Something the matter?"

"The drunks are staggering home."

"You could wait a bit," he suggested with feigned casualness.

Molly sternly repressed the urge to agree. "No, better not. Who knows when the last of them will go past."

He sighed. "True."

"But I'll bet I can get out your window." Better that than risk giving in to temptation.

With Pete happily clicking after them, they retreated to his bedroom. Molly was grateful for the darkness that hid the rumpled bed.

She pressed her ear to the window. No sound came from the alleyway. It wasn't likely the saloon patrons would stagger around back here when they had Main Street all to themselves.

Witt pulled her to him, starting a fresh, unsettling wave of heat surging through her. "I don't like you going out in the night like this unescorted."

"I can't wait till morning, when half the town would see me."

"I know." His hand cupped her face, his callused palm warm and rough against her cheek.

"I'll be all right. And I do have Pete if I run into anyone."

"Damn dog." A moment's silence, then, "Sorry. I didn't mean—"

Molly laughed. "I agree completely."

The dog, seated on the floor between them, gave a little bark of encouragement.

Witt reluctantly let her go, then pulled aside the blanket that served as curtain and slid up the sash. It grated against the warped frame, disconcertingly loud in the night's silence. They both froze, listening.

Nothing. The alleyway was empty.

Molly cautiously poked her head out the window. The buildings across the way loomed, black shadows in the darkness. Not one showed so much as a hint of lamplight through a shuttered window. She gathered up her skirts and swung a leg over the windowsill.

"You'll be careful?"

He was so close, his whispered demand came as a brush of warm air against her ear. A shiver shot through her, rousing desire. She was in a sad way if so simple a thing could set her aching. No matter. Witt might have his doubts about marriage, but he'd come round—she make sure of it—and once he did...

She laughed and jumped. It was a longer drop to the ground than she'd expected, but she stumbled only a little when she landed. Witt ducked back inside, then leaned out a moment later with a squirming bundle of fur in his hands.

Molly clamped her hand over Pete's muzzle before he could bark. The little dog gave a wiggle of protest, then obediently settled into her arms.

"As if you've never done anything wrong in your miserable little life," she whispered to him, and kissed that flyaway ear.

Keeping to the darkest shadows close to the buildings, Molly cautiously made her way down the alley. She glanced back once and saw Witt's head sticking out of the window. When she looked back again, just before she reached the street, his shadow was gone and she was alone.

She didn't let Pete go until they were safely back in the house and the door was bolted behind her.

She didn't fall asleep until shortly before dawn.

Witt didn't get to sleep at all.

Chapter Nineteen

Grown-ups sure talked a lot. Bonnie sighed and fidgeted on the rough plank bench that was one of dozens set out around the bandstand so people could sit while the mayor and old Reverend James and a bunch of long-winded old men droned on and on about Elk City and the vision of its founders and the great things that lay in its future.

The parade through town this morning hadn't been too bad, but you could *die* waiting for those old fogies to stop talking.

If it hadn't been for having to keep an eye on Dickie, who fidgeted ten times worse than she did and who'd managed to sneak some bread for Pete into one pocket and his slingshot into the other, she'd probably have keeled over an hour ago from sheer boredom.

At least watching Dickie meant she didn't have to watch her mother and the sheriff making stupid sheep eyes at each other. They thought nobody noticed, but if there was anyone over six years old who *hadn't* noticed, Bonnie hadn't spotted them. They were worse, even, than Crazy Mike and that silly Louisa Merton, and those two were bad enough.

It was embarrassing to see her mother act this way. No, it was downright, die-in-your-shoes *humiliating*. Her own *mother* for Heaven's sake! Blushing and smiling and just as silly about it as Mary Sue Mandelbaum had been when Jimmy Jacobs had been courting her, and *everybody* in town had talked about how silly Mary Sue had been.

At least the endless yammering from the folks in the bandstand was coming to an end. The band played something loud and unrecognizable—that new tuba player Mrs. Trainer was so happy about couldn't hit one right note in ten—then everybody cheered and clapped and started getting to their feet. Judging from the expressions on the faces of some of them, the cheering was mostly relief that the ceremonies were over and now they could focus on the picnic lunches they'd brought and look forward to the afternoon's entertainments.

Dickie was one of the first off the bench. "Come on, Pete."

"Don't you go running away and getting lost in the crowd, Dickie Calhan," Bonnie warned him. "We're going to have lunch pretty soon!"

"And don't you go bossin' me around, Bonnie Mae Calhan. Me'n Pete are goin' t'do just what we want, and you can't stop us. So there!"

He was off like a shot, worming his way through the crowd. Shoving sometimes, even, which would upset Mother no end because she was always lecturing about good manners and consideration for others.

Not that her mother had even noticed, Bonnie thought sourly, setting off after him. *She* was too busy smiling at the sheriff.

* * *

As she always did, Molly had brought enough food for a dozen. She bent to retrieve the heavy wicker basket she'd shoved under the bench only to find that Bonnie and Dickie had disappeared. A quick scan of the crowd revealed no trace of them.

Ah, well. No sense worrying. When it came to eating, they always found their way back.

With the basket bumping against her leg, she slowly worked her way through the crowd toward Witt. If she'd had any sense, she'd have invited him to share their lunch last night. But last night she'd had other things on her mind. It was only while she was dreaming over the skillet of frying chicken this morning that she'd remembered that a well-fed man was much more likely to be reasonable than a hungry one—and she was determined to make Witt Gavin see reason if she had to feed him the whole darned chicken to do it.

Once free of the crowd, Dickie broke into a jog trot. He'd heard some of the older boys talking about firecrackers and some bottles of beer snitched off a delivery wagon carelessly left unattended behind Jackson's saloon. He wasn't quite sure what they planned, but he was determined to find out. After all, mother wouldn't be laying out lunch for hours and hours and *hours*— once they got going, grown-ups always ended up talking for forever—and he'd listened to about all the talking he could take for one morning.

"Dickie Calhan, you come back here!"

Dickie briefly considered running faster, then decided that would only make things worse. To his disgust, the minute he stopped, Pete raced back to Bonnie, tail wagging.

"Traitor," he said when the two of them caught up. Pete just plopped his bottom on the ground and grinned.

"You shouldn't be running off like this," Bonnie scolded. "We're going to have lunch soon."

"How soon?"

"*Soon.*"

"I'll be back by then," Dickie said. "Come on, Pete."

"I'll tell Mother!" Bonnie reluctantly fell into step beside him. "She says I'm supposed to watch you 'cause I'm the oldest, but *you're* the one who's always getting into trouble, not me!"

Dickie didn't bother listening. He glanced down a side street, hoping to spot the older boys with the firecrackers, and stopped dead. "Holy cow! Look! The bank robbers are back!"

Bonnie almost tripped over the dog. "Who? Where? What robbers?"

"See? Those guys disappearin' round that corner." He was almost bouncing he was so excited. "Didja see 'em?"

"There's nobody there." Bonnie frowned. "And there are *no* bank robbers."

"Are, too, and *I'm* gonna catch 'em!" said Dickie, starting after them. "Wait 'n' see if I don't!"

"I'm telling Mother."

"Go ahead," Dickie retorted. "I don't care."

"You'll be sorry!"

"Hah!" Dickie said.

"Hah yourself!" Bonnie pointedly flounced away.

The street suddenly seemed awfully empty without her. Dickie's steps slowed. For an instant, he debated going after her. On the other hand, maybe he ought to find the sheriff. But the last time he'd spotted these guys the sheriff had said he was busy and maybe he, Dickie, ought to round them up since he seemed to be the only one who ever saw them.

Rounding them up sounded good. Dickie considered it for a moment, caught between burgeoning excitement at the possibility of adventure and a stomach-squeezing doubt. After all, they were grown-ups as well as bad men. He'd never managed to make grown-ups do what he wanted, ever.

Maybe he really oughta get the sheriff.

Pete decided for him. His dog emerged from a good sniff under a bush halfway down the street and barked as if wondering what was keeping him.

The streets were empty—everyone up at the park, for sure—yet there were two horses tied in the alleyway that ran behind the bank. Dickie had read enough to know what that meant.

Heart hammering, but with every sense alert in the very best detective tradition, he crept around the building. To his delight, the bank door was open a crack.

Dickie started up the steps, then hesitated. It was one thing to read about guys like Nick Carter and Frank Meriwell, quite another to act like them when faced with real, live bad men. But someone had to stop those bank robbers and right now there was no one else in sight.

Screwing up his courage, Dickie pushed open the door to the bank and walked in.

Nothing. The place looked like it always did. Pete whined unhappily.

A scuffling sound came from the back, then a very masculine curse.

Cautiously, Dickie crept forward, through the wooden gate, past Mr. Goff's desk and the door to Mr.

Hancock's office. All the way to the back room where the big safe was kept. For a moment, he simply stood in the doorway, heart pounding, struggling to remember what Nick Carter had done in a similar situation.

"Hey!" he said. "What do you think you're doing?"

The two men abruptly stopped what they were doing and turned to face him.

He shouldn't have agreed to this, Witt told himself grimly as he helped Molly spread a worn checked tablecloth in the shade. He wouldn't have come at all if it hadn't been his responsibility to keep an eye on things.

You would have crawled here on your hands and knees if it meant being able to see her, a silent voice in his head chided.

Witt glanced at Molly, who was setting a stack of enameled tin plates on the cloth, followed by forks and napkins, and food in a variety of jars and covered bowls. Without looking up, she filled a plate with baked beans and potato salad and spiced tomatoes and a hunk of fried chicken, then handed it to him.

Reluctantly, Witt took it. "People are going to talk. About me having lunch here with you, I mean."

Molly nodded. "Probably, but wait till you hear what they say about Louisa and Mr. McCord picnicking all by themselves like that." She glanced up, eyes sparking with mischief. "I think he's going to propose."

Witt stabbed the chicken with his fork.

"Or maybe he already has." She lowered her voice to a secret-sharing level. "I saw them kissing this morning. Right over there by that pine tree. Kissing! Can you imagine?"

Witt abandoned the fork and simply ripped off a hunk of meat with his teeth.

Her voice lowered still further, soft and intimate. "I must say, he looked like he was a very good kisser, though not anywhere near as good as you."

The chicken stopped halfway down his throat. He choked, then thumped his chest once, twice, until he coughed and swallowed it down.

Molly calmly dug another jar out of her basket. "Pickles?"

"No!"

"No pickles?"

Witt angrily shoved his plate aside and leaned forward, close enough so no one else could hear him. "Molly—*Mrs. Calhan!* This is crazy. We can't just pretend that—that last night never happened. Your reputation—"

Her smile almost blinded him. "You know, I wouldn't have dreamed of being half this bold when Richard was courting me. On the other hand, I wasn't anywhere near so sure of what I wanted, way back then."

He just stared. He didn't know what to say. Bandits, he could have dealt with. Drunks and bullies and disasters were easy as falling off a log. But this wild, confusing mix of love and hunger and a thousand doubts— he didn't even know how to begin to sort it out.

It was her turn to lean close, so close she seemed to steal his air, making it impossible to breathe.

"Last night I said all you had to do was tell me you didn't love me, that you didn't want to marry me," she said. "You couldn't say it last night, but maybe it wasn't fair to ask right then."

Her clear gaze locked on his, pinning him in his

place. "If you can say all that *now,* in the clear light of day, I'll believe you and I will never say another word about the matter."

She leaned closer still, eyes narrowed in unmistakable challenge. "But you have to *say* it first."

Witt opened his mouth, then closed it without breathing a word.

She gave a little crow of triumph and sat back. "I knew it! I *knew* you couldn't say it. You couldn't say it last night and you can't say it now because you know that you'd be lying if you did."

"And I told you I don't have much talent for being a husband."

Molly nodded agreeably, smug in her conviction that she'd won. "That's what you said. I still don't believe you, though."

Her face was alight with laughter and something far more dangerously tempting.

Witt groaned and shifted position so she couldn't see the effect she was having on him. He'd almost gotten his breathing under control when he spotted Bonnie storming across the park toward them.

Molly looked up, and sighed. "Where's your brother?" she said when Bonnie threw herself down on the cloth, clearly disgusted.

"Off getting into trouble. Said he saw those bank robbers of his again."

"Here? Right now? Well, you just go find him and tell him if he wants any fried chicken, he'd better leave the bank robbers alone and get back here where he belongs."

Witt couldn't help but grin, grateful for the distraction. Somebody'd better rob the bank soon or Dickie was going to pop from frustration.

"I *tried*," said Bonnie. "He didn't listen to me. He *never* listens to me! Anyway, I think he's really gone off to watch Tom Seiffert and his friends set off all their firecrackers."

"Firecrackers! I've told him not to play with firecrackers." Molly glanced at him, then at the picnic she'd laid out on the cloth. "I suppose I ought to go get him."

"Boy'll be all right," Witt assured her. It was dangerous being so close, but he didn't want her leaving him, either, not even for five minutes. "He's like a cat. Always lands on his feet no matter what he gets into."

The sharp *tat-tat-tat-tat-tat-tat* sound of a string of fireworks going off brought a sudden silence to the throng of picnickers. For a moment, everyone craned, trying to see where the sound came from. Then someone laughed and the crowd came back to life. No one blinked when the second round of fireworks went off, or the third.

Molly sighed and reluctantly got to her feet. "I suppose I'd better go find him. If you'll watch the lunch…?"

Witt nodded. He didn't dare stand for fear the whole world would see what kind of effect she had on him.

"I'll show you where he went!" Bonnie offered, jumping up to follow her.

To his dismay, Witt found matters just got worse when he watched Molly walk away, head high, skirts gracefully swaying.

The flags mounted on the telegraph poles along Main Street waved gently in the breeze while the heavy banners strung on ropes across the street flapped and swayed and billowed. Everything else was still and utterly silent. Without a brass band playing, without the excited crowds that had lined the street this morning, the place seemed oddly empty and forlorn.

"Why would he come this way?" Molly glanced up and down the street, irritably searching for any sign of her son. She wanted to get back to Witt, not waste time looking for Dickie.

"He said the bank robbers were headed this way," Bonnie said. "If they really are bank robbers," she added darkly, "then I guess they'll be at the bank."

Molly glanced at her daughter, then laughed and gave her a quick hug. "I guess they will. Shall we go see if they are?"

They were two doors down from the bank when the explosion hit.

The heavy *boom!* coming from the center of town sounded absolutely nothing like firecrackers.

After a moment's frozen surprise, Witt spat out his half-eaten mouthful of chicken and sprang to his feet. He was already running when the crowd in the park buzzed back to frightened life.

"Dynamite!" he heard someone shout. "That was dynamite!"

"The mines!" someone else cried.

"No, no! It was downtown! Dynamite downtown!"

Molly and Bonnie had headed downtown, looking for Dickie.

Witt grabbed the nearest saddled horse. Without stopping to find the stirrups, he swung into the saddle and kicked the beast into a gallop. Behind him, he could hear the sounds of men shouting, of people running, but he didn't wait to see who followed.

Outside Elk City State Bank, hell repeated itself.

There was the bank, its windows blown out. There were the robbers—two of them, both armed and dangerously frightened—running from the bank carrying big, well-stuffed canvas money sacks.

And there were the children. Only this time, the children were Dickie and Bonnie and they weren't fifty feet away, wondering what was going on.

The first robber had a cursing, kicking Dickie by the collar—Witt could see the barrel of a deadly .45 poking up by the boy's ear as the man tried to hold on to both gun and boy even as he struggled with the cumbersome money sacks and the dog clamped around his right ankle. Despite the mouthful of trouser and boot, Pete was growling and snarling enough for a dozen dogs.

The second man was trying to fight off an enraged Bonnie, who'd grabbed hold of one of the three money bags and dug in her feet. He kept cursing and swinging the heavy bag, trying to shake her off, but she was hanging on as tenaciously as Pete. She didn't seem to be doing as much damage—the first robber was starting to limp.

"Let my brother go!" she screeched. "You let him go!"

Witt swung out of the saddle, then, with a hard slap to its rump, sent the horse trotting off. No one had yet noticed him. He pulled his gun and cautiously moved forward.

At least they weren't shooting. If he could stop them before the crowd caught up, maybe they never would.

He forced aside the ugly memory of two other robbers who had. He didn't dare let those memories influence his judgment now.

Molly suddenly appeared in the bank doorway. Her

hat was half off and Witt could see a thin trickle of blood staining the side of her face.

"Stop them!" she cried. "Stop them! Let my son go!"

The first robber let Dickie go, then turned toward the bank and Molly. His arm came up.

Witt raised his gun and fired, then fired again and again and again.

Chapter Twenty

The shots shattered the bank's wooden flagpole, freeing the rope that spanned the street and sending it and the heavy banners tied to it tumbling down on top of the robbers' heads. The first man's gun went flying. The second man dropped one of his money bags, then tried to pick it up again and dropped his gun instead.

"Bonnie! Dickie! Run!" Witt roared, diving for the free end of the rope.

Swinging wide, he dragged the rope in a circle, sending the two men tumbling. Pete got thumped, cursed, kicked, smashed and pounded, which only seemed to make him bite down harder.

Dickie dashed in and snatched up the first robber's gun. Holding it two-fisted, he waved it menacingly in the thieves' general direction.

"Put 'em up! We got ya covered! Put 'em up or I'll shoot!"

To Witt's immense relief, he'd forgotten to cock the thing. "Dickie—"

The gun's owner got one hand free and clouted Dickie on the ear, sending him tumbling, too. Dickie hadn't stopped rolling when Bonnie launched herself at the man like a mountain lion at its prey.

"Don't you dare hit my brother!" she shrieked, pounding on the hapless robber. "Bully! Meanie! Pick on somebody your own size!"

The man cowered under the furious rain of blows, futilely trying to protect his head. She slapped him, socked him and punched him, then landed a solid kick to the ribs for good measure. "Stinking pile of dog poop!"

"Hey, hey! That's enough!" Witt grabbed her around the waist and swung her away.

"Don't you ever hit my little brother again!" She lashed out with her foot, clobbering the fellow on the side of his head and sending him sprawling. "Nobody hurts my brother! *Nobody!*"

She was still swinging and kicking when Witt set her on her feet in front of Molly.

"Hold her!" he shouted over his shoulder as he plunged back into the fray.

Another loop with the rope and a couple of well-aimed punches settled things so that by the time Elk City's citizens charged onto the scene, matters were pretty much under control.

Mike McCord was one of the first to arrive. He eyed the bank's broken windows, the crudely trussed robbers with Dickie standing guard over them, and grinned. "Keepin' all the fun to yourself, are you?"

Witt frowned at him, then snatched the big .45 out of Dickie's hands. "Give me that gun."

"I almost shot 'im, didn't I?" Dickie said, near bursting with pride.

"Almost." Witt gave a silent prayer of thanks that

the boy hadn't managed more. "Now call off your dog."

"And I stopped 'em from robbin' the bank, didn't I?" Dickie insisted.

"That, too. But next time you decide to pull a stunt like that," Witt said sternly, *"don't!"*

He left the job of untangling the robbers to Mike and crossed to where Molly stood at the edge of the crowd, watching them anxiously and trying to keep a still furious Bonnie under control. She'd wiped the blood from her face, but a bruise was already starting to form at her temple.

He didn't have a chance to ask how she felt because she threw herself into his arms first, laughing and crying. And then she kissed him, right there in front of God and everybody.

After the first moment of stunned surprised, he kissed her back. And then he kissed her again. And again. And again.

If it hadn't been for McCord tapping him on the shoulder, he might never have come up for air.

"What you wanta do with these two?" Mike inquired with a grin, cocking his thumb at the prisoners.

Witt managed to stifle the first three suggestions that came to mind.

"Talk to them," he said, regretfully letting Molly go. He couldn't walk away, though. The memory of her in that bank doorway and the sight of that purpling bruise had toppled the last of his defenses. He took a deep breath, then slowly let it out.

"I love you, Molly Calhan," he said, and gently touched her cheek. "We'll talk about the rest later. All right?"

And then he bent to kiss her again, heedless of the rude, good-natured cheering from the gathering crowd.

By the time Witt got back to the business at hand, five armed miners were standing guard over the collected mailbags, Mike was guarding two very unhappy would-be thieves with the help of Dickie and his dog, and Gordon Hancock had stormed onto the scene, full of outrage and bluster.

"You're fired, Gavin," he shouted. "Do you hear? Fired! How could you let this happen? It's your responsibility—"

"Hancock?" said Witt.

"What?"

"Shut up."

He said it mildly, in an almost conversational tone, but the banker must have seen something in his face. Hancock shut up.

The crowd edged closer, clearly pleased with this new development.

Witt turned to the two robbers, studying them thoughtfully.

"Gotta tell you boys," he said, "it's gonna be a job fillin' out all the paperwork for the judge."

The first robber, the one who'd grabbed Dickie, sneered and tried to look tough. Number two didn't bother to try.

"There's armed robbery," said Witt, calmly ticking off the items on his fingers. "Attempted kidnapping, assault and battery—"

"What?" said number one.

"You hit Mrs. Calhan. *And* the boy."

"He hit me first!"

"Attempted murder—"

"The hell you say!"

"You were going to shoot Mrs. Calhan."

"I wasn't gonna shoot her," the man objected, indignant. "Just wanted t'scare her, make her shut up."

"Intimidation…"

The man's eyes bulged, but this time he kept silent.

Witt frowned, then casually rubbed his bruised knuckles. He glanced at Hancock, who was following the conversation with growing impatience. Out of the corner of his eye he could see Hiram Goff slinking around the edges of the growing crowd.

He turned his attention back to the thieves. "I might consider dropping a couple of those charges if you tell me how you knew the mine payrolls had been delivered early."

The robbers looked at each other, then back at him. Robber number two was the first to crack.

"That fella from the bank was the one set us up," he cried. "He was the one told us what t'do!"

"What?" Hancock's face turned red. Suddenly, a pistol was in his hand. "Why you miserable swine—"

Witt's fist connected with Hancock's chin with a satisfying thud. Hancock's head snapped back. Witt hit him again, harder this time. Like a tree felled by a lumberjack, Hancock toppled backward, unconscious before he even hit the ground.

"Not him. *Him,*" said the robber, pointing.

At the edge of the befuddled crowd, Hiram Goff gave a panicked squeak and tried to run. An instant later, he dived nose-first into the dirt with one small boy wrapped around one leg and one small, nondescript brown mutt nipping at the other.

"Got 'im!" Dickie crowed, cheerfully dodging Goff's furious, thrashing kick. "I *got* 'im!"

Pete barked and wagged his tail in approval.

"Is it all over?" Molly demanded a few hours later when Witt was finally settled at her kitchen table with the remains of lunch on a plate in front of him.

She'd spent the intervening hours scolding her two children in between bouts of crying and hugging them and checking one more time to make sure they were all right. And whenever she wasn't doing that, she'd thought of Witt and all the wonderful years that lay ahead, and almost danced with the sheer joy of it.

But now she wanted answers to a couple of nagging questions. "What have you done with the robbers?"

Witt added extra sugar to his coffee. "Goff and the two thieves are well on their way to Gunnison. Bigger jail there," he explained when she looked surprised. "Bigger and a whole lot more secure. Everyone figured it'd be safer that way."

"And you didn't go with them?"

He shook his head. "I'm stayin' here to keep an eye on things. Hancock's moved that payroll money into the other banks until Friday and got somebody to board up the windows until he can get them fixed, but he insists I gotta watch the place, just in case."

He took a sip of coffee, then signed in satisfaction. "Now *that's* good coffee."

She waved the compliment aside. "I'm surprised Gordon Hancock hasn't demanded your resignation after you hit him like that. I thought he'd never come to."

Witt tried to look contrite. "There was something said about needing a new sheriff," he admitted, "but I don't think anyone else paid much attention in the confusion."

"He'll bring it up at the next town council meeting," Molly warned.

"I expect he will. Say! You got any more of that potato salad?"

"Don't change the subject!" Molly dumped a generous heap on his plate, anyway. "If you're staying here, who went with the thieves?"

"The mayor deputized Mike McCord and four other men to watch 'em. Guess he figured Goff was such a slippery fellow that he might escape, otherwise."

Something in the way he said it, in the laughter she could hear just beneath the surface of the words, put Molly on the alert.

"You knew it wasn't Hancock," she said accusingly. "All the time you *knew*."

For a moment, she didn't think he was going to answer, then a slow, tantalizing grin spread across his face.

"Yeah, I knew but I've never been a man to pass up an opportunity."

"Is that so?"

He nodded. The twinkle in those changeable eyes was almost irresistible.

Molly eyed him suspiciously. "*How* did you know? Did you really believe Dickie's story about the bank robbers?"

"No. Wish I had. But I *was* interested in Mrs. Thompson always arguin' over her account."

"But she argues over every penny she ever spent!"

"True. But I doubt even the penny-pinchin'est fool in the world would accuse a bank of stealing her money unless she had pretty good reason to believe they had. Hancock didn't strike me as the type to fiddle with a small account like that, but Goff did."

"And Mrs. Thompson was right?"

Witt nodded. "Goff really was stealing. Once we got him talkin', he confessed to everything. How he's been 'borrowing,' as he likes to put it, a little bit here and there for years. But eventually it started getting away from him. He knew a careful review of the books would show what he'd been up to, so he found two fellows who were just stupid enough to agree to rob the bank for him. They'd blow up the books when they blew up the safe, then give him a share of whatever they got away with."

"And if they didn't get away, then you'd be there to shoot them. They'd be dead, the records would be destroyed, and Goff would still be safe."

Witt's smile vanished. "That's what he figured."

For a moment their gazes locked across the table, then somehow she was out of her chair and in his arms, shaking and fighting back tears.

"I was so scared," she said. It was scarcely more than a whisper. "Dickie and Bonnie. You."

"Not half as scared as I was," Witt said softly, rocking her and cradling her against him. "When I saw you come out of that bank with the blood tricklin' down your face..."

His hold on her tightened convulsively.

"I love you, Molly Calhan," he said, voice tight with remembered fear. "I love you and I know damn well I can't live without you no matter how many times I've tried to convince myself I can."

She gave a choked, tearful laugh and shifted in his arms so she could look up into his face. "Does this mean you'll marry me, Witt Gavin?"

"I—I guess it does." He laughed, too, and his voice

was just as shaky as hers. "If you're fool enough to have me."

"I guess I am, because I don't have any intention of letting you get away, you know."

"I know," he said, and kissed her.

It was a long, long kiss, and it carried the world in it.

"Do you—" Witt said when they finally came up for air. He swallowed, then tried again. "Do you think Pete might possibly escape again tonight?"

"He might," Molly said, and laughed. "I can't say for sure, but there's a very good chance he might. A very, *very* good chance he might."

* * * * *

MONTANA MAVERICKS

MONTANA MAVERICKS HISTORICALS
Discover the origins
of Montana's most popular family...

On sale September 2001
THE GUNSLINGER'S BRIDE
by **Cheryl St.John**
Outlaw Brock Kincaid returns home to make peace with his brothers
and finds love in the arms of an old flame with a secret.

On sale October 2001
WHITEFEATHER'S WOMAN
by **Deborah Hale**
Kincaid Ranch foreman John Whitefeather breaks all the rules when
the Native American dares to fall in love with nanny Jane Harris.

On sale November 2001
A CONVENIENT WIFE
by **Carolyn Davidson**
Whitehorn doctor Winston Gray enters into a marriage of
convenience with a pregnant rancher's daughter, only to
discover he's found his heart's desire!

MONTANA MAVERICKS
RETURN TO WHITEHORN—WHERE LEGENDS ARE BEGUN
AND LOVE LASTS FOREVER BENEATH THE BIG SKY...

Harlequin Historicals®
Historical Romantic Adventure!

HHMM

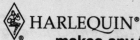

Harlequin invites you to walk down the aisle...

To honor our year long celebration of weddings, we are offering an exciting opportunity for you to own the Harlequin Bride Doll. Handcrafted in fine bisque porcelain, the wedding doll is dressed for her wedding day in a cream satin gown accented by lace trim. She carries an exquisite traditional bridal bouquet and wears a cathedral-length dotted Swiss veil. Embroidered flowers cascade down her lace overskirt to the scalloped hemline; underneath all is a multi-layered crinoline.

Join us in our celebration of weddings by sending away for your own Harlequin Bride Doll. This doll regularly retails for $74.95 U.S./approx. $108.68 CDN. One doll per household. Requests must be received no later than December 31, 2001. Offer good while quantities of gifts last. Please allow 6-8 weeks for delivery. Offer good in the U.S. and Canada only. Become part of this exciting offer!

Simply complete the order form and mail to: "A Walk Down the Aisle"

IN U.S.A
P.O. Box 9057
3010 Walden Ave.
Buffalo, NY 14269-9057

IN CANADA
P.O. Box 622
Fort Erie, Ontario
L2A 5X3

Enclosed are eight (8) proofs of purchase found in the last pages of every specially marked Harlequin series book and $3.75 check or money order (for postage and handling). Please send my Harlequin Bride Doll to:

Name (PLEASE PRINT)

Address   Apt. #

City   State/Prov.   Zip/Postal Code

Account # (if applicable)   **097 KIK DAEW**

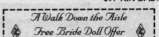

A Walk Down the Aisle
Free Bride Doll Offer
One Proof-of-Purchase

Visit us at www.eHarlequin.com

PHWDAPOPR2

COMING SOON...

AN EXCITING
OPPORTUNITY TO SAVE
ON THE PURCHASE OF
HARLEQUIN AND
SILHOUETTE BOOKS!

*DETAILS TO FOLLOW
IN OCTOBER 2001!*

YOU WON'T WANT TO MISS IT!

PHQ401